Precious Memories

The Winsome Ways of Miz Eudora Rumph

Volume Two

To Elvera,
Here's to your own precious memories!
Catherine Ritch Guess
"Miz Eudora"
July 16, 2010

BOOKS BY CATHERINE RITCH GUESS

EAGLES WINGS TRILOGY

Love Lifted Me
Higher Ground

SHOOTING STAR SERIES

In the Bleak Midwinter
A Song in the Air

SANDMAN SERIES

Old Rugged Cross
Let Us Break Bread Together
Victory in Jesus

- - - - -

In the Garden
Church in the Wildwood
For the Beauty of the Earth
Tis So Sweet
Be Still, My Soul
The Friendly Beasts
In the Sweet By and By

CHILDREN'S BOOKS

Kipper Finds a Home
Rudy the Red Pig (Rudy el Puerco Rojo)
Rudy and the Magic Sleigh

MUSICAL CDS

Musical Sculptures
This Is My Song

Precious Memories

The Winsome Ways of Miz Eudora Rumph

Volume Two

CATHERINE RITCH GUESS

CRM BOOKS
Publishing Hope for Today's Society
Inspirational Books~CDs~Children's Books

CRM BOOKS, PO Box 2124, Hendersonville, NC 28793

Visit our Web site at www.ciridmus.com

Printed in the United States of America
ISBN (10 digit): 1-933341-27-0
ISBN (13 digit): 9781933341279
LCCN: 2008909557

To

Amy and Sarah,

who met Miz Eudora in person
and married my sons anyway!

May your marriages be filled
with many years of laughter!

and

to women (and men) who for years
have told their stories and shared
their legacies through quilting,
and to those who continue to share
that art form with the world

ACKNOWLEDGMENTS

"The Winsome Ways of Miz Eudora Rumph" would not be the same without some very special people for whom I am most grateful. You are all very near and dear to me and I give thanks for you daily!

To those of you who allowed me to "borrow" your personna for one of my characters, MANY THANKS! You'll find yourselves "in the funny pages!"

To the residents and business owners of Smackass Gap and Clay County for your acceptance and support of Miz Eudora, I love you as much as I do her.

To my friends who helped with the Paducah segment - Ada Herndon, Susan Marlier, Carol Selepec, Orion Burns and Quilt in a Day, Serenitea owners Erin and Cameron, and the gracious police officers; also to the Delta Queen passengers, John and Bettie Russo, and crew who gave me a "crash course" on cruising the Mississippi during your steamboat race. Congratulations on winning the Golden Antlers and may the memory of the Delta Queen live on forever!

To Dort and Charly of Leicester, NC, for allowing me to tag along and see a Paducah winner "first-hand" at the Expo, and for allowing me the visit to your home and quilting room. Dort, you are an artist extraordinare! I expect to see many more of your winning entries at Paducah.

To Handy Dandy Railroad engineer John Barden and his wife, Kim, the Sage Brush Six Guns and Rawhide, Ken, Cheryl, Meghan, and especially Brown and all the fine folks at Denton - you made making a fictional setting there for Miz Eudora easy - let's do it again next year!

To Pastor Mark and my choir members at St. John's Lutheran Church in Concord, NC who have to endure Miz Eudora way too often. Pastor Mark, you'll recognize the joke and Mr. Grover Swicegood, you know who you are! And a special word of appreciation to Jane Cress for pointing out ***Immoral, Invisible***. It has served Miz Eudora well, as you'll see.

To Miz Eudora's Sparklin' Shiners, all my "red and purple sisters" and "beach sisters," here's to many more excursions. That is, if those of you who survived Smackass Gap with Miz Eudora can stand another one!

To Chris Williams Efird, Deb Rodgers Farris and Barbara Brooks Taylor for their willingness to share our childhood memories with my readers. Yes, our friendship will last forever, even if it's in the left lane or exit corridor of the toll road!

And most especially, to Mama and Daddy, Josh and Amy, and Jamie and Sarah for allowing me to be like Miz Eudora, exactly who and what I am, and still loving me - ***and Miz Eudora***. Without your constant help and encouragement, Miz Eudora Rumph would not be able to share the gift of laughter with so many. And to C.J., you're the best "book toter" I know!

And as always, to Mark Barden for stories, ideas and inspiration, as well as the "Miz Eudora-ish" Miz Eudora photos and covers.

Most importantly, to all of my readers who've spurned me on during the writing of this second "ride" with Miz Eudora. From all the books you've had me sign and send to people in hospitals, rehab centers, and who are enduring crises in their lives, obviously "laughter ***is*** the best medicine!"

A Note from Catherine

For those of you who read ***In the Sweet By and By***, I'm sure your seatbelt is handy and ready. For those of you who've not had the "experience" of Miz Eudora Rumph, all I can say is "Hold on!"

Hopefully, Miz Eudora will continue to help you discover the bright spots in everyday living, inspire you to find humor in the simplest things in life, and show you how to view life through the eyes of a child. Most of all, may she release you from taking yourself too seriously and give you the ability and self-confidence to laugh at yourself and the world around you, finding great pleasure in ***all*** that surrounds you.

May your each and every day include a "Miz Eudora" moment, ***and*** may you use those "Miz Eudora" moments to light up the world of others around you!

Sit back, take a relaxing breath, kick your feet up, and take a big swig of iced tea – sweetened or unsweetened, as your locale fancies – as you prepare for one wild "joy ride"of fun and hilarity. Oh, and don't forget to buckle up. You may fall in the floor from laughing!

Blessed travels,
CR?

IN MEMORY OF

LA UNA FULLILOVE,
"THE ONE FULL OF LOVE"

WHO EXEMPLIFIED THE SPIRIT
OF BEING A TRUE RED HATTER,

AND WHO,
ON 10-11-08 WENT TO
SHARE IN HER WELL-DESERVED
"CELEBRATION" WITH THE LORD

PROLOGUE

THANK YOU FOR joining me for another breath of fresh air as we set sail – oops, it was a steamboat – scratch the sail, with my dear friend and neighbor, Miz Eudora Rumph. To make sure you fully understand what you're getting yourself into before diving – well no, she didn't dive at the beach – scratch that, too, as you won't be diving in the pages. Just be prepared that there's far more than "just one" breath of fresh air in this book. You'll be breathing the air all the way from Smackass Gap to New Orleans, to up the Mississippi, to the beach, to the Threshers' Reunion and back to Smackass Gap before you leave this second excursion with Miz Eudora. You'll get lots of fresh air along the way. ***And*** meet a couple of people who got a little "too" fresh!

So you can grasp the full flavor of Miz Eudora and Smackass Gap, I'll continue to do my best to tell the story using her vernacular.

Best wishes,

Sadie Callaway

GLOSSARY OF MIZ EUDORA'S SPEECH HABITS

afraid - a'feared

because - 'cause

can't - cain't

could of - could'a

going to - gonna

I came to - I come to

ing - in'

seen - see'd

sure - shore

that's going to - what's gonna

was - wuz

wasn't - wadn't

we were - we was

would of - would'a

You get the picture!

JWB

ONE

Yes, It's a Real Place!

EVER SINCE THE news arrived that Miz Eudora's ***Precious Memories*** quilt won the International Quilt Show and Contest, and that she and three guests were off to Paducah, Kentucky, all of Smackass Gap and most of Hayesville "was all abuzz." In fact, it wasn't only Smackass Gap and Clay County that felt the ripples of her sudden "stardom." It seemed, in her exact words, "the news just trickled out and down the mountain. I wish I had an outhouse that worked that good. I'm thinking I might just get myself one with the prize money."

Those prophetic words to the press became my all-time favorite quote – ***or "Eudoraism,"*** as I had begun to call her memorable sayings that I was now collecting in a notebook.

What's more, Miz Eudora Rumph had put Smackass Gap on the map with her instant notoriety.

People were calling Chinquapin's from all over the country to see if there was really such a place or whether it was a gag. People were traveling from Massachusetts to California to drive through our tiny community, which did them no good since the signs that read "Smackass Gap" and "Peckerwood" stayed gone all the time, thanks to the people who kept stealing them. Cyberspace was filled with "Googlers" checking it out online. And suddenly, the local "paparazzi" was having a field day with Miz Eudora, the quilt, her house, her land…, even poor Clyde, the mule. Everything except her sister-in-law, which is probably because Miz Eudora informed one reporter that "Mabel Toast Jarvis is the real '—' of the family, not Clyde."

That lone statement – which I considered "well thought out" and "precariously executed" by Miz Eudora – worked, for it kept Mabel from being mentioned in any of the media. As Miz Eudora later confided to Hattie Crow and me in private, "I hated to say that, but it was the only way I knew to 'execute' her from the press. I didn't want people all over the country thinking I have anything to do with her." Her logic worked, for as far as the public eye knew, there was no such thing as a Mabel Toast Jarvis.

As for the prophetic words about the new outhouse, Miz Eudora did "one better than that" with the prize money. She bought a new ***motorized*** outhouse, which served no purpose except to attract even more media attention. I would have wagered that she had her picture taken more times in a week than Madonna as she "scooted" through town in her new vehicle that was built on top of a go cart.

The reality of the situation hit me one day as I was driving her to Ingle's, since there wasn't much room for groceries in the small space under the "one-seater," when I saw a bumper sticker of her on the vehicle in front of us. There she was, poised and smiling in her purple "fopher" coat, wearing her red hat and holding her "new used red leather pocketbook," for all the world to see. Along with her picture were the words "Smackass Gap, NC – Home of Miz Eudora Rumph." There was even a small caricature sketch of Clyde in the corner of the bumper sticker.

"Just wait until you see the other one," she stated proudly when I quizzed her about it.

"You mean there's more?" I asked in total bewilderment. And "just wait" I did, for when I found out it had come from Chinquapin's, I made a beeline there instead of Ingle's.

People were lined up at the counter, eating ice cream and purchasing T-shirts with her caricature on them. The front of the shirt showed a front view of her standing next to Clyde; the back showed the rear view of "the couple" with her handprint on the mule's rump.

"I wanted everyone to know how Smackass Gap got its name," she defended when I asked her what she thought she was doing.

"It's her!" someone exclaimed, rushing over to get Miz Eudora to sign their newly-purchased T-shirt.

People dropped everything they had, including the ice cream, to dig for cameras in their purses and backpacks. There were so many flashes going off that they could have turned off all the lights in the establishment.

"Sign it?" Miz Eudora asked. "What for?"

I hurriedly pulled Miz Eudora aside and gave her the five-cent pep talk about "stardom," after which Rob Tiger, the owner of Chinquapin's, handed her a Sharpie pen and she started writing. People began pulling out everything from sales receipts to napkins from their ice cream for her to "put her 'John Henry' on."

"That's your 'John Hancock,'" I corrected.

"I like the song ***John Henry*** better," she shot back, sounding like a child making an argument for which kind of candy bar or cereal they wanted in the grocery store. Considering she was the one getting requests for her autograph, I let her call it anything she wanted as long as she wrote her real name on the item being signed.

While she finished the private autograph party with her "fans," I busied myself looking for the other bumper sticker. I found it without too much difficulty, for there was a display of them on a nearby table. I'd seen the oval decals bearing initials of all the exclusive "hang-outs" in areas, such as Hilton Head and Jekyll Island, but here was that same white oval with the letters "SAG" in bright purple. I was rather amused when some fellow picked up one of the decals and showed it to his wife. "It says 'SAG,'" he stated questioningly, the tone of his voice indicating he had no clue what those letters represented.

I was more amused by Miz Eudora's reply as she hollered across the store, "Yes, sir, that's what most of us women in Smackass Gap do!"

My head lowered immediately, to hide my face turning the same color as Miz Eudora's hat, as I joined the laughter that erupted. Hands flew from every direction to grab one of the decals, which now came with a story that would be shared many times over.

I rescued Miz Eudora, pulling her out of the store by her coat with her holding onto her hat with one hand and her purse with the other. "Bye, ya'll," she yelled as I opened the car's passenger door and shoved her in. Never did I realize that so many people would be capturing my car on film that day or I would have bothered to wash it before our run to the grocery store.

After that incident, I stayed home as much as possible until it came time for the cruise on the Delta

Queen, one of the components of Miz Eudora's winning package. Thirty-five thousand people were expected to converge on Paducah the week of the International Quilt Show and Contest. It would be a lot easier to hide out in that crowd than in Smackass Gap, I told myself, hoping I was right in my prediction.

Hattie and I had been asked to go on the trip from the day news of the winning quilt arrived, but we had no inclination as to whom Miz Eudora would "bestow her good graces on" with the remaining spot for the cruise and ticket to the quilt show.

Mabel, on the other hand, was certain the ticket had her name on it. Three weeks before the trip, she arrived, uninvited, at the Rumph residence during one of our morning coffee chats when Hattie was also there. "I need to know exactly what day we're leaving for Paducah," she informed us. "I want to make sure I've checked my social calendar for those dates."

"And just what makes you think you're going, Mabel?"

"Admit it, Eudora, you need one sane person to go."

Hattie's eyes and mine both flashed at Mabel at the same time.

"Well, you know what I meant. I… I… It's just that you two have spent so much time with Eudora that you don't see her as strange anymore."

"Strange, no, charming, yes," I replied.

"Don't forget, Mabel. I knew you when you were nothing but a little Toast," Hattie reminded her. "I went to school with Melba, Milton T. and you. You weren't the 'head of the class,' you know. Huh! Everybody used to joke that you triplets only got one brain between you."

"Surely they didn't," sulked Mabel.

"Oh, surely they did," Hattie said. "If you ask me, Miz Eudora's got more common sense than anyone I ever met."

"P'SHAA! The only one that's sane, I reckon," said Miz Eudora, shaking her head in disgust. She turned to Hattie. "And if you ask me, Mabel got the short end of the brain. At least Melba and Milton T. had an ounce of sense. They at least made something out of themselves. All Mabel made was a fool out of my baby brother, John G.

"A little Toast," she added with a snicker. "Look at her now. She's a whole loaf of bread!"

I turned my head so quickly, trying to hide my own snicker, that I heard my neck pop.

Mabel started to rebuke, but Miz Eudora stopped her. "I'll think about it, Mabel, but it's only because there's no telling what kind of a mess you'd stir up here in Smackass Gap before we'd get back home that I'll even consider letting you go. I've got to protect John G.'s memory as much as I can."

I glanced back to see Mabel literally biting her

tongue. It was obvious that she wanted to get the last word, but she feared losing her "possible" spot on the trip if she did. I concluded that might be the only time in history I'd see Miz Eudora button up that woman's lips. She couldn't have done a better job if she'd used her quilting needle and thread.

So that's how it turned out, at the end, that Mabel "held claim" of the third ticket. Miz Eudora felt an overwhelming sense of guilt over leaving Mabel at home for the rest of her friends to look after, fearing she'd be banished from "our fair community" upon her return. Given that, she crumbled the week before we were to leave and told Mabel she could go to Paducah. ***Which means that an ample supply of Horace's "special blend" will also be going to Paducah.***

So much for the public eye! I decided, knowing that in that one decisive moment, "Smackass Gap" and "Mabel" were about to become household words along with "Miz Eudora."

Yes, it's a real place, I said to myself the night before our departure, getting in practice for the thousands of times I would say those five words in the next two weeks. Little did I realize, at the time, that those five words would become the most used expression in my entire vocabulary.

TWO

Are We There Yet?

BLAM!...BLAM!

I hit the latches on the suitcase again, trying to get them to stay closed. A glance at my palm, whose bruise was beginning to take color, made me wonder whether I had been out of my mind to look forward to "a road trip" with Miz Eudora Rumph and what had become her "entourage." Had I not been so generous with my wheeled luggage, and allowed her to borrow it, I was sure my belongings would have already been zipped up and in the car, ready for the first leg of the trip.

Oh, well. At least Miz Eudora will be packed and ready when I get there. Suddenly, a flutter in my stomach told me that I was as unprepared for this day as I had been the morning eighteen months earlier when I arrived at her door, an unsuspecting soul with a basket of food in hand, to convey my well wishes for Horace. I guess you could say that day was the beginning of all that had transpired up to this point. It was the beginning of the "celebration."

Ha! I laughed to myself. ***"Celebration" has taken on several new meanings for me since that day.*** I laughed again. ***At least where Miz Eudora is concerned.***

Having no hammer handy, I found a screwdriver - which I'd learned was a handy tool to have around for a variety of needs - and used its handle to give the latches a good whack.

PING! As pretty as you please, the first latch popped into place. ***PING!*** The second latch followed suit, as if right on cue.

Why didn't I think of this earlier? I asked when the suitcase was securely fastened. As I dragged the suitcase from the bedroom recliner and lugged it to the car, that insecure feeling of a second ago rippled through me again. I knew why I felt insecure.

When the prize packet had arrived months earlier, Miz Eudora passed it along to me since it was my job to drive them to the dock for the Delta Queen, which would then take them to Paducah, Kentucky, for the city's noted International Quilt Show and Contest. I don't think she ever computed the fact that the Delta Queen was any more than the pontoon boat that took passengers for rides on Lake Chatuge. Call it selfish if you wish, but I feared she'd not take the trip if she knew we would be floating up the river for nine nights before arriving in Paducah. Furthermore, aware of the threat that this was, more than likely, the last season the Delta Queen would ever run, I really wanted to cruise the mighty Mississippi on it. And then, there was that last small detail that this particular cruise was a race between three steamboats and the winner would proudly hang the Golden Antlers over the captain's wheel for the next year. This was a trip I had coveted taking with Leon for years before his passing. Not only that, but I was afraid Miz Eudora might consider New Orleans too "wicked," for lack of a better word, and have nothing to do with going there. Therefore, I hadn't bothered to inform the other three that to get to Paducah, Kentucky, we were first heading south.

Far south…very far south. That's right. The river cruise on the Delta Queen started out in New Orleans. I would have suggested we fly, but they'd have had no part of that. Therefore, I'd seen no other way out than me driving there, catching the steamboat that would carry us to Paducah, and then renting a car to get us back to Smackass Gap once the show was over. Then I'd worry about getting back to my car in New Orleans. That tiny dilemma could have explained my state of insecurity that morning.

But for then, I was banking on the fact that Hattie, Miz Eudora and Mabel would become so engrossed in conversation that they'd never realize we were on our way to Louisiana until we were halfway there. In the end, it turned out that I banked halfway right.

Now if I can just get this thing in the trunk, I thought, hoisting the suitcase with all my might and giving it a big toss. Once that task was completed, I checked the house to make sure all the doors and windows were locked and that all the appliances were off. It was funny how this simple routine reminded me of all the fun road trips I'd shared over the years with Leon. ***Perhaps that's why I have this strange feeling. This is the first time I've taken an overnight trip since he's been gone.*** I smiled contentedly as I closed the front door behind me.

That's it, I told myself confidently as I started the car's engine. I could still see his warm, gentle smile in my mind's eye, the same one that he'd always flashed at me as we began all our trips. It was the same one that allowed me to believe that all would still be well and safe upon our return. What I didn't sense was his laughter of all that was going to happen ***before*** that safe return on this particular road trip. That would come later.

Much later and many times, I was to learn.

"WHERE'S THAT MABEL when I need her?" Miz Eudora asked while trying to zip the large suitcase I'd loaned her, as Hattie and I held it down.

None of us had to offer an answer, to her question for which we had no answer, for Mabel's silver Buick came flying up the driveway, billowing huge clouds of dust behind it. Miz Eudora rushed for the front door as speedily as the car's approach and threw open the screen.

"Mabel Toast Jarvis!" she yelled at the top of her lungs. "Where in tarnation have you been? You're always hanging on my cuff when I don't want you around and the one time in my life I actually do need you, you're not here." She burst into a fit of coughing. "And land sakes! You didn't need to throw up that mess of dust. I just got my house all cleaned in case we got killed before we got home."

My eyes shot toward Miz Eudora. ***And all I'd ever worried about was clean underwear when we went on a trip. Mama must have forgotten this part.*** I swallowed. ***No wonder I had a strange flutter in my stomach.***

Miz Eudora missed the steps on her way to the ground from the porch as she yanked open the driver's door of the car, pulled out Mabel – who was hanging onto her "fur critters" with one hand and her hat with the other – by her left elbow and drug her all the way into the bedroom where the suitcase lay perched with the lid stuffed open in all directions. There was no "Hello!" or "How are you?" or "Isn't this going to be a fun trip?" or any kind of greeting.

Instead, Miz Eudora commanded Hattie to grab the other arm and help. With that they plopped Mabel right up on top of the open suitcase. I didn't even have time to alert them that there was an expandable pocket. It didn't much matter, though, for when Mabel's "dead weight" - as Miz Eudora called it – hit the top of the suitcase, the expansion blew open as the contents went poufing out in every direction, but at least the lid was then in close proximity to the zipper.

I didn't realize that I was standing there gaping until Miz Eudora ordered, "Sadie, you come over here and cram all these things back in the sides and then zip the lid closed while we've got it down." Afraid I'd be the next one lunged through the air if I didn't obey, I quickly set about the task I'd been assigned.

"You hold that leg up, Hattie, and I'll hold this one up," instructed Miz Eudora. "That way Sadie can get the thing zipped all the way around. You'd better put a hand on her back, too, so she don't go spilling over on the bed. It would be a shame to have to do this all over again."

Why didn't I give Miz Eudora the suitcase with the old latches? I wondered, thinking that Mabel's legs could have simply dangled over the side of it. The bruise on my palm reminded me that either way, it would have been bruised. I counted my blessings that things weren't worse, all the while remembering that the zipper on the expandable pocket was probably broken.

The minute I finished with the zipper, Miz Eudora gave a big yank of the suitcase, which sent Mabel flying over the back of the bed. I was surprised she wasn't already squawking, but I'm sure she'd been in too much shock. Not to worry, turning a back flip over the bed brought her instantly back to her senses.

"Eudora Jarvis Rumph, if this is the treatment I'm going to receive, I'm going to stay home."

Miz Eudora set the suitcase back on the bed and began to unzip it. "C'mon, Hattie, you grab that arm and I'll grab this one."

Not again, I silently begged.

"You're not getting rid of me that easily!" exclaimed Mabel. "Someone with some sense has got to go on this trip…," She paused and looked at me. "Begging your pardon, Sadie, I didn't mean to imply that you're 'one of them,' but someone has to go along that can handle Eudora. She's never been outside the state, except for Hiawassee, Georgia, and we surely don't want to turn her loose in Paducah, Kentucky with 35,000 quilters from all over the world. I know it's not Boston or Chicago, but still, it's an old historical river town. Those people have a lot of pride and they just wouldn't know what to make of her."

"What they've already made of her," I wanted to say, "is a winner. She's the reason we're all going there." But rather, I looked at my suitcase back on the bed with a huge indention, the size of Mabel's backside, on the top of it. ***Look at it this way, Sadie. You've always admired impressionistic art. That shape is definitely impressed upon your luggage***.

I sneered as I again zipped the corner Miz Eudora had unzipped. ***Designer luggage, that's exactly what I've always wanted***. Lest I had thought otherwise, I reminded myself that this was going to be "one doozy of a trip" as I carried the luggage to the trunk.

Just as I was about to give the instruction for everyone who was "riding in my chariot" to come on, Mabel piped up with, "Miz Eudora, I thought it might be better if we take my Buick. I'm not sure Sadie's Honda has enough room for us to ride all the way there comfortably."

"We'll be quite comfortable," was the reply she got. "You just mind you don't eat like a horse while we're gone, Hattie can sit in the back seat with you since she's smallest, and we'll be fine.

"In that case," Mabel continued, "perhaps I should sit in the front seat with Sadie and navigate."

"The only way you know to navigate us is straight to the grave, and an early one at that. Besides, Sadie's done pulled up the directions on her computer. All you have to do is sit back and enjoy the ride. It would help a great deal if you'd keep your mouth shut, too," Miz Eudora added.

I knew that was like giving an open invitation to be a chatterbox to Mabel Toast, "Mrs. John G." – she was always quick to point out – Jarvis. ***Are we having fun yet?*** I asked myself as I watched them all settle in place and fasten their seatbelts. ***Our only casualties thus far are my bruised palm and the big black mark that Mabel's heel left on the bedroom wall when she took the back flip over the bed.*** I drove down the driveway in silence, not sure whether I was too shocked or too afraid to think of what lay ahead. ***Oh, and my suitcase,*** I thought as I recalled the enormous indention on its top flap. ***Since everything always happens in threes, maybe we're done with casualties for this trip.*** But even I wasn't naive enough to buy that.

Once Mabel saw that she was irrevocably ***not*** going to be the chauffeur of this trip – ***which is a good thing since they have no clue that New Orleans is a "short" side trip!*** – she immediately turned her focus to her sister-in-law. ***Or rather, her sister-in-law's appearance.***

"Eudora Rumph," that is without a doubt the ugliest skirt I have ever seen."

"It isn't ugly," Miz Eudora informed her, "it's crazy."

"Well, that's one time we agree precisely." Mabel gave her sister-in-law a scrutinizing once-over.

"Honestly, Eudora, I didn't think I'd ever see anything that looked more ridiculous than that crazy concoction of an outfit you wore to Horace's service. But now, this? Whatever were you thinking? You're supposed to be accepting an award, not looking like a scarecrow."

"Those celebratin' clothes weren't crazy. That was a fopher coat, not a crazy quilt. And the dress, purse, hat and shoes came from that nice chain named Goodwill. They were ***not*** a concoction. You think you're so much smarter than everyone else. Well, you don't know ***anything*** about medicine, even though John G. was a doctor. A concoction is something Ma used to brew up to make us feel better when we were sick. You know, like that rectal paste concoction of John G.'s."

"Personally, I think you'll be the star of the show," defended Hattie. "When those women in Paducah see how clever you were to wear an outfit that looks like a quilt, they'll all be jealous. I wouldn't be surprised if they didn't all want one."

"Only if they're farmers and their scarecrow has bitten the dust," complained Mabel.

"Too bad ***you*** haven't bitten the dust. You keep this up and you might before we get out of Smackass Gap," challenged Miz Eudora.

"Eatin' dust is more like it," Miz Eudora leaned in and whispered in my ear. "If we threw her out of the car, she'd be chasing us in that new silver Buick so fast that she'd be eatin' your dust all the way to Paducah."

Glancing to my side, I caught her give Hattie a huge grin.

"On second thought," she leaned toward me and whispered, "that might not be such a bad idea."

I gave her a reprimanding scowl, trying my best to keep from smiling, but I could tell she knew I was actually agreeing with her and merely being kind to Mabel. The days of playing peacemaker were getting more and more difficult between those two. Some days I considered letting them have it out, but figured my life would be wretchedly gloomy and boring without the pair of them.

"Really, Miz Eudora, how ***did*** you come up with that idea for the quilt?" I asked.

"I kept thinking how proud Ma would have been to know that I'd won an international contest doing something she'd taught me as a child. Then I remembered how she was always warning me about being wasteful, so I got the notion to make myself a skirt and jacket using the scraps I had left from the winning quilt. I knew she'd have been doubly proud of me then." A momentary bittersweet tear formed in her eye, and then she gave a cheerful smile.

"I nearly worked Ma's old Singer into a convulsion, I was pedaling that treadle so fast." She revved up the decibel a notch as she concluded with, "Obviously Mabel is not as good a judge of fine art as she thinks she is."

"HMMPH!" was Mabel's only comment.

I could tell that Mabel was in for a most enlightening lesson once we hit Paducah. This was one time Eudora Rumph was right. Quilting was a fine art form, and she was about to find out how much in demand it was. I firmed my grip on the steering wheel and settled back in my seat for what I knew was going to be one wild ride. And prayed that they didn't soon start asking, "Are we there yet?"

THREE

Up the Lazy River

BEFORE WE HAD barely gotten out of Clay County, Hattie and Miz Eudora were already "singin' up a storm." They'd done everything from ***Blue Moon of Kentucky*** to ***My Old Kentucky Home*** and were now giving me their own rendition of ***Wildwood Flower***. Had there been an autoharp handy, I do believe Miz Eudora could have put Mother Maybelle Carter, herself, to shame.

"Miz Eudora," I said, complimenting her, "I didn't know you were so musical. Wherever did you learn all those songs?"

"A body had to do something to pass the time when you worked in the field all the time. No offense, Sadie, but your generation missed out on a whole lot of life. All this stuff these youngun's do now, why, that don't take any imagination at all. Their brains are sittin' up there unchallenged and unmotivated while all they do is sit on their rumps and push buttons. What a sad life is that!"

Lucky for me, her body had learned to pass the time so well. Those songs had kept them busy for nearly the first two hours of the trip. It didn't matter that they were singing everything in their repertoire that mentioned Kentucky. ***I guess to get them in the mood for Paducah.*** I debated on whether I should suggest they croon out a few choruses of ***Shrimp Boat a-Comin'*** in honor of going to the Gulf, but since they didn't know we were going there yet, I saw no point in breaking the news yet.

Mabel, refusing to lower herself to their standards of taste in music, had covered her eyes with the mask she used at night and put in her earplugs. In no time, she was out like a light until she got the urge for a pit stop.

Realizing that rest stops would have signs denoting what state we were in, not to mention all the maps and brochures, I chose to stop at a gas station, thinking my chances of being discovered might be less. I was right. Mabel went straight to the business at hand, while Miz Eudora and Hattie made a list of songs, to occupy their time for the next leg of the trip, while they waited their turn for the restroom.

It helped my cause considerably when Miz Eudora's glasses fell off in the back seat while she was getting a drink from the cooler. Her hands were full, since she'd also gotten a bottle of water for me, so she went ahead and placed our bottles in the cup holders of the front console.

About that same time, I heard a big "Whoop! What is that under me?" from Mabel. She reached her hand back and pulled out Miz Eudora's glasses, only one of the arms was broken off.

"Oh, my!" observed Hattie. "Where's the other arm?"

"I don't want to know," answered Miz Eudora. "Just give me what's left. I'm not about to go reaching for that other arm."

Trying to keep the situation from turning into an episode, I offered, "I'm sure there's an eye doctor in Paducah that can have you a new pair of glasses in no time."

"Yes, it would be a shame not to be able to see your own quilt when we get there," said Hattie.

"I didn't look with the arm. The lenses are fine, no thanks to Mabel. I'll be able to see everything I need to see."

I hope that doesn't include the road signs, I commented to myself.

Hattie, seeing a bit of humor in the situation now that it was over, added, "I've heard of eyes in the back of your head, but this is ridiculous."

"You know," replied Miz Eudora, "Mabel thinks it's her job to pass inspection on everybody. She's so intent on it that you'd think she believes it's her calling from the Good Lord. I guess this way she can keep a check on people in both directions."

Hattie and Miz Eudora gave a large chuckle and went back to singing while Mabel returned to her snoozing, which I found most irregular. It wasn't like her to be so passive.

So far, so good, I mused, thankfully, wondering whether Miz Eudora had slipped a few drops of paregoric in Mabel's water bottle.

AFTER ANOTHER HOUR or so, Mabel removed the mask from her eyes and began rifling through the picnic basket to see what she could find to eat. She set about handing out sandwiches and apples, after I told them I thought it best to keep moving instead of stopping at a picnic table. ***Due to my goal of reaching New Orleans before dark*** – a tidbit I didn't bother to share.

I looked in the mirror at Mabel's mild manner, making sure we'd not left with Melba instead. I'd become so concerned about her abnormal behavior that I missed the spitting and sputtering of the engine for the first few minutes. That is, until I saw the engine light come on. By the time I got the car off the road, it literally died.

"Don't worry," I said. "I have AAA."

"Sadie," replied Miz Eudora sympathetically, "you poor dear. All this time you've been living across the street from me and I never knew. How'd you keep a thing like that a secret?"

"Maybe because I never needed roadside repair before?" I replied quizzically.

"Roadside repair?" she repeated, shaking her head. "Mabel, maybe we should have let you drive the Buick."

I fully expected that comment to set off an explosion of fireworks, but instead, the only reply I heard was, "I'd have been glad to drive."

Wonder what was in the bottle with the paregoric? I asked myself, making a note to quiz Miz Eudora on the subject later.

I reached for my cell phone to discover that I had no signal. "Okay, ladies, it looks like calling AAA is out. Someone should come along soon to help us."

Miz Eudora leaned toward me and whispered, "If you need a little nip to settle your nerves until you can get some help, I brought along a small stash for Mabel."

"Oh, no, Miz Eudora," I responded in no uncertain terms. "I would never consider drinking and driving."

"Drinking and driving?" asked Hattie. "Miz Eudora, what did you think AAA is?"

"Alcoholics Anonymous, of course."

Mabel laughed aloud. “Eudora, that’s only 2 A’s. AAA is three.”

The paregoric must be wearing off.

“AAA is an organization that comes out and helps drivers when their car breaks down,” explained Hattie. “They do lots of other things, too, but that’s what we need now.”

“Just because Mabel sat on my glasses and broke them, she didn’t need to sit on the car and break it.”

“Why not?” I nearly blurted out, along with, “She’s already sat on my suitcase and broken it this morning.”

A new pick-up truck with a back seat stopped in front of us. The driver hopped out, came back to the car and asked, “Which way you going?”

Before I had a chance to respond, Miz Eudora yelled out, “Paducah, Kentucky.”

“That’s a long way,” he replied, causing me to give a sigh of relief that he’d not blown my secret. “I’m headed toward New Orleans and thought if you were going that direction, I might be able to give you a lift.”

I opened my mouth, thinking that being rescued was worth having the secret blown, but Hattie said, “Thanks for the offer, but we’re not going anywhere near there.”

“Too bad. That truck has plenty of room. I could have dropped you off anywhere along the way. I’ll call for some help for you." He took off so fast that I didn't have a chance to stop him.

"That feller must be in a real big hurry," stated Miz Eudora. "Too bad he wasn't going our way. We'd have been there in no time flat."

I bit my tongue and sat silently waiting for another car to pass. ***And another, and another, and another.***

"Hey," called Miz Eudora, "look what's comin.'"

I saw a truck carrying six portable toilets coming from the opposite direction.

"What good is that going to do us?" asked Mabel. "We've already had a rest stop."

"We can hitch a ride on it," offered Miz Eudora.

"Miz Eudora, this is no time for jokes," scolded Hattie.

"Who's joking?" defended Miz Eudora. "Look at the truck. There's six Porta-John toilets and only four of us. We could each get our own seat."

"You're not serious?" I asked, appalled at her suggestion.

"Of course, I'm serious. There's no difference in that than there was on the fully-equipped bus those Red Hatters were on last year. It had indoor plumbing. This way, we all get our own one-seater."

"Good gracious alive!" exclaimed Mabel. "She ***is*** serious! She doesn't have enough sense to make up something this ludicrous."

Miz Eudora jumped out of the car and started waving her arms in an effort to flag down the driver.

"I have no intention of riding the rest of the way to Paducah on a portable toilet," stated Hattie.

"I have no intention of riding ten feet on a portable toilet," insisted Mabel.

Welcome back to our world, Mabel! I didn't know whether to cheer or to cry.

"Riding on the back of the Porta-John truck is the best way to go," explained Miz Eudora. "No one slams on brakes in front of you. Nobody rides too close to your back bumper, and everybody gives you a wide berth when they pass you. The best ride I ever had to Franklin was on a Porta-John truck. It was the best view of those mountains I'd ever had. There wasn't anybody in my way."

I glared at her in disbelief. As much as I found it impossible, Mabel was right. The whole story was too ludicrous to be made up.

Obviously, the driver of this Porta-John truck had never had any passengers. ***Or even people who wanted to be.*** All he did when he passed Miz Eudora was give a big wave and blow the air-horn.

"I guess the drivers here aren't as friendly as the ones back home," she said, deflated.

"We've no choice except that you two are going to have to go find us some help," instructed Mabel, looking directly at Hattie and Mabel. "Sadie and I will stay here and take a look under the hood."

Which meant that I would stay there and take a look under the hood while Mabel helped herself to another sandwich and a piece of apple pie.

"Are you sure you can't use your cell phone to call for help?" inquired Hattie, not thrilled at the option of going for help.

"This place is so far off the map that I can't get a signal," I told her. "I can't call anybody from out here."

"Then what's the use of having it?" asked a confused Miz Eudora. "What in tarnation is the good of it if you can't call somebody when you're broke down in the middle of nowhere? You don't need to call anyone when you're close to people. Why, you can give a holler and get help then."

I had no response to that for she was entirely right. "We'll wait right here for you until you get back, even if someone comes in the meantime," I told them.

"Just don't stay gone all day," added Mabel.

"We'll stay gone," stated Miz Eudora, "until we have a way to get us on the road again."

With that, Miz Eudora and Hattie set out on foot – going north, which was really south, but they didn't know that because I'd still failed to share that we were on our way to New Orleans – and were singing ***On the Road Again*** to the top of their lungs. They left with the promise of either finding someone, or a phone to call for someone, while Mabel and I waited with the car in case someone should pass.

Sadie, my brain kicked in as I watched them disappear over a distant hill, ***you just sent those two poor defenseless souls out when neither of them know where they are or where they're going.*** In spite of my recklessness in that decision, it proved to be a good thing, for as they say, "ignorance is bliss."

"HERE COMES A car," Mabel called excitedly. "Maybe they'll be a little more cordial than the other three that passed.

I had my doubts and was, frankly, getting concerned about Miz Eudora and Hattie. ***Perhaps I should have gone and left the three of them here.*** My spine tingled with fear at that thought. ***No, that wouldn't have done at all. There would have been need for a funeral by the time I returned!***

Feeling more anxiousness about those two than the car, I saw that there was an old "battleship-type" vehicle from the 70's coming toward us. It was still far enough away that I couldn't tell what color it was, but I could tell it was big enough to hold all of us. If only Miz Eudora and Hattie would hurry up and get back, maybe we could actually hitch a ride with this person.

As it came closer, I could tell that it was a convertible with the top down.

"Look!" exclaimed Mabel. "Eudora and Hattie must have brought them. I see Eudora's big old red hat."

She was right, I noticed. ***At least those red hats are good for something. You can see them a mile away.*** I tried to make out the make and color of the car. ***Well, maybe not a mile away***, I corrected myself.

Please do not tell me that is a purple car, I pleaded, not sure to whom, as it continued toward us.

My plea went unanswered, for here it came, a purple Cadillac convertible, its red top crunched down against the trunk.

"Good gracious alive, Eudora!" announced Mabel. "You've done gone and stolen a pimp car."

"A pimp car?" repeated Miz Eudora questioningly. "I'm not right sure what that is."

I wasn't right sure I wanted to explain that to her, either, so instead, I asked, "Miz Eudora, how is it that you came across this car?"

"You told Hattie and me to find someone to help ***us***, but instead we found someone that we helped."

That told me a whole lot. Sorry I asked.

"There was this nice-looking young fellow broken down alongside the road and as we came up to him, Miz Eudora asked if she could help. He told her she sure couldn't hurt and handed her a wrench. She fiddled for a little bit with this piece under the hood and then asked him for the gum he was chewing. He handed it to her and she put it on some part that was causing the problem. She told him it would hold him for a while."

"Then he wanted to know what a couple of sweet ladies like us were doing walking alone down the highway," Miz Eudora took over. "When I told him your car had broken down, he asked where we needed to go. I told him Paducah, and he was going there, too."

"How's that for luck?" asked Hattie.

Looking around for the "nice-looking young fellow," I started to ask about his whereabouts, but Mabel beat me to the draw. "What did you do with him, stash him in the trunk?"

"Of course not," answered Miz Eudora. "He told us that he had to go take care of a gig, and that if we'd ride with him there, we were welcome to take the car and he'd meet up with us in Paducah. I told him where we'd be staying and gave him the phone number there. He's going to call us the day after the quilt show starts so he can pick up the car.

"Anyway, he took us to some place about thirty minutes away where there were a whole bunch of women and he got out," she further explained.

"I told you it belonged to a pimp," stated Mabel emphatically.

"Then he tipped his hat and he wished us safe travels," continued Miz Eudora, nodding her head for emphasis of how nice the young man had been.

"We tried to pay him for the use of his car," added Hattie, "but he told us it was his privilege to be able to help a couple of little ladies, saying that if his sweet little old grandmother ever got stranded, he hoped someone would do the same for her."

"How in heaven's name is he going to get to Paducah without his car?" asked Mabel, for the second time beating me there. "I'll bet one of those scantily-dressed women takes him."

"One of the women ***was*** going to take him," snapped Miz Eudora, "but she wasn't scantily-dressed. She was red-and-purple-dressed."

"She's right," seconded Hattie. "It was a big conference center in Birmingham, Alabama, and he was the entertainment for a huge event by the Red Hatters down there."

"Entertainment?" asked Mabel. "Scratch the pimp, he's a stripper."

"You mean he quilts, too?" asked Miz Eudora. "I knew I liked that boy from the time I laid eyes on him."

"I hope you didn't lay your eyes on too much of him," said Mabel.

"I sure enough did," bragged Miz Eudora. "He had a bright red suit with white pin-stripes and a red derby hat to match."

"Don't forget the purple satin shirt, the red satin tie and the purple socks," reminded Hattie.

"And you should have seen his red alligator shoes," said Miz Eudora. "Talk about a sharp dresser."

"He said he had a purple suit with red accessories, too," continued Hattie. "Said the ladies really liked him on stage and he liked them, too."

"Goodness gracious! He was a pimp ***and*** a stripper," insisted Mabel. She shook her head in absolute disgust until she suddenly jerked her entire body to a frozen position. "Birmingham, Alabama? You two walked all the way to Birmingham, Alabama?"

"I surely reckon we did," answered Miz Eudora, "'cause that's what the sign said when we got to the convention center."

Suddenly the fact that we were farther – ***much farther*** – south than everyone had suspected came to fruition. All eyes turned to me and I wondered how far away I was from a lynch mob. I told them the whole story of how I was afraid they wouldn't accept the trip if they'd known they had to ride to New Orleans first, and that I'd hope once they got there, they'd be so tired of riding in the car, and so impressed by the Delta Queen, they'd be glad to cruise up the river to Paducah.

My mother had taught me that truth was always best, and I listened. I really did, but I guess you never get too old to stray from your mother's teachings. For there I was, now with two cars instead of one to get back to after the trip to Paducah. That still left the predicament of getting back to Smackass Gap after the quilt show.

"It appears I have gotten us into a real dither," I confessed apologetically.

"A dither, my foot," expressed Miz Eudora. "We'd have never met the Purple Stallion if you hadn't brought us here."

"The Purple Stallion?" repeated Mabel, aghast. "Is that what he called himself? I told you the car belonged to a pimp!"

"Whatever he is, he has a sweet grandmother," declared Miz Eudora, "and you'd better thank your lucky stars for her, or we couldn't have this nice roomy car right now."

"I've always wanted to go to New Orleans," said Hattie, thinking about the trip ahead of us.

"I must admit, I do love the pralines and beignets there," added Mabel, letting her stomach distract her concern over the car and its owner.

"Would you listen to that?" asked Miz Eudora. "And here she was two minutes ago squallin' 'bout me gettin' tangled up with a pimp."

"Enough talk," I pronounced, once the smoke had cleared enough to realize we were no worse for the wear, as I began to move suitcases from my car. "I'm ready for some Cajun food. We'll have to hurry so we can get there in time for embarkation of the Delta Queen tomorrow."

"What'd she say we were going to do to the Delta Queen?" asked Miz Eudora, looking at Hattie. Then without waiting for an answer, she turned to her sister-in-law. "Oh, and you're welcome, Mabel," she added, putting the last of the suitcases in the trunk, which still had room for at least twenty urns full of ashes should we come across any good yard sales.

I closed the trunk and walked to the driver's door.

"I always did want a Cadillac convertible," said Hattie. "May I drive?"

"Well, somebody had better drive," belted Mabel, "because Eudora doesn't even have a driver's license."

"What?" I gasped in disbelief. The fact that I'd never seen Miz Eudora drive had never indicated to me that she couldn't drive. It just indicated to me that she'd always had Horace to take her places, and after his death, I'd been her "designated driver." ***Not to mention that she just drove this Caddie from Birmingham which is a good twenty miles away.***

"I can drive a tractor better'n anybody in Clay County," Miz Eudora said defensively. "They've never stopped me on the road there."

"You don't ***have*** to have a driver's license to drive a tractor," replied Mabel, like she knew what she was talking about.

"If you can drive a tractor, you should be able to drive a car," Miz Eudora continued.

"Thank goodness, you were able to fix this car, Miz Eudora," I noted. "I must admit, I'm amazed."

"It was nothing," she replied. "Horace always said if you could fix a Massey Ferguson, you could fix anything."

"Then why couldn't you fix Sadie's car?" Mabel asked.

"Because I didn't have a wrench or any bubble gum."

I knew better than to ask any more questions after that comment, so I took my place in the back seat beside Mabel as Miz Eudora handed Hattie the car keys. With no success, I tried the cell phone again, hoping to have AAA call someone to tow the car into a garage for us.

"Where's your purse, Hattie?" I asked once we reached the interstate. "We'd better make sure you have your license handy in case we get pulled over in this 'inconspicuous' car."

"I don't have it," she replied, hitting the gas a little harder as she came off the ramp.

"I thought you said you had a driver's license," I commented politely.

"I do," she said with her usual pleasant smile. "I just haven't driven in twelve years, so I don't see the need to keep it in my wallet."

"Land sakes!" exclaimed Miz Eudora. "At least I've driven in the past year. You'd better pull over and let me back under the wheel."

"Why don't you let Sadie under the wheel?" Mabel asked. "She has a license with her ***and*** she's been driving lately. I'd feel a lot safer if she was to drive."

"You didn't get the car, and you didn't do the fixin,' so you just hush up and sit in the back seat. Besides, I'll bet that nice young Purple Stallion would tell you it's okay for me to drive," argued Miz Eudora.

"Well, of course that's what a pimp would…oh, never mind," cajoled Mabel, realizing she was at a stalemate as she covered her eyes again with the mask and laid back against the plush leather headrest.

Perhaps I should ask Miz Eudora if there's any more of what Mabel had at the beginning of the trip. Rather, I decided it best at the moment to adhere to the bumper sticker on the back of the convertible that read, "Sit down, shut up, buckle up and hold on!"

Compared to what we'd been through to get there, the Delta Queen was going to be smooth sailing. ***Or cruisin' up the lazy river***, I concluded, thinking of the gentle lulling of the paddlewheel churning the massive expanse of water, known as the "mighty Mississippi," as I imagined myself on the riverboat's deck, stretched out and floating the days, ***and nights***, away.

Up the lazy river…was my last thought as I fell to a peaceful afternoon's slumber filled with precious memories of my Leon and how much he loved the water.

FOUR

If I Had a Rich Man

I'D BEEN RIGHT about the Delta Queen being smooth sailing compared to the road trip to New Orleans. The women were so excited about hitting the French Quarter that they were in rare form the entire rest of the road trip, which meant they actually behaved themselves. For Miz Eudora, who'd never left the state of North Carolina, except for the few times she'd been over to Hiawassee, she was getting a view of a good chunk of the Gulf and southeastern states, on land and water. ***And loving every minute of it.***

Being aboard the riverboat had proven to be the most relaxing time I'd experienced in a long while – since the week Leon and I had discovered Smackass Gap, to be exact. At least that was the case for the first day. After that, the "trio" became acclimated to the Delta Queen so it was an all-day, all-night ordeal keeping up with them; it seemed I should have brought along a leash for each. There were no episodes, there were just three little ladies – ***well, one not so little!*** – that were having the time of their life. In that respect, I guess you could still say it was smooth sailing. Or, at least eight out of out ten days wasn't bad. It wasn't actually until the seventh evening that we had a slight problem. Naturally, it waited until I'd already gotten dressed for bed to happen.

Ah! I thought dreamily as I slid on my old, comfy silk pajamas, relishing a few minutes of uninterrupted reading time before falling into a much-needed deep slumber. Somehow I had not anticipated how taxing keeping up with a group of three older ladies could be. ***Especially when they're boxed up on a riverboat with nowhere to go!*** I couldn't remember being this tired in years. "Or ever," I mumbled softly as I slid under the covers, my back to the headboard and my book in hand.

The tranquil setting of a prairie farm, taking me mentally and physically toward my own soothing serenity of dreamland, was horrifically interrupted by a loud rap on the door of the next room. "Miz Eudora, come quick!" I heard, recognizing the voice to be Hattie's. "You've got to help me with Mabel."

"Why in tarnation do you need to help Mabel?" Miz Eudora responded quizzically, her words penetrating the wall.

"C'mon! I'll explain on the way back down to

the lounge."

"The lounge?" Miz Eudora's ears obviously perked with those two words. "Don't tell me that Mabel's down there tormentin' people with her voice!"

"It's worse than that!" Hattie's voice was now a plea of desperation.

"P'SHAA! That woman's big enough, old enough ***and*** ugly enough to help herself," fumed Miz Eudora. "I've had more of her than I can stand for one day. I'm going to bed. Besides, I already got on this nice new flannel gown that Sadie gave me."

"Well, just throw on a robe and get out here or we'll never get Mabel out of this mess."

"Maybe we ought to just leave her wallowing in her mess, whatever it is, and we'd be rid of her once and for all."

"Eudora Rumph, honestly! I thought you were my friend. You're worse than the three of those Toast triplets put together."

"Oh, aw-right," moaned Miz Eudora as she gave in, shamed that she might be worse than the Toasts. "I'm a-comin'. Just let me get my fopher coat on."

I decided to quickly dress and follow, more concerned about seeing what Mabel had managed to get herself into than how I might offer help with the situation. The book's tranquil setting was left open and upside down on the bed, where I knew it would be more necessary upon my return.

As I followed the pair down the hallway and then the stairs, I got a charge out of the game of suspenseful secrecy as I imagined myself portraying a character in an old Dick Tracy comic. ***Maybe I should change my book of romance to a mystery***, I thought, steadily and silently keeping my pace behind the two. That idea was quickly blown down by the realization that I had more suspense and mystery - caring for the three women with me, and playing sleuth - than even Mary Higgins Clark could write into a bestseller.

All I could hear in front of me were muddled whispers going from Hattie and gasps of "Land sakes!" coming from Miz Eudora. I had no clue as to what we were about to find, but I already knew this had the makings of a good caper, fully worth leaving my world of tranquility on the prairie behind. The mystery was sounding better all the time.

By the time I hit the door of the lounge, I saw the problem with my own eyes. I needed no explanation, but I placed a hand on the back of each Hattie and Miz Eudora in support. Truthfully, I think the hand was to hold them up in their shock of the sight before them. For there stood Mabel – well, actually she wasn't standing. She was waddling all over the stage, the top two buttons of her dress undone, and slinging the "fur critters" around her head like a lasso as she attempted to give her best Marlene Dietrich imitation.

The sight was sickening enough, but to make

matters worse, she was singing ***If I Were a Rich Man*** to the top of her lungs, which for Mabel's lungs, was unusually loud.

"What on earth is she doing?" shrieked Miz Eudora, the vision before her more appalling than even she could imagine of Mabel.

"You know that flask of Horace's special blend you slipped into your 'new, used red leather pocket-book' in case you needed to put Mabel out of our misery?" asked Hattie.

"Yes," Miz Eudora answered slowly as her eyes shifted from the monstrosity in front of her to her friend. I could see the horror written all over her face as she knew what was coming next.

"It appears she obviously got her hands on it because it's over there on the table beside her purse."

"What is that she's bellowin' out up there?" Miz Eudora asked.

"It's a song from a Broadway musical," I offered.

"Only it's intended to be sung by a bass, not a woman," explained Hattie.

"Well, with all that 'digga, digga, digga' she's doing up there, all she's doing is digging all our graves deeper," observed Miz Eudora. "We've got to get our hands on that flask."

"First, we've got to get Mabel out of here," Hattie insisted. "She'll make a laughing stock out of all of us."

"I'm afraid it's too late for that," I said sympathetically, watching the crowd watch Mabel.

"Hey, honey," yelled a woman from the back of the bar, "don't you think you should change the words to 'If I ***had*** a rich man?'"

I should have anticipated what was coming next, but by the time I did, it was too late. For I caught sight of the back of Miz Eudora, her fopher coat thrown over her bright purple-and-red flannel gown and her striped, chenille socks hanging out of her red orthopedic shoes as she dashed for the stage.

"You obviously don't know Mabel," Miz Eudora answered before her sister-in-law had time to think about the question. "She'd come nearer to being a rich man than having one. Of course, she did have my baby brother, John G., but I don't have time to tell you about that now. It's past Mabel's curfew." She jerked Mabel up off the stage and slung the limp body – fur critters and all – over her shoulder, making a mad dash back past the table where her sister-in-law's purse lay.

I saw Miz Eudora's hand reach for the flask, but before she could get it, a man picked it up. "What's she got in this thing? I'd like a shot of whatever she's had."

"Me, too."

"Count me in."

"Pass that thing back here."

"Wonder how much it cost to buy a whole jug of that stuff?"

Shouts of agreement from "wanna-be partakers" came flying from around the room. ***How are we ever going to get out of this?*** I asked myself, aware that I didn't really want to know.

"You can't be whisking that woman out of here like that," yelled a man from the back corner, his voice bursting through the din of cacophony now in the lounge. "I've asked her to marry me."

I peered closely through the crowd to make sure Miz Eudora didn't pass out and drop Mabel, or worse, have a heart attack right there on the bar's floor. ***How would I ever explain that to Preacher Jake?*** I wondered, pinching myself to make sure I wasn't caught up in a nightmare. Sadly, I pinched myself until I bruised, but the nightmare was still there.

"An…I…sai…yeh…," came Mabel's slurred response as her head came up off Miz Eudora's shoulder and went spinning around in lasso fashion like her fur critters had been minutes earlier.

"Lady, you're about ten minutes too late," called one of the members of the band. The captain of the ship already came in here and performed the ceremony. He's already pronounced them man and wife."

"P'SHAA!" barked Miz Eudora. "I thought there was already a movie called ***Dumb and Dumber***."

Where'd she come up with that? She has no knowledge of movies.

Although I thought my words had been uttered in silence, they must have been louder than I realized, for Hattie answered, "She can read the newspaper, you know."

"Read the newspaper?" I gasped. "Oh, no, this will be all over Clay County after next week's edition."

"Not if no one mentions a word of this," Hattie assured me with a secretive wink.

"But, Mabel...we're talking about Mabel Toast Jarvis...whatever her last name is now...she can't ever keep her mouth shut," I wailed quietly.

"And Eudora Rumph owns enough property to buy that newspaper. Besides, the editor is a good friend of hers. Firstly, she'd never run a story like this. Secondly, the readers would think she's the one who'd been in the 'special blend' if the story ever ran."

I took a deep breath and looked at the sincerity written all over her face. "I guess you're right."

"Of course, I'm right," she said, wiping her brow with a hankie. "Now get over there and help Miz Eudora out of here before we both have to go over and throw her over our shoulders. I'm afraid this is more than even she can stand."

I made my way over to Miz Eudora and helped her set Mabel in a chair at the table where the purse and flask were.

"Land sakes," she said slowly, as if she were lost in another world, "if I'd known all this was going on down here, I'd have put on my black dress and mourning veil. Actually, I'd have given it to that groom of hers. That poor fellow won't know what hit him by morning."

Miz Eudora looked painfully back at the stage where the repulsive event had taken place. "She was singin' the right song, at least. Or at least she would have been if she'd have changed the words like that lady suggested. She surely didn't get a rich man, for he's the poorest soul I know right now. Can you imagine being hitched up to that thing for the rest of your life? I hope for his sake that he has something terminal."

Hattie looked at Mabel, who was now slung over the table and quiet. "I think he does."

"Aren't you going to take that flask with us?" I asked as Hattie and I turned and followed Miz Eudora toward the door.

"Nope," she answered simply.

"Surely you're not going to leave that for Mabel to get back into?" I asked again, this time in shock.

"It ain't for Mabel, it's for him. And I warned him about the whale of a headache he'd have when he wakes up after a snort of Horace's special blend." Miz Eudora looked sorrowfully back across the room at the two newlyweds. "In fact, there are no words to describe the kind of headache he's going to have when he wakes up with Mabel."

As hysterical as that comment was, it was also sadly true, making it impossible for me to laugh. I went back to the table where the "groom" now stood, looking over his "bride," and ridded him of the flask. "I'll be right back," I assured him. I took the flask to where Miz Eudora and Hattie waited, opened it and took a big swig, and then handed it to each of them. "You'd better down one. You'll need it by morning."

After we'd each chugged one down, I took the flask back to the "groom" and then ushered my two friends back to their cabins.

"Too bad she really ***wasn't*** a rich man," Miz Eudora finally said, as she opened her door. "Neither John G. nor us would have had to deal with her."

Suddenly she wheeled around, her face as bright as the stage lights of the Lounge. "Do you know what this means?" she asked. "We won't ever have to deal with Mabel again. That poor soul down there, he's got her – lock, stock and barrel – for the rest of his life."

I think she was ready to lunge into the "Mighty Mississippi" and swim ashore to make sure she'd never have to see Mabel again. But I could tell from the look on Hattie's face that she was no more optimistic about this being over than I was.

No one said another word as I made sure Miz Eudora and Hattie were each safe in their own cabins before returning to mine.

I'm afraid the morning is going to hold more than mourning, I warned myself as I pulled the covers over me, the untouched book on the pillow beside me.

FIVE

Here Comes the Bride, There Goes the Groom

"SADIE..., SADIE..., ARE you awake in there?"

Had I been in a casino instead of on a riverboat, I'd have laid my every dollar on the bet that I'd gotten exactly the same amount of sleep the night before as Miz Eudora. I had lain awake, staring at the same spot on the ceiling, the entire evening. I'd not moved, the book was still upside down and untouched, and my head had tossed and turned with so many thoughts that I didn't think my brain was capable of another thought.

"Sadie...,"

"I'll be right there," I answered groggily, but sure I had to get myself completely alert in the few seconds it would take me to get to the door.

"Sadie," Miz Eudora proclaimed again as I opened the door, "Horace got us into this mess and Horace is going to get us out!" She burst into my cabin and took a seat.

Before she had a chance to explain, I asked, "Were you able to sleep a wink last night?"

"Slept like a baby, I did," she replied, full of enthusiastic vigor. "They always did say that stuff would knock you right out, and it worked. That was a good idea you had passing that flask around a-fore we left the Lounge last night."

Dismayed and distraught, I stared at her in disbelief. ***Obviously I didn't take as big a snort as she did!*** I glared at her face, showing no signs of sleep loss. ***It's a good thing I was shut up in my room instead of a casino. I'd be penniless right now,*** I reminded myself. That's when the effect of her earlier words hit me. "Horace…?" I repeated slowly.

I began to wonder how big of a snort she really had taken the night before. ***Maybe her sleep was filled with dreams, so realistic she mistakenly perceived they were real. That's got to be it,*** I convinced myself. ***She had visions of Horace last night in her dreams and now she thinks he's still alive and with her on the riverboat.***

Suddenly I was totally alert. ***Oh, no! Now I don't know who's in worse shape – her or Mabel!*** I stood there with the thoughts of everything that had transpired, just from the time she'd entered my cabin, racing around in my head. ***Where's that flask? I need to go back to sleep!*** I chuckled to myself before my rest-deprived body reminded me, ***Back to sleep? You never got there to start with!***

"Why don't I get dressed," I asked, "and we'll talk about this over coffee?" I wasn't sure which one of us needed to have our head cleared, but I didn't think it would hurt either one of us at this rate.

"That's a great idea. I'll go fetch Hattie and lay out the plan. If Horace was here, I'd bake him the biggest apple pie he ever did see!" Miz Eudora headed for the door. "In fact, I think I'll bake it anyway when we get home and we'll all have a healthy-sized slice to celebrate. I didn't know Horace's celebration was going to last so long. Preacher Jake was right!"

I was in such shock that I had to force my eyes to blink. I pinched myself, as I had the evening before, and found that I was still stuck in the same nightmare. Although I had no inkling how Horace was going to rescue us from this, I was hoping he'd do it soon. ***And the sooner, the better!*** I surmised as I splashed cold water on my face and attempted to find attire appropriate for whatever episode this day was going to hold. I wasn't sure my wardrobe was ready for this kind of activity.

"Relax, Sadie," I seemed to hear. "How many times has my memory spoken to you from the grave?"

Leon? I asked mentally while peering around the cabin. Then I realized what had just happened. My Leon had led me to Smackass Gap. My Leon had led me to this wonderful creature named "Miz Eudora." My Leon had led me through many predicaments and situations – ***mostly predicaments!*** I concluded with a lighthearted laugh – since his passing. And it was all done through the memories I had of life with him.

I smiled as I threw on my best outfit. ***And now you're telling me that it's okay if Horace is having the same effect on his dearly beloved.*** With that, the smile that had formed on my face developed into a full-blown belly laugh for as hard as I tried, I couldn't imagine Horace fitting the mold of "dearly beloved."

But he must have been, Sadie, for the situation – excuse me, PREDICAMENT! – that you're in right now started out with the words, "Dearly beloved...,"

A welcome realization that my body no longer hurt, from the lack of sleep or the fear of what was coming next, spread throughout me like a wave of calm. Heaven only knows why, for whenever Miz Eudora and Mabel are in the same room, there's anything but calm. But for whatever reason - I think largely due to the feelings I'd held for my own "dearly beloved" – I knew that I was going to make it through this "occurrence."

"Occurrence?" That's a good one, Sadie. These experiences with Miz Eudora really are more from the world of the "occult" than they are from everyday life, I realized, still laughing, as I answered the door to see Miz Eudora and Hattie, who was still bug-eyed.

Too bad Leon wasn't around to talk to her, I thought as we headed for the dining room – the same room that had been the Lounge the evening before.

"NOW HERE'S WHAT we're gonna do," Miz Eudora began as we sat at the table, near where all this had happened the previous night.

Her words, combined with the voice in which she said them, brought to mind a John Wayne movie where he had all his cowpokes around him at the campfire and was telling them "what we're a-gonna do." The visual image of Miz Eudora on a horse, with Hattie and me following closely behind on our own horses, tearing into a campsite to "shoot 'em up and take the hostage back," was more than I could stand. An outburst of laughter accompanied my conclusion of ***Too bad I really didn't bring my boots and saddle.***

"Don't laugh yet," warned Hattie. "She hasn't told us the game plan. It might not be so funny."

Obviously she isn't seeing this through my eyes! I thought, imagining the exact same scenario, only this time with Miz Eudora holding up a flag of red and purple. ***The final touch***, I envisioned. ***Nobody would mess with an army of us Red Hatters and our Ragin' Hormones!***

"What I see here," our fearless leader continued, "is that Mabel's done gone and got herself hitched to some old coot." She hung her head. "Oh, my poor old baby brother, John G. Thank God, he's not here to see what a spectacle Mabel has made of herself."

I don't think I'd ever seen Miz Eudora so close to tears, as she pulled out a black piece of see-through fabric from her purse.

"What is that for?" I asked, wondering whether I really wanted to know, which was the same reaction I had often with her.

"It's a mourning veil. I borrowed it from my other cabin neighbor, Mrs. Bettie, to use as a part of the costume for my plan, except talking about John G. made me feel like I need it now instead of later."

"Now what we've got to do," she continued, pulling a hankie from her purse, "is to get her 'unhitched.'"

Back to the boots and saddles, I see. I imagined the scenario from before materializing in my mind's eye again, complete with a hitching post for the horses this time.

"Since this is largely Horace's fault...,"

I didn't bother to inform Miz Eudora that had she left the special blend in the cellar where Horace left it, we wouldn't be in this "worse-than-sour pickle."

"...we're going to let him get us out."

"Just exactly how do you propose to do that?"

asked Hattie.

"Hopefully better than that man who proposed to Mabel last night," she replied, indicating that she wanted the two of us to "shut up and listen." "I saw Horace trying to persuade one of his buddies not to marry a girl once and when he'd tried every tactic he could unsuccessfully, he started making things up about the gal so's the man would picture what she'd look like fifty years down the road. It worked. The man dropped that girl right then and there like a hot potato. Never even bothered to take her home. Since Mabel's already sixty more years down the road than that girl was back then, this ought not to be too hard."

Sounds logical to me! I concluded while chuckling inside.

Hattie, on the other hand, made a totally different recommendation. "Look at the bright side of this, Miz Eudora," she said cheerfully. "If she's married, then she's somebody else's worry. You won't have to deal with her all the time anymore."

Miz Eudora's eyes grew wide as that thought took shape in her mind. "Hey, you've got a point there. Maybe this is our just reward for having to put up with her ever since Horace's celebration." A huge smile spread across her face as she whipped the black mourning veil off her head and stuffed it back in the purse. "C'mon, ladies, this is going to be a ***real*** celebration. Even bigger and better than the one Preacher Jake had for Horace's passing."

I had no idea what was going on inside Miz Eudora's head, but I knew that whatever it was, I wasn't going to miss it, any more than I'd missed Horace's funeral service. It was sure to be memorable, whatever it was.

"Instead of telling him all the bad things, we'll make up good things. That'll be a whole lot harder in Mabel's case, but we're all three intellectual women. We'll go knock on the door and I'll start first. You ladies jump in wherever you want to with whatever you want to say. Got it?"

I nodded, feeling a "powerful urge" to reach for my imaginary lasso.

"But how do we know which door it is?" asked Hattie, being way too "intellectual" for "my liking."

"Honey, I can smell that brew a mile away," responded Miz Eudora. "Follow me."

We did as instructed and sure enough, Miz Eudora looked like a bloodhound going up and down the hallways until she came to the right cabin. Only she forgot to knock and bolted right in the door. She also found it impossible to find anything good to say, so she started with, "That woman's got more warts than a witch. You could put her on display at the county fair and make a bundle. Her cooking's so bad that the neighbor's dogs won't eat it. She's more stubborn than my mule, Clyde."

I stood there, my mouth gaping, as she whirled out insult after insult, wondering "where in tarnation" she came up with all of them.

Hattie was also watching, enjoying the spectacle of seeing a bit of what Mabel gave to others in grade school – since they'd grown up in the same school – until she could stand it no longer. "And she's had so many face lifts that her belly button is her mouth. Just don't ask what those bags under her eyes are!"

My mouth dropped nearly to my own belly button. I couldn't believe the tongue lashing these two women were giving Mabel. A rare occurrence, I actually felt sorry for "the old bag." That thought, though – combined with the calamity of what happened next – quickly relapsed into the comical scene I was caught up in.

For until that moment, I'm not sure Mabel had an inkling as to where she was. She got a glimpse of the person beside her, gave a gigantic gasp in the same breath as a thunderous "Ahhh-Whooop!", and pulled the covers up around her neck. "Who are you and what are you doing in my bed?"

"The old coot" didn't get an opportunity to answer, for Miz Eudora blurted out, "He's your husband and it's his bed, not yours. Honestly, Mabel Toast Jar...Jar...Jar...,"

She paused, finding it impossible to "muster up"

the strength to even add her family's name onto that of Mabel's. "You're an embarrassment to our family name, that's what you are!" she finally managed. "What would poor John G. say? And worse than that, what would Pa, the poor thing, say? I'm sure he's up there on that mountainside turnin' from side to side in his grave. Why, I bet's he's a-churnin' so hard that he's layin' in a tub of butter instead of a coffin!

"Besides," she went on, not even allowing me time to laugh, "you're the one that said, 'I do,' to him and you don't know his name, how do you expect us to? Land sakes, you done gone and married a man without a name. Ain't that a fine 'ne'er-do-well?' Saying, 'I do,' I reckon!"

She reared back for what I foresaw as another round. And believe me, I was ***not*** disappointed.

"P'SHAA! And what about you going on with that 'To have and to hold!' How could you want to 'have' something like him?" she asked, pointing at the man whose eyes were now bulging out of his head. "If you'd have told us you'uz in the market for an old goat, there was plenty of them back behind Smiley's Funeral Parlor. Luther Smiley would have probably let you have one for free. Not to mention that business of 'to hold.' Land sakes, Mabel, I doubt you could hold it even if you wanted to! You probably forgot how."

At that point, my laughter not only erupted, but

became so uncontrollable that no one was able to speak over it until I finally gathered myself, imaginary boots and saddle and all.

"You have nothing to worry about, my dear lady," assured "the man without a name." "I took one look at her, this Mabel person this morning, when I regained my…my...uh…composure and lost my appetite," he said. "The goods are untouched. You may have her back, no harm done."

"No harm done?" Miz Eudora continued to rant. "I have to drag her home and try to explain to Preacher Jake, let alone Grover Swicegood, what happened aboard this wooden fish. I'll be lucky if they ever allow me to darken the door of the church again, and I'm as good as booted out of our family plot in the church cemetery. Sadie'll have to coerce the neighbors to plant me next to one of my fields on the side of the Chunky Gal Mountain."

"Why don't we sit down and talk about this like grown men?" the man asked, reaching to throw back the sheet.

"NO!" screamed Miz Eudora, throwing her new purse up over her eyes. "You just stay right where you are and we'll talk about this all we need to. I don't want to see any more of you than I already have. And furthermore," she said, pausing to get a fourth wind, "I don't intend to talk to you like a grown man. Just because Mabel parades around the stage and bellows out about wishing she was a rich man doesn't mean I do!"

She halted her speech and glared straight at Mabel. "And while we're on the subject, you hussy, I've wished you were a lot of things in my lifetime, but a rich man wasn't one of them! Where in tarnation did you come up with wantin' to be a rich man? Even Horace knew he couldn't drink enough of that stuff to make him think he was a rich man. P'SHAA! A rich man, I reckon!"

"I'm sure we can speak to…'the groom'…about an annulment," I opted, offering everyone a mite's reprieve, but also afraid I might spew out blood from my tongue having been bitten so many times during her tirade.

"An annulment? What's that?" she asked, slowing down for a second.

"You know, where you get out of it as fast as you got in it," answered Hattie.

"Is there really such a thing?" Miz Eudora asked, looking to me.

I nodded my head, trying not to laugh aloud again.

"How do we go about doing that?" Miz Eudora's question was directed at Hattie since she seemed to have the right explanation.

No one got to answer the question for a loud banging started on the door.

"Who in the world?" asked Mabel. "Somebody do something. I can't be seen like this. What would my friends at the Myers Park Country Club say?"

I wanted to inform her that some of them might actually pay her to advise them on how she'd gotten into this predicament, but decided that opinion was better left unsaid.

"Excuse me," called a man's voice, equally as loud as the banging on the door. "I must speak to you right away."

"Which one of us?" Miz Eudora called back, causing all eyes to shoot straight at her, some of them filled with poisonous darts.

"Which ***one*** of you?" the voice replied in panic. "You mean there's more than one of you in there?" The banging on the door came to an abrupt halt as he asked, "Oh dear, what kind of monster have I created?"

"Don't worry about that, Mister," answered Miz Eudora in a reassuring tone. "Mabel was already a monster before she got herself in this mess."

Seeing as I was closest to the door, I walked over to it – mainly as an escape from another laughing bout – slipped it open and stepped outside, indicating for the others to stay quiet while I did so. Within a few minutes, I realized the web was much more tangled than it seemed, even from inside the "honeymoon" cabin, yet laced with a much easier resolution than seemed possible. I breathed a sigh of relief as I motioned for the man to follow me into the cabin.

"Mister...," I began and then paused, turning toward him. "I'm sorry, but I didn't get your name."

"Doesn't anybody on this boat have a name?" huffed Hattie, making it hard for me to attempt a reasonable and serious remedy to the situation.

"Swicegood," he said. "My name's Swicegood."

Miz Eudora gulped and I thought we were going to have to pick her up off the floor.

"Did...you...say...'Swicegood?'" repeated Hattie in horror.

Maybe this would have been easier if he* hadn't *had a name, I deduced, feeling more like a detective again than one of John Wayne's cowpokes.

"Yes, ma'am. Swicegood. Julius Swicegood."

I bowed my head and covered my mouth, pretending to cough.

"Do you by chance have relatives in North Carolina?" Mabel asked in a quiet and fearful tone, something I'd never known her to possess.

"Yes, ma'am," Mr. Swicegood answered with an eager Boy Scout kind of nod, "my daddy's brother, who is my Uncle Grover, but I'm sure you wouldn't know where he lives," he continued solemnly. "It's a tiny community in the mountains, in Clay County. He told us what it's called, but I'm sure he made it up. There can't really be a place named Smackass Gap."

If I'd had any smelling salts, that would have

been a good time to reach for them. Luckily, there was a bed for Miz Eudora to fall onto. I thought, from the look on her face, that at this point she was ready to crawl under the covers with Mr. "Whatever-his-name-is."

"Why don't you proceed with the story?" I suggested.

"First I must apologize," he began, looking directly at the newlyweds. "I must have had a little too much of whatever that was you were passing around last night," he said to Mabel. "Anyway, I got to feeling a little too, shall we say, 'comfortable...,'"

"If you had a little too much of that stuff," blasted Miz Eudora, "we shall say 'plastered!'"

"Yes, well," he went on, cowering a bit, "your real wife came up to me," he said to the groom, "and,"

"My real wife?" the groom interrupted. "My real wife is back home in...,"

He paused when he saw Mr. Swicegood shaking his head in disagreement.

"She's on the Delta Queen," Mr. Swicegood informed him. "She wanted to teach you a lesson for going on your 'business trips' and having too much fun without her. When she saw how you were behaving last night, she devised a plan to teach you never to do it again."

"You mean his wife devised a plan to get him married off to Mabel so she wouldn't be married to him any longer?" asked Hattie.

"Oh, no, ma'am," answered Mr. Swicegood. "She loves him alright. She wants to keep the flame alive in their marriage, so she's trying to make sure he takes her along on his trips instead of leaving her behind."

"Leave her behind?" stormed Mabel. "I'll kick her behind from here to yonder if I get my hands on her."

"You'll do no such thing," said the groom in what was the couple's first marital spat. "She's the best thing that ever happened to me. I've never pulled a stunt like this in my life. I don't know what you had in that flask last night, but it was worse than any 'Love Potion #9' that I've ever tried in New Orleans."

This time it was the groom who bowed his head.

I've never seen this much head-bowing in one room, even during Preacher Jake's revival services, I thought to myself. ***It's a good thing, too,*** I surmised, ***for after this trip, there's quite a few people that better be asking for forgiveness!***

Mr. "Whatever-his-name-is" took a deep breath and stated, "Like I said, my wife, my Tootsie, is the best thing that ever happened to me. I've never taken her on business trips with me because, frankly, I didn't want her to be bored while I was sitting in offices all day long. Then it got to be fun to fool around with the guys…I don't mean ***really*** fool around, just have a good time. I guess this good time got a little out of hand."

"A little?" asked Hattie. "I'd hate to see what you'd call a lot where you're from!"

"Maybe he's from Texas," commented Miz Eudora. "I've always heard they do things in a big way out there."

Remind me never to take this crew to Texas, I thought, making a mental note.

Mr. Swicegood cleared his throat in an attempt to regain everyone's attention. "The bottom line is, I'm not really the captain and you're not really married. I'm just the bass player of the band and happened to be dressed like the captain last night. Your wife said you were too…uh…'out of it' to do anything wrong and she was sure that when you woke up beside this woman, you'd never again leave her at home."

"Does this mean that Mabel's ours again?" Miz Eudora asked, stupefied as she stared back and forth from Julius Swicegood to "the groom." "I think I'd better put the mourning veil back on," she said, reaching into her purse. "It's not bad enough that we're stuck with Mabel, but that was the most pitiful story I ever did hear tell of."

She looked at the "newly un-newlyweds" and ordered, "Mabel, get yourself up and together. Well…, as together as you can get. I'll wait out in the hallway for you to make sure you don't get lost on the way to breakfast."

Hattie and I followed our fearless leader out the door – ***minus the horses, boots and saddles*** – as did Mr. Julius Swicegood, who bowed his head in respect to us and then quickly made his way in the opposite direction from that which we were going. It wasn't any time until Mabel joined us, saying not a word, as she straightened her hat and put on her bright red lipstick, dabbing a little on her cheeks and rubbing it in.

Rubbing it in, I thought to myself. The urge that followed was too strong to resist. ***Either that or you've been around Eudora Rumph too long, Sadie Calloway!*** "Well, look at it this way, Mabel," I said calmly. "At least you won't have to go home with a horseshoe trophy!"

"Honey, there wasn't any chance of that," noted Miz Eudora, completely serious. "Horace would have come nearer landing one of those than Mabel."

"Now you listen here, you…you…," started Mabel.

"Yes, Miz Eudora, Mabel's ours again," I wanted to say.

I glanced at Hattie, who uttered softly so that only I could hear, "Things are back to normal."

Normal? I asked myself and then laughed. "As normal as it gets with those two," I replied, causing Hattie to also enjoy a good laugh. "Who wants to be normal when you can spend your days with that pair?"

It was then that I realized this was our last day on the riverboat and how much I was looking forward to getting back to Smackass Gap and my own home with these ladies. ***And thanks to "that pair," the trip ended with a bang.*** I smiled. ***Or at least the banging of a door!***

We took a few more steps. "I don't know about you, Hattie Crow, but I'm ready for a good night's sleep. Do you reckon Mr. 'Whatever-his-name-is' has anything left in that flask?"

"Honey, you'd better leave that with him. I've got a feeling he's going to need more 'special blend' than Horace made his entire life when he sees his wife."

"Do you realize we escaped that entire escapade and never did find out the name of the man Mabel 'married?'"

"That's probably a good thing," Hattie replied. "It means less chance of anybody ever getting wind of this."

"Especially Grover Swicegood," I chuckled. "I have a feeling his nephew would as soon die as to have his behavior trickle out in the family gossip."

"I have a feeling you're right," Hattie seconded.

I put my arm through hers and hummed the *Bridal March* from Wagner's "Lohengrin" for a few seconds before singing, "Here comes the bride, there goes the groom…,"

SIX

Monkey's Eyebrow and Possum Trot

"WELCOME TO PADUCAH, ladies," greeted a man in a robust voice as we strolled down the ramp from the Delta Queen. "I'm delighted to see that you have a real Southern Belle in the group."

"Oh, thank you," replied Mabel, doing her best to give a demure blush and smile.

"Land sakes, Mabel!" exclaimed Miz Eudora. "He's not talking about you. He's referring to Mrs. Bettie in her hooped skirt."

We all four watched as the man, dressed in a bright red blazer with a brass tag that read "Ambassador to Paducah," took Mrs. Bettie's hand and bestowed a kiss on it while she curtsied and gave a "real" demure blush and smile, one befitting of a true Southern lady.

"Why, I feel exactly like I'm in the pages of ***Gone with the Wind***," said Hattie. "Watching Bettie and her husband, John, dressed so finely and seeing the Delta Queen and the Mississippi River in the background, why I could swear that I'm staring straight at Scarlett O'Hara and Rhett Butler. It's like Margaret Mitchell wrote us right into her novel and Mark Twain took us over. I fully expect to see Tom Sawyer and Huck Finn any minute now."

"You have to go on up to Hannibal, Missouri, to see those two," advised the man in the red blazer.

"This place is incredible," I added. "Take a look at the facades of all these buildings along the riverfront. They look as if they haven't changed one bit since they were first built."

A woman, also dressed in a red blazer that bore the brass Ambassador tag, stepped forward. "I, too, would like to welcome you fine folks to Paducah, Kentucky. I heard you talking about our buildings," she said, looking in the direction of our small foursome. "Many of them have been restored to look exactly as they did back in the days the businesses were founded. Our motto here in Paducah is 'Preserve, Not Rebuild.'"

"That's a great way of thinking," roared a man from the back of the crowd who'd exited the boat. "All our town wants to do is tear down everything and see how big and odd they can rebuild something, and all you see is a tall mass of glass and steel. Huh! Nine times out of ten you're looking at it wondering what shape it is or what it's supposed to represent."

Sounds of a common understanding swept through the crowd of river cruisers as the woman went on to give a brief history of the market area and the characters who had been instrumental in the shaping of Paducah. In agreement with Hattie, I felt like I'd stepped into the pages of another era rather than stepping off the riverboat into a city.

"This is the very first building ever built along the riverfront," explained the tour guide. "Because we are located at the confluence of many waterways, Paducah, originally called 'Pekin,' has always been known for its commerce. There are only two cities named Paducah in the United States. The other is in Texas and it was named after us.

"And for those of you interested in our historically beautiful architecture, Paducah has twenty downtown city blocks on the National Register of Historic Places." Both well-informed and courteous, the woman held the attention of everyone in the group, but I could tell that Miz Eudora was "itchin'" to get to the quilt show and see her winning entry.

Not that I blamed her, I was "about to bust" myself at the thought of this precious lady and her ***Precious Memories*** quilt winning an international award. It was already exciting enough to have won a cruise on the Delta Queen – ***even without Mabel and her proposition of marriage...or should I call that***

supposition? I laughed to myself – but to see your hours of long, hard work hanging for the entire world to see. I didn't know what thrilled me more, knowing the unassuming lady who won, or knowing that an international winner had come out of "little old Smackass Gap," as had been the scuttlebutt back home.

Miz Eudora was at least polite enough to listen to the tour guide's presentation, but the minute the woman paused and asked, "Any questions?" Miz Eudora grabbed Hattie and me, hauling us away from the group as quickly as possible.

"What about Mabel?" Hattie wondered aloud.

"She's on her own now," Miz Eudora replied, wasting no time. "If she can get herself married on board a riverboat, she can surely take care of herself in Paducah.

That perception bothered me more than I cared to think about, for it was exactly right. There was no telling how Mabel could take care of herself here. "What happens if she gets lost and gets back on the Delta Queen?" I asked, trying not to sound too overly concerned.

"Maybe she'll get married again!" was all the answer I got. It was the only one I needed, for back down the street behind us, I heard, "W—A—I—T…, Wait…for…me!" There was no mistaking that voice.

"Keep running!" ordered Miz Eudora. "We should be able to lose her in this mob of people." Our fearless leader darted in and out of people like a first-string halfback as I heard Mabel's screams get farther and farther behind. She stopped only when she came to a police officer who was directing people.

"How do we get into the Quilt Expo at the convention center?" she asked.

"Slow down," he said pleasantly, "it isn't going anywhere. At least this week."

I immediately liked his demeanor. So far I'd only met three residents of Paducah, and thus far, the town was on a roll, as sure as if it had been the big paddlewheel of the Delta Queen churning the waters of the Mississippi.

"It might not be going anywhere, but Mabel sure is. If we don't hurry, she'll catch up."

"Who's Mabel?" the officer asked.

"My sister-in-law," answered Miz Eudora, but…,"

"Say no more," he interrupted. "I've got one of those, too."

"Does yours wear fur critters around her neck?"

"Nope," he said, shaking his head, "worse. She wears…,"

"Eudora…Eudora Rumph!"

"I've gotta go," shouted Miz Eudora. "Which way?"

"Straight over there and take a right through those doors. I'll lose her for you. What does she look like?"

"You can't miss her," Miz Eudora yelled behind her, dragging Hattie and me as she went.

We got inside the building and found a spot to hide while watching Mabel with the officer. He pointed in a direction opposite from where we were and she took off as hard as she could go.

"You did it, Miz Eudora," I said, congratulating her. "Let's go see the quilt now."

"No, that man's the one what did it," she replied. "I want to go back out there and find out exactly what he did for the next time I need to lose her."

Hattie and I followed her, suspecting we might also find the information in question handy at some point down the road. ***Literally and figuratively!***

"What in the world did you say to her?" asked Miz Eudora.

"When she asked me if that was the location for the quilt show, I told her, 'No, it was the tractor pull.' I informed her that the quilt show was ten miles down the road the other way."

"And she fell for it?" Hattie asked, finding it hard to believe that even Mabel was that out of touch.

"You wouldn't believe how many people fall for it," he said. "I love telling people that. You'd think when they see a thousand women in front of them all heading toward the front door like it's the 'After Christmas Sale,' they'd know what it is, but then they stop to ask me if that's the quilt show. You just wouldn't believe how many people stop and ask me foolish questions."

"How do you like that, Sadie? And I thought I got all the foolish questions," Miz Eudora commented with a huge guffaw.

"But it wasn't a lie," he defended. "There is another quilt exhibit down the road there. In fact, there are several all over town. You might want to also catch some of them while you're here. By that time, your sister-in-law will have discovered that the real quilt show is back here and you'll miss her."

"Thanks for the help," offered Miz Eudora. "This is the most excitin' thing that's ever happened to me in my entire life and I didn't want her here to ruin it for me."

"It's quite alright," said the police officer. "I pretty much figured that. Comes with the territory after all the dumb questions."

We headed back for the front entrance of the convention center when he called behind us, "Hey, if you get home and anyone asks you where in the world Paducah is, you tell them it's between Possum Trot and Monkey's Eyebrow."

"Monkey's Eyebrow?" repeated Miz Eudora, stopping in place. "Is there really a place with such a strange name?"

"There surely is," he answered proudly.

"Why, I never heard of such a funny sounding name for a place to live," she replied, her comment causing people to stop and listen to their conversation amidst muffled laughter.

"And where, if I might ask, do you live, ma'am?" the officer asked.

"Smackass Gap, North Carolina," Miz Eudora answered equally proud. "It's at the bottom of Chunky Gal Mountain."

I watched with great amusement at the man's reaction as the crowd now burst into a roar.

"Smack...," he repeated slowly, hesitant to say the last half of the word.

"Yes, Smackass Gap," Miz Eudora said again, filling in the blank for him.

"There's really a place named that?" he asked, disbelief in his eyes.

I could hardly wait to see his face by the time Miz Eudora finished filling in "the Gap" for him, giving him the history of the name and the area. I felt certain she had a bumper sticker to share with him. ***In fact, after giving Mabel the slip the way he did,*** I wagered, ***she might even give him half a mountain.***

"We all live there, Mrs. Hattie and Sadie and myself," Miz Eudora continued. She leaned toward the man. "Mabel thinks she lives there, but she's not really one of us. She's just a Smackass 'wannabe.' When she found out how high-uppity the people was just across the Georgia border from us, she decided to come, her fur critters around her neck in tow, and try to horn in on the high society on the other side of the lake. You see, we've got a large body of water at home, too, and it separates the 'haves' from the 'haves not.'"

Miz Eudora gave one of her robust cackles. "The only thing is, them folk on the other side of Lake Chatuge think they're the ones that's got it, but what they don't know is that we got everything in the world right there in Clay County. And we had it back way before the "big wigs" came in there and dammed up the lake.

"Monkey's Eyebrow," she said again, punching me. "Ain't that about the funniest place you ever heard tell of?"

I smiled at the policeman, whose face was nearly as red as the ambassador's jacket had been, and who was still shaking his head in utter disbelief. ***Well, she's done it***, I said to myself. Miz Eudora had little more than "stepped off the boat" – ***literally*** – before she'd made her mark on the town of Paducah, Kentucky. Truth is, I'd not thought about it, but if I had, I'm sure I'd have expected nothing less. My smile grew in anticipation of how big that mark would be by the time we left town.

Suddenly, I felt a huge swell of pride at sharing the name of my home and my friendship with the character that was the "pride of Smackass," as the ***Clay***

County Progress had dubbed her. It was the first time I had been away "from home" since my move to Clay County and somehow, in my settling there, I'd not once considered what it would be like to tell people where I was from. This was going to be a wonderful vacation. I simply hated that Leon wasn't along for the ride. ***Or the 'trip,'*** as I was sure this was going to be "a trip and a half," as they said in the South. ***In more ways than one!*** I chuckled quietly to myself as I looked at Miz Eudora and Hattie and thought of the busload of Red Hatters who would descend on Paducah, Kentucky – between Monkey's Eyebrow and Possum Trot – in a couple more days.

SEVEN

Puffy, A Girl's Best Friend

THE LOOK ON Miz Eudora's face as she turned the corner and saw the ribbon and certificate hanging on her prize-winning quilt made the entire trip, including the bruised palms, worth every mile. Never had I seen such pride, masked in humility, in my life. I stared at her in sharp contrast to all the other women lining the aisle and making the rounds to see the submissions, and the winners, and take in new ideas for their own projects.

It was obvious from the looks of the spectators that many had machines to do their work and cut their hours. They, having traveled from all over the world to claim their greatly-deserved stardom, were surrounded by reporters and flashing cameras. Yet here stood this sweet, unassuming little elderly lady, the winner in the original handwork category, by her simple means.

Once Miz Eudora overcame the initial shock of seeing her work displayed in such an ominous fashion, she walked leisurely and methodically toward it and placed her hand on the quilt, looking like someone reaching out to a concrete "thing" to make sure they're not caught up in a dream too good to be true.

"Ahhh!" gasped a woman behind her.

"I can't believe she did that," balked another woman.

"You can't touch that quilt!" exclaimed yet another. "Can't you read the sign?"

Miz Eudora, without removing her hand, slowly turned her head. Without anyone saying a word, whispers sifted through the crowd as people put the work, the name and this common woman's appearance together to realize they were looking at one of the best quilters in the entire world. From the looks on their faces, I half expected some of them to bow down to her as if she were majestic royalty.

***Sadie Calloway, in this moment and in this hall, she* is *the queen*.**

I wondered if there was that same magical moment for each of the winners and suspected that, in their own right and way, there was. Maybe not the same as it was for this woman though, for this was the first time she'd seen the world outside her own little circle. Outside Smackass Gap.

Except for that mistaken trip to "Hotlanta"

where she was nearly exposed to the Chippendales. I grinned at the play on words that had just romped through my mind. ***Or rather, were nearly "exposed" to her!***

Although I'd seen the quilt upon its completion, it took on a spectacularly unique splendor under these lights, where it hung so majestically, the various narrow strips of red and purple fabrics culminating into the perfect border outlining the hand-sewn work of art. The simple objects of each of her many hand-stitched appliqués came to life as ***Precious Memories*** did exactly what it was supposed to do for this contest, and that was to tell a story in pictures.

Miz Eudora's story included the beautifully serene mountains of the Great Smokies, her farmhouse with its bright green roof, an apple pie piled high with "the morning's pickin's", ice cream cones – one each of butter pecan, strawberry and lime sherbet, a stately Christmas pine, a red hat, her red self-painted eyeglasses, a busload of Red Hatters with their little heads sticking out the windows, Horace's tombstone on the hillside of the church cemetery, and yes, even a couple of horseshoes. I had shared enough of life's experiences with this dear lady, in the short time I'd known her, to understand the significance of each of the appliqués, all except for one. It was of an adorable pink pig which, unbeknownst to me, I was to learn more about in the next few minutes than a body needed to know.

As I watched the crowd - that seconds earlier had been ready to "crucify" this lowly creature for her wrongdoing – mellow into an adoring audience, people reached out to shake her hand and congratulate her.

"How long did it take you to make this?"

"Did you have a pattern?"

"Who taught you to quilt like this?"

The air was suddenly filled with a barrage of questions as the crowd settled around Miz Eudora, their cameras now zoomed on her and her award-winning work of art. It was then that I noticed a familiar voice rising above the others, as its owner attempted to plow her way closer to the star.

"This is Eudora Rumph, my sister-in-law, you know. She's the older, ***much*** older, sister of my late husband, Dr. John G. Jarvis. It was him who taught her everything she knew. The women of their family have been known as the best quilters in those Great Smoky Mountains for generations. Why, their mother...,"

I watched as Miz Eudora's head gradually turned from again admiring the ribbon and certificate hanging on her quilt to staring a hole straight through Mabel. ***And to think I laughed at the trivial notion that the yellow "crime scene" tape downstairs had been due to a murder caused by quilting needles.*** Now I was about to see that very thing happen in front of my eyes.

Mabel dropped her words in mid-sentence as she read the expression on her sister-in-law's face. It didn't take "much smarts" to see that the words, "If you say one more word, you'll find yourself sewn inside my next quilt!" were written all over Miz Eudora's face. However, the look on her face hinted that she had also many more words to offer on the situation. I actually found it amusingly comical that the one time Mabel found anything good to say about Eudora Rumph was the time that she was told to keep quiet.

Of course, any time she opened her mouth was a bad reminder for Miz Eudora that now, not only did she bear the brunt of being a widow, she bore the brunt of putting up with her "dear baby brother's" widow. ***Isn't there some verse in the Bible like that? Something like "to those with little, much is given?"***

Mabel didn't move from her position of assumed honor, in close proximity to the cause of all this commotion, but she at least kept her comments low enough that Miz Eudora was unable to hear her over the din of other questions and comments flying at her. She had no intention, warned or not, to miss this opportunity to bask in the glory of being the "next of kin" to this international star.

Next of kin? I repeated to myself. For whatever reason, it was the first time that reality had crossed my mind and I instantly prayed that I'd be far from the scene if Mabel ever dared to verbalize that fact in front of Miz Eudora. Cringing down my spine from that scary thought, I focused my attention back to the warm reception Miz Eudora was receiving from all the other quilters. Seeing her so accepted by her own, tens of thousands of women who also excelled in the art of quilting, turned the cringes into a warm fuzzy ripple as I listened to her exchange ideas with her comrades.

I was about to suggest that Mabel join me for a bite of lunch when I noticed a woman approach Miz Eudora. There was a purpose about the woman's stature and her movements that told me there was something more to her than an adorning fan. My ears attempted to hear the woman's words but all I caught, between Mabel's rantings of being left out of the loop, was a glimpse of her handing Miz Eudora a card and looking down at her watch.

Either she's making an appointment with Miz Eudora or she has an appointment. I intended to find out which and make sure that someone wasn't planning to take advantage of my dear neighbor.

Cool it, Sadie! She got here by herself, she can get out of here by herself.

I decided it best to leave the "sleeping dog" – Mabel – lie and pretend that some noteworthy person had not just introduced herself to Miz Eudora. Knowing Mabel as I wished I didn't, she'd "hightail it off" after the woman to make her acquaintance and share the fact that she was responsible – in who knows what way – for this ***Precious Memories*** quilt and quilter being in Paducah as one of the winners of the world-renowned Quilt Contest.

The winning quilt wasn't the only thing about Miz Eudora receiving attention. "I've been admiring your beautiful quilted jacket," commented a woman donning a red hat. "I would give anything to have one like it. I'd be the envy of all my Purple Mountain Majesties."

"I love the skirt," said another. "Look," she pointed out to a third friend dressed in purple and red. "It's a real quilt."

"Well, not exactly," explained Miz Eudora. "It's only pieced like a quilt top. It is a crazy quilt design. I'm glad you noticed." She took off her jacket and demonstrated, adding, "This jacket, though," she said while turning it inside-out, "has the batting and the backing, and has been stitched just like a full-size quilt."

"Would you look at those beautiful stitches?" admired one of the onlookers. "What kind of machine do you use to do that?"

"Machine?" repeated Miz Eudora. "Honey, I did every one of those stitches by hand."

"You don't use a long-armed machine?" asked another woman in shock.

Miz Eudora held out her arm and gave it a scrutinizing look as if determining its length. "Honey, I've never been blessed with a long arm in my whole life. Why, even my Horace didn't have very long arms." She blushed. "But they were long enough to snuggle up to me before he went and forgot how." Her blush turned into a somber glare at the ground. "I surely do wish at times that Mrs. Phoebe could have been around back then and brought that horseshoe trophy to our house. It might have joggled his memory a bit." She grinned as the blush returned. "It might have joggled something else, too."

Determined that was a path we didn't need to travel, I suggested, "Miz Eudora, would you be willing to make a few of these skirts and sell them?"

"Sell them?" she asked, getting back to the subject at hand. "Who in the world would want to buy these things? Why, we made them simply because we didn't have anything else to wear. You rich kids might have had your fancy duds, but we were lucky to have Ma find us some garments at the Rag Shake."

"Rag Shake?" repeated someone from the back of the crowd.

"Whatever is a Rag Shake? Is that what you called your thrift store back then?"

"It's where someone ought to have taken Eudora Jarvis and shook some sense into her when she was a child. Lord knows, she could have surely used a good dose of it." Mabel's comment went unnoticed, except by me, as all eyes focused on Miz Eudora for the answer.

"Thrift store?" asked Miz Eudora in shock. "P'SHAA! Why, none of us had any money to go to the store. And there was no such thing as a thrift store. Those that had anything wore it until there was nothing left. Leastways, not enough to sell at a thrift store. Not a thread was wasted. Even the scraps were used for something.

She turned her body so that she was facing the crowd, and went on like a great orator. "When Pa killed a hog, he'd take either John G. or myself into town to Chinquapin's store and buy us a pair of shoes from that nice Mr. Tiger who ran the general store. We never got a pair of shoes at the same time, though."

"Mrs. Rumph," called a voice from the crowd. "I heard someone ask if you'd be willing to make and sell your handiwork. I'd love to have a skirt like yours, and I'd be willing to pay whatever it costs."

"Well, the first thing," Miz Eudora answered, "is that people don't call me Mrs. Rumph if they know me. You call me 'Miz Eudora' like all my other friends." Her eyes sent a firm message in the direction of Mabel, who had never once called her "Miz" Eudora. "The second thing is that I've never charged a person for anything in my life. All my handiwork has been done as gifts for others. I wouldn't have a clue whether to charge a dollar or five dollars."

A loud gasp wafted through the crowd.

"Clearly this woman has no business sense," spoke Mabel, moving toward Miz Eudora and throwing her right arm toward her sister-in-law like an attorney defending a client. "I'll be happy to talk to you about this project, should it materialize. My husband, the late ***Dr.*** John G. Jarvis, had a professional business and I know all about taking care of customers and charging them."

"You know all about swindling them," Miz Eudora accused. "Pa told me one time how much John G. made for sticking his hand up…for seeing his patients. It was highway robbery, I tell you, and it had your name written all over it."

"I'll have you know that your brother did a lot for the advancement of proctology." Mabel turned to the crowd. "He had the most prestigious office and examination rooms in all of Charlotte, making him the envy of his circle. Why, he was even laid for viewing in his favorite examination room upon his passing."

"Land sakes, Mabel, the next thing you'll be telling them is how he concocted that 'special rectal paste' that sounded like something you'd coat fried chicken with instead of sticking up your…,"

Seeing visions of peppermint patties on the crest of the horizon, I quickly asked, "Hattie, did they have rag shakes where you grew up?"

"No, they did not!" fumed Mabel. "She grew up in Hickory where I did and we most certainly did not need to have rag shakes. We're the very ones who sent those poor ragamuffins our hand-me-downs and leftovers."

"While you're going on so, Mabel," Miz Eudora informed her, "you need to know that John G. grew up wearing clothes from the Rag Shake, too. For all you know, he was wearing hand-me-downs that had come from your brother, Milton T. Toast. So don't you go getting all high and mighty. He growed up the very same way I did and had a good life until you got your grubby ole hands on him. We all know you must have bushwhacked him or he'd have come to his senses long before he went down the aisle with you."

"May I try on your jacket, Miz Eudora?" asked one of the onlookers who'd obviously been so enamored with the crafter's work that she'd missed all the flying sparks.

Miz Eudora handed the jacket, which she was still holding, to the young woman. It was a perfect fit as the fan twirled around to give the full effect to the crowd.

"That would look good on any one," noted one of the women. "Look how it falls on her body."

"I want to try it," said another.

"Me, too," chimed yet another.

Before long ladies were lined up to try on the jacket.

"I'd love to see the skirt on me," spoke another voice from the crowd.

"That's where I draw the line," replied Miz Eudora. "I'll not be seen standing here in this crowd in my petticoat." Her eyes darted toward her sister-in-law again. "Mabel's the only person I know who shows her 'hiney' by going out in public without her skirt on. Would you believe she showed up at my Horace's funeral in her black slip and no skirt? Preacher Jake had said it was going to be a celebration, but it was all but that when Mabel pranced herself down the aisle that a way."

I heard snickers lightly ricocheting off the walls, muffled by all the quilts hanging in the room.

"If I knew the owner wouldn't mind, I'd invite all you ladies over to where we're staying at Ada's Bed-and-Breakfast for a private fitting this evening."

"I wouldn't mind a bit," shot a reply from the back of the hall. Heads turned to see Mrs. Ada standing there. "There's a beautiful parlor in the front where there would be plenty of room to try on the skirt."

"But would you make them and sell them to us, Miz Eudora?" pleaded one young woman. "I think you can see from all of us congregated here that we'd love to have a Miz Eudora original."

Hattie stepped forward. "I'll bet Sadie would

help me do the paperwork and you could take measurements for orders."

"How much do you think a skirt would cost?" asked the woman who'd wanted to try it on.

"Tell you what," I offered. "Anyone who is interested can drop by Ada's Bed-and-Breakfast between say…seven and nine and we'll have a price for you by then."

Mrs. Ada began giving directions to her home, otherwise known as her lodging establishment, as the spiral of interest in Miz Eudora's new line of clothing continued.

"In that amount of time," added Hattie, "Eudora could have a couple of other ideas for original handcrafted items. She's a real whiz at drawing up things in her head."

"She draws up things in her head, alright," mumbled Mabel, but not nearly low enough to keep Miz Eudora from hearing it.

"Mabel, the only thing that needs to be drawn up right now is your,"

"Miz Eudora, why don't we run back over to Eleanor Burns' store and let you start getting some ideas together for your fans."

"…mouth," Miz Eudora finished, much to my relief.

"Are you really going to allow us to give you orders this evening, Miz Eudora?"

"I'm going to call all my friends and tell them," said one lady.

"Not me!" exclaimed another. "I want to be the only one wearing her outfit."

Each comment seemed to set a new idea in motion in Miz Eudora's head. I watched the gears begin to turn as I saw what I suspected might be the beginning of a new shop in Smackass Gap. She'd been bitten by the excitement generated from the crowd.

"I do believe I'd like to do that," she agreed. "I've already got a plan in mind. We can have sizes from small to extra large, and then 1-X, 2-X, 3-X, all the way up to Mabel-X." Her eyes darted in Mabel's direction, her astute mind taking mental measurements. "On second thought, I'm not sure they allow that many X's. How would I ever find a table big enough to cut the pattern?" She smiled, the light bulb going off in her mind as she proudly announced, "I know. We'll simply lay her out on the ground and cut around her."

"Eudora Rumph, you'll do no such of a thing!" Mabel retorted. "I only buy my garments from the best clothiers there are. You obviously have no clue as to style ***or*** fashion design."

"I know that those expensive stores make big sizes and put smaller size labels in them to make you feel better about yourself. I learned that from Hattie when she told me about Spainhour's in Hickory where you used to buy your clothes."

"That is not so!' stormed Mabel. "I was always a perfect size 12 until recently."

"Well, I guess I can't argue with that," replied Miz Eudora. "A twelve on this leg," she said, demonstrating by holding her hands around one of her own thighs and then moving her hands to the other thigh, "and a twelve on this leg."

"Eudora Rumph, you are absolutely impossible!"

"I'm not impossible. I'm just truthful and sometimes the truth hurts."

"You know what they say," spoke Hattie matter-of-factly. "It's only the ones who love you that will tell you the real truth about yourself."

At least there was some agreement between the sister-in-laws for they each glared straight at Hattie with a "That was enough!" look. There was little doubt about which one would come back out swinging first.

"And that 'until recently' must have been when you turned twelve. Why, it would have taken two feed sacks to cover you the first time I laid eyes on you. 'Course I must admit, I didn't look long enough to make a good assessment. I know we raised hogs all my life, but even us Rumphs and Jarvis' weren't accustomed to seeing that much lard in one place at one time."

"HMMPH!" snorted Mabel, making the scene even more ridiculously animated as she began to sound like a sow. "Your baby brother surely didn't think that way. He loved me from the time he first met me."

"I do declare," Miz Eudora said in a solemn tone of voice that indicated she'd just been privy to a "light-bulb moment" of realization. "No wonder poor John G. took to you so. The only thing we worried about him being homesick for on the farm, when he went away to Carolina, was his pet sow, Puffy." He named her that 'cause she was always puffed up from carrying little piglets. That old sow certainly did keep our family and all the neighbor folk rich in pork and lard."

Seeing where this verbal battle was headed, I debated on whether I should run for cover but I was too slow.

"Pa was awfully glad the freshman college classes started up in the late summer so that John G. wouldn't see him fattening up Puffy for the next winter's slaughter. I can still remember my poor brother's face when he came home that first Christmas, though, to find that Puffy was nowhere around. Ma made a point not to serve any ham for Christmas dinner that year and she went awful light on the seasoning. Reckon that was the first time I ever ate green beans without fatback cooked in 'em."

Miz Eudora looked around at all of us with big, pitiful sympathetic eyes while Mabel's cheeks continued to expand like a "puff-belly toad." "Looky there!" she pointed out, as if any of us needed any help in noticing the resemblance. "See what I told you? Now she really looks like John G.'s Puffy." She shook her head in sorrowful pity. "I'll tell you, Pa would have died a much happier man if he'd ever realized that his poor son only took to you so because you reminded him of Puffy. It shamed him every time he thought about one of his own going out and marryin' some half-breed."

"Half-breed?" retorted Mabel. "Half-breed? I'll have you know that I am most definitely ***not*** a half-breed."

I could tell from the glances around the room that I was not the only one relieved that Mabel had chosen only that accusation to rebuke. I could also tell that we all knew there could still be more to come.

"My family came from the finest stock," she added, a choice of words that I did not feel helped her cause. "They were Irish and Dutch."

"I told you that you were a half-breed."

"HMMPH!" Mabel again snorted. "My great-great grandfather arrived on one of the first ships to come to the American colonies."

"Was he a-whippin' or a-rowin'?" asked Miz Eudora, causing more snickers to erupt from around the room.

Mabel, in an effort to back out of that subject, retreated. "And about what you were talking about earlier, I know absolutely ***nothing*** about a Rag Shake, nor what your brother might have worn that belonged to my brother."

"Mabel Toast Jarvis, that's the biggest lie you ever told. Your rags shake every time you take a step. You just ought to see yourself from the backside. Why, there's ***A Whole Lotta Shakin'*** goin' on!"

All the Elvis fans broke into a roar of laughter combined with a round of applause, while one of the quilters' husbands broke out into his best imitation of "the King."

"Are you sure you never went to Memphis before our stop on the Delta Queen?" Miz Eudora asked, continuing to grill Mabel and having a good time doing it. "Maybe that's where he got the idea for that song." Miz Eudora laughed herself this time. "I don't know who could shake their hips the most, you or that good-lookin' feller. Too bad you didn't get paid as much as he did for it, though. Then maybe ***you'd*** be livin' in Graceland and we wouldn't have to be puttin' up with you in Smackass Gap!"

With that, everyone joined the Elvis fans for a bout of laughter. Miz Eudora didn't know too much about some things, but she surely knew enough to set Mabel straight on just about any subject. To beat that, she took great pleasure in doing it. It was almost as if she saw that as being her just reward for having to "put up" with her sister-in-law and "those blamed fur critters."

Mabel ignored the comment as she "commenced" to rattling off her genealogy at great length, a point I could see was getting her nowhere with her sister-in-law. What I did see happening in her sister-in-law, though, was a summing up of her size.

"I've got it," Miz Eudora finally interrupted. "We'll have every size from small all the way up through 2X, 3X, 4X, 5X and Puffy. That's much kinder than calling them a Mabel-X and it's such a nice tribute to my baby brother, John G." She beamed with pleasure at her solution to the problem. "Not to mention that I won't have to think about that confounded Mabel while I'm making clothes for all the sweet, lovely Puffy ladies."

She hastily made a beeline for Eleanor Burns' Quilt in a Day store a couple of blocks over, stopping only briefly to share a final recollection with us. "You know, the finest pair of shoes Ma ever got was when Pa slaughtered Puffy. He went down to Chinquapin's and ordered her very first pair of heels as a present to help her overcome missing her baby boy so."

As she passed me, I heard her softly add, "Too bad she didn't use them to stomp that ole Mabel into the ground!"

Mabel, who should have given up the ghost, unfortunately followed Miz Eudora for the next round. Her effort backfired when the increasingly-popular quilter responded with, "You don't have to go and get all huffy and puffy for the crowd."

Mabel immediately spewed words of retaliation but to no avail, for Miz Eudora continued walking.

"Besides, I was ***not*** puffy," Mabel insisted, still lagging behind as she looked at her waist and smoothed her jacket down with her gloved hand. "I may have been a ***little*** pleasantly plump," she then admitted.

"You're not ***'pleasantly'*** anything, Mabel, and little has never been within a hundred feet of you. Just admit it. If the cloven foot fits, wear it!"

Miz Eudora barely let the laughter die down before she continued. "And what makes you think there's anything wrong with being 'puffy?' John G.'s Puffy was the prettiest pig you ever did see…not that you're pretty, too. But everybody loved her. So see, Mabel, don't take it so hard. You're not totally like Puffy, but one out of three similarities was enough to turn John G.'s head."

Miz Eudora finally halted her rampage as she turned to the person, a complete stranger, standing next to her and leaned in with that habit of hers – the one where she pretended to whisper but said the next words just as loudly as all the others. "It's just too bad his head didn't keep on a-turnin' like one of those dolls you see whose heads make 360-degree turns."

With that statement, she made a 180-degree turn and kept on a-walkin' herself. "See you ladies tonight!"

she called behind her. “Remember, 7 to 9 at Mrs. Ada’s!”

Hattie and I followed her, trying our best to keep up and taking no heed of what was happening behind. We’d see enough of that later, when Mabel showed up for the fittings.

The rest of the day was spent with Miz Eudora scanning the aisles of the Quilt in a Day store, choosing skirt and jacket fabrics with the aid of a salesclerk whom she dubbed “Southern Belle Susan.”That pair hit it off like they were soul sisters, with Susan offering suggestions for color combinations and my neighbor offering her usual fun and laughter to everyone who crossed her path in the store.

“I sure do wish I could take Southern Belle Susan home with us and leave Mabel here,” Miz Eudora shared on the way back to Ada’s Bed & Breakfast. “I won’t waste my breath to ask whether you think anyone might notice.”

What I ***did*** think everyone would notice was the shirt Miz Eudora bought in the store that read “Eleanor Burns Made a Stripper Out of Me.” That was enough to turn the heads of even Smackass Gappers!

EIGHT

Christmas in April

MY FAVORITE THING about the Paducah Quilt Show was the fact that we met so many people – multicultural and multigenerational - woven together by a common thread, ***or quilting thread***, in that particular case. Miz Eudora had moved outside her safe, little serene circle of Smackass Gap into a huge circle of many people, all with different interests. It was remarkable to me that such an unassuming, down-to-earth seemingly-unimportant creature wound up attracting endless numbers of friends and, because of her talents and abilities, fell into the likes of artistic masters from around the world. Add to that the attraction of people to her purple "fopher" coat and she was like the Pied Piper, her contagious laughter and dry wit serving as the mode of music instead of a flute. The one thing that stuck out, even though she had moved into what was swiftly becoming a giant orb, was that she still walked the same safe, serene path of the little circle. That – I was certain – was because she was surrounded by angels whose only job was to take care of her. And, believe you me, I'd learned it was a full-time job caring for her. In fact, there were days that I wished we had half the residents of Clay County caring for her. That was before I "come to know" that God had His own army shielding her.

I think that "holy army" was encamped at the grocery store, for that is where we met many of the people, at least those closest to her, who came into her circle. By this time, I should have learned to "put the pedal to the metal" when we passed a grocery store, but no, I had to give a signal and turn into the local Food Giant when Miz Eudora and Hattie asked if they could "go in for a minute." ***Guess I had not learned the definition of "a glutton for punishment" yet.***

What's more, it seems I had not learned to prohibit the two of them from going in unchaperoned. Forever playing the role of the gracious hostess, I drove them right up to the front door, let them out and went to find a parking place, glad that Mabel had stayed back at the B&B.

What I missed while parking the car was Miz Eudora introducing herself to some stranger on the baking needs aisle, going right up to her and starting a conversation. Not merely a "How are you? Nice day, isn't it?" conversation, but a whole "three generations back" conversation. By the time I reached the front door of the Food Giant, another "victim" had been added to her personal entourage.

"Sadie...," I heard as I passed their aisle, not in a polite "inside voice," but the one I was sure she had used to call across the mountain to Horace. "Sadie..., we're over here in front of the chocolate chips and nuts."

Well, at least they stopped on the right aisle. They ought to feel right at home with the nuts. For if they don't, I do. Now everybody in the store knows where they are. I don't know why they didn't just go ahead to the front office and announce their whereabouts over the store's intercom.

"And I don't know why you let the two of them talk you into stopping at the grocery store." There went that voice again. ***Bless dear Leon's soul. Even from the grave***, I learned, ***hindsight has 20/20 vision***.

I tried to pretend I wasn't with them as I sacheted down a couple of other aisles before getting to theirs. Picking up two jars of marshmallow cream, I scanned their back labels, trying to give the impression of comparing them. Heaven only knows why I did that, for all that did was cause Miz Eudora to yell out, "Sadie, put that down. We don't need any marshmallow cream for what we're doing."

My face then as red as the writing on the blue label of one of the jars, I replaced them and walked speedily to join the "nuts" and chocolate chips, thinking all that was missing from this picture was the dried fruit.

"Would you look at this, Sadie? I've found us a new friend. Can you believe that she's moving to Clay County next month? Imagine that!"

All I could imagine was the manager calling over the intercom, "Price check on Aisle 9, we need a price check on new friends."

"I walked right up to her," explained Miz Eudora, "and told her she looked like she could pass for someone from a family back home. She asked me where I lived and when I told her, she said she'd never heard of that town."

Imagine that!

"I told her we're just a little community and not a town, but I did tell her about us getting our second traffic light recently. She'll need to know not to go barreling down Highway 64 when she moves there."

Glad to hear we covered all the important bases, I noted, wondering whether Miz Eudora was ever going to give this petite little lady a chance to speak for herself. "Hi, it's a pleasure to meet you," I said, introducing myself and acting like someone in Clay County had manners. "My name is Sadie Calloway. I moved to Clay County myself around two years ago. It's a good choice."

"My name is Theona Rouette," she replied in a

politely pleasant, yet extremely quiet voice.

Too bad she wasn't the one who called down the aisle for me, I thought, judging the situation. ***With a name like that, she surely won't have any trouble fitting in. She already sounds like a local. And from her quiet demeanor, she's probably glad to have Miz Eudora doing all the blabbing for her.***

"Hayesville is where we go when we have to get groceries," shared Hattie. "There's a really nice Ingle's there. You wouldn't believe it, but that's where I met Miz Eudora and Sadie and we've all been best friends ever since."

"But that's not where she met Mabel," interrupted Miz Eudora, "and she's not one of our best friends. She's my…well, never mind, it's not important. But if you're lucky, you won't have to meet Mabel, in the grocery store or anywhere else."

"There's also a general store in town called Chinquapin's where you can find unique gifts and nice clothing."

"And ice cream," added Miz Eudora. "Don't forget the ice cream. That's how I met all my Red Hatter friends. They stopped in town, 'cause Hayesville ***is*** a town, you see, and that's where Chinquapin's is, right in the heart of the square. I was sittin' there eatin' my butter pecan ice cream and celebratin' Horace's passing when they picked me up and took me with them 'cause they thought I was one of them."

She was so excited that she'd met a new friend who was moving to her neck of the woods that Miz Eudora had turned into a "regular Chatty Cathy doll." ***The way she's goin' on, I can't imagine anyone mistaking her for one of them***, I observed, not sure whether to be embarrassed or amused. ***Or at least admitting it! Now***, I ventured, ***I understand what it's like to take a three-year-old shopping.***

"If they don't have what we need at Ingle's or Chinquapin's," Hattie concluded, "then we go to Franklin or Hiawassee or somewhere else. But we do have pride in our community. It's not everybody who can live in such a nice place with such a unique name."

"Don't forget to tell her about Clay's Corners. That's where we have the New Year's Possum Drop and then there's the Fireworks on July 4th at the Dam and the...and the...and the,"

She went on and on, giving Theona Rouette the whole scoop on the entire county. ***Forget Chatty Cathy. Call her Gabby Hayes.***

"What made you decide to relocate to Clay County?" I asked curiously, but also as an effort to hush Miz Eudora.

"I have roots in the North Carolina mountains," Theona replied timidly, not meeting my eyes, "but my family lived over on Brush Creek and Sawmill Hill."

"Why, that's in Swain County," blurted Miz

Eudora. "I know exactly where that is. Never been there, you see, for we kept close to home all our lives, but I do know about it. That's to Bryson City what Smackass Gap is to Hayesville. And it's not too far from Cherokee."

"You're right," said Theona, a sudden spark in her already-beautiful bright-blue eyes, glad to see that her new "friend" knew something about her area. "My grandmother was a Cherokee princess. Princess Fa Fa La Da."

"A princess?" asked Hattie. "I didn't know they had Red Hatters back then."

"They didn't," I answered, intrigued by this lovely evenly-tanned woman who stood in front of me with such iridescent blue eyes. It was hard to picture that those eyes had come from an Indian grandmother.

"If she was a princess back then," Hattie continued, ignoring my words, "she was probably a pink hatter. I think she'd have been a queen by the time she graduated to a red hatter."

"Wait a minute!" blared Miz Eudora, causing everyone to look at her – which I was glad about because I was totally confused with all the conversations going on. "Princess Fa Fa La Da doesn't sound like a Cherokee name at all."

"It isn't, really," admitted Theona, her eyes still not looking directly at any of us. "That wasn't the

Cherokee name she was given at birth. She got the name from missionaries in the area who called her that because she liked to sing all the time. Even when she was a baby, it's said she made syllables in rhythm, sort of like the "Fa-la-la-la-la" part of the ***Deck the Halls*** carol. So the missionaries nicknamed her 'Princess Fa Fa La Da' and it stuck because everyone liked it. They said it had a fun kind of ring to it. Rumor is, she even called her father, 'Fa-Fa-Da-Da.'

"The story goes that Grandmother Rouette liked the song, and the name, so much that she was forevermore singing it. I'm sure her parents must have been sick of it."

"Especially if the chief had to hear her call him 'Fa-Fa-Da-Da'" all the time," replied Miz Eudora. "Oh, well," she then observed, "at least she didn't have to worry about gettin' trench mouth since her front two teeth and her tongue got such a good work out from pronouncing all the syllables. She'd have had no worry of contractin' hoof-and-mouth disease."

Which you're going to do if you don't shut your mouth, I noticed.

"So do you sing?" asked Hattie.

"Oh, yes!" exclaimed Theona enthusiastically, straying from the shyness I'd witnessed up to this point. "I love music and love to sing anything."

"Did I hear someone say, 'sing?'" I heard coming behind me in an all-too-familiar voice.

Quick, call the manager! I thought in cartoon fashion. ***Unidentified inventory has been mistakenly placed on the wrong aisle. Stock clerk needed for assistance immediately.*** I stopped my silly thoughts long enough to realize that Mabel was, in fact, on the right aisle. ***The dried fruit has arrived!*** I announced to myself, turning just in time to see Mabel's prune face.

"What are you doing here and how did you get here?" asked Miz Eudora in a huff.

"I rode with Ada. She was being a hospitable hostess and asked if I'd like to accompany her to the grocery store. When I saw Sadie's car in the parking lot, I decided to come in and make sure you weren't creating a scene."

Too late for that, I rationalized, while foreseeing another scene brewing on the horizon.

Fortunately, it was Hattie who gave a brief introduction of Theona. I prayed that she'd skim over the part about Grandmother Princess Fa Fa La Da, but no such luck. The brewing scene lost no time in blowing in. It blew in, however, in the form of Mabel singing ***Deck the Halls with Boughs of Holly.***

I watched poor Theona's face shrivel up to the point that it nearly matched Mabel's. We quickly glided up the aisle and out the front door of the Food Giant. Luckily, the soloist was so busy "fa-la-la-ing" that she didn't even miss us. For once, I was relieved that

Mabel was so caught up in her egotistical self.

Maybe the stock clerk will hear her and "reshelf her" to the bread aisle with the rest of the toast, I thought, unlocking my car door. ***Now where are they?*** I wondered, looking around to see what had happened to the other three. I finally spied them on the other side of the parking lot at what I assumed to be Theona's car. Deciding to save time before Mabel discovered our disappearance, I drove over to where they were.

"Look, Sadie," Miz Eudora said, pointing to a late model blue car. "Theona has a car just like the one Hattie used to have."

"Isn't that something?" I asked, looking in the rear view mirror to make sure Mabel wasn't on my trail.

"I bought a car just like this when it was brand new," Hattie said, running her hand along the front left fender of the Buick Century. "It sure was a good car."

"That's nice," I commented, still watching the front door of the store. "Why don't we get out of here before Mabel gets out here? Theona, I know these ladies would love to...,"

"That's why you look so familiar!" announced Theona to Hattie, sounding more like this motley crew all the time. "Your picture is on the driver's license in the glove compartment."

"My driver's license?" repeated Hattie, dumbfounded. "You must be mistaken. I kept my driver's license in my wallet and I still have...,"

She stumbled for words for a moment while I waited for Mabel to stumble out the front door.

"Why don't you finish this subject at the conference center? I'm sure Miz Eudora would like you to see her...," I said, using the same voice that had been used to summons me inside the store.

"Is that what happened to that license?" Hattie asked. "I remember now. I thought I had lost it at the grocery store and had a duplicate one made right before I sold the car."

"We can lose Mabel at the grocery store if we hurry," I pleaded.

"So that's where it was," Hattie said, her mind replaying the day she'd misplaced her license.

"Sure is. It was in a clear plastic sleeve that contained your grocery store cards."

"How do you like that?" Hattie replied, shaking her head. "I must have hurriedly placed it there as I tried to get the groceries in the car before I got soaking wet. It was raining up a storm that day."

"IF YOU LADIES DON'T HURRIEDLY PLACE YOUR CARCUSES IN THE CAR BEFORE MABEL GETS HERE, IT'S GOING TO BE RAINING MORE THAN A STORM OUT HERE!" I yelled at the top of my lungs.

"Oh…,Mabel!" exclaimed Miz Eudora, finally remembering why we were in the parking lot in the first place. "Hattie, you ride with Theona in the Hattie-mobile and I'll ride with Sadie. Follow us to the…,"

"…la, la, la," we heard, sounding like a cannon going "Ka-BOOM, Ka-BOOM, Ka-BOOM!" instead of a joyous carol.

"…Quilt Expo-o-o-o-o," echoed Miz Eudora as she slammed the door shut while I screeched out of the lot, Theona on my tail.

"Hattie-mobile?" I asked once we were well out-of-sight. "Where did you come up with that?"

"What else would we call it?" Miz Eudora asked. "When Hattie and I came back with that purple Caddie convertible, Mabel said it was a pimp-mobile because it belonged to a man she called 'Pimp.' Only we discovered that he wasn't really named Pimp. He was somebody's sweet young grandson dressed up to entertain a group of Red Hatters. Now we have a car that belonged to a woman that we know is named Hattie, so that naturally makes it a Hattie-mobile."

"Oh," I accepted, reluctant to ask for further explanation.

"Hattie tells me you have a quilt in the show," Theona said to Miz Eudora, once we arrived at the conference center's Expo. "I do, too."

The two quilters had already begun comparing notes before we hit the entrance of the convention center. I laughed lightly, wondering if the "holy army" got paid overtime for instances such as this, and whether they had any part in bringing these three women, all strangers, yet divinely connected, together. Wondering about my role in this "entourage," I finally decided I was the horse that pulled the chariot of the "holy army." I didn't have to wonder what that made Mabel.

By the time the afternoon was over, and we'd shared strawberry shortcake with ice cream from the Boy Scouts' booth, we learned that Theona Rouette was a retired librarian – ***which would explain the quiet disposition***, I determined. I'd seen her type before and figured that she, like them, was capable of throwing a verbal punch that would hit you right in the gut if you pushed her too hard the wrong way. "A zinger," Leon had called that. Yet she seemed the kind of person who walked the earth quietly and made no enemies. I also pondered about her Native American background and whether she still had connections with the tribe's medicine man. If so, I wondered whether she could coax him to blow that same kind of dust on Mabel.

"Do you have an Indian name, too?" I asked.

"Yes," Theona answered, again too shy to meet my eyes. "I'm called Smiling Spirit because those who know me say I never lose my smile."

"That's beautiful," I replied, touched by its loveliness. ***But they obviously never saw her when she***

was listening to Mabel sing.

"There you are," said Mabel, approaching us. "I knew this is where I'd find you."

What is it with this woman? Does she have some kind of radar that goes off every time somebody mentions the word, 'sing?' I didn't even have to mention it. I just thought it and, POOF! here she is. QUICK! Where's that medicine man with his medicine bag?

Mabel, too, had a bowl of strawberry shortcake topped with ice cream as she headed toward the outside picnic table where we sat, next to all the food vendors. I had to do a double-take. She was calm, cool and collected. ***The stock clerk must have chilled her a while in the cucumber aisle***, I reasoned.

She paraded herself right up to Theona, ignoring the rest of us, and said how pleased she was to meet another person in Paducah who shared a background of royalty.

"Since when are you anything royal?" asked Hattie, having known Mabel's background.

"I'll tell you what she is royal," said Miz Eudora. "She's a royal pain. And she does that royally!"

"If you're moving to Clay County and you love to sing," Mabel went on, ignoring both Hattie and Miz Eudora, "you might want to consider joining our choir at the church. I'm the designated soloist," she was quick to inform Theona, "but they're always looking for new talent." She paused and looked in our direction. "That's why Miz Eudora doesn't sing in the choir. She has no talent."

"Somebody has to sit in the congregation with the shotgun to make sure everyone else doesn't run out the door when you start singing. Preacher Jake works too hard on his sermon to let you scare them all out the church door."

Miz Eudora took another bite of ice cream. "Furthermore, Miss Royal Pain, if it weren't for my 'no talent,' you'd not be here eating ice cream and shootin' the breeze right now."

Mabel, looking back to Theona, concluded, "I'm sure you'd be a lovely asset to our group."

"You've got the market on assets in the choir," insisted Miz Eudora. "This poor little thing wouldn't stand a chance beside you."

"Pay her no attention," instructed Mabel. "She's just jealous because she isn't the songbird that I am." With that pronouncement, she proceeded to sing the familiar carol again, "Fa, la, la, la, la, la, la, la, la," this time with her full cheeks jiggling in time to the words as she nodded both her head and purse in rhythm, while spraying ice cream in every which direction.

Once she reached the second strain of "Fa-la-la-la-la-la," Miz Eudora blurted out, "We're here for the International Quilt Show, Mabel, ***not*** a Christmas in April Exhibition. And these customers don't want you exhibiting anything, especially your voice. Besides, they've all already paid admission to get in here and if you don't stop that caterwauling, they're all gonna want their money back."

"I'll have you know, Eudora Rumph, that I was the highlight of the Christmas cantata last Christmas. Everyone loved my solo rendition of ***O Holy Night.***"

"That was an act of God," replied Miz Eudora, who then turned to me and quietly whispered, "It was really an act of Horace's special blend, but we won't tell anybody." She gave me a playful wink which caused me to think how all that was missing from this scenario was her dressed up as Mrs. Claus.

I had an odd sensation as I stood watching the foursome and admiring the diversity between them. I wasn't quite sure what to make of it, but my mind retraced its steps back to the time I took her to that first yard sale. Now I realized what it was. It seemed that every time I took Miz Eudora out in public, we wound up with one more body in the car. There was that time at Ingle's that she met Hattie Crow, the time at the yard sale – ***Well, it was a body of sorts!*** – and now. I decided that taking Miz Eudora out was like taking in stray cats. With that thought, however, I decided I might as well get used to running a kennel, for I was sure there were going to be many more times of taking her places. There was too much fun to be had on the way to finding the "stray cats."

From the looks on the faces of Miz Eudora and Hattie, this might as well have been Christmas Day. Whether we had been given a "stray cat" on this day, or a stocking filled with chocolates, nuts and fruits, I wasn't sure. But I did know that our circle of best friends had just grown to include Theona Rouette, granddaughter of a Cherokee princess, and what a lovely present she was to find under the Christmas tree.

Even if that Christmas tree was Aisle 9 at the Food Giant. In April.

NINE

Treasured Heirlooms

THEONA STOOD, BEAMING, the next day as people in the Quilt in a Day store stopped to ask about her winning antique quilt. A Sunbonnet Sue design, she explained how different people used to do one square each and then put the squares together to make a keepsake quilt for a special individual. She proudly shared the significance of each person whose name was on one of the "Sunbonnet Sues" of her quilt.

It reminded me of a quilt that belonged to my own mother. Actually, the one that belonged to my mother wasn't even a quilt, only a quilt top. ***And not much of one at that, in my opinion***. She'd saved it ever since I could remember, a fact which had always puzzled me since it looked like it should have been thrown away years before. What's worse, it somehow wound up with my belongings, so it had made the move to Smackass Gap and was there, hidden away in its ugliness – as I saw it – in its original storage box.

As I thought of the quilts in the antique section of the Quilt Expo, with their various intricacies, patterns and designs, my appreciation for them shot up a couple of notches. Especially when I recalled the price tags hanging from the ones for sale.

Suddenly, I had a brilliant thought. I hastily called Preacher Jake and inquired as to whether he, or Mrs. Grover Swicegood, might go to my house and find the quilt top that had belonged to my mother. I knew exactly where it was because I had run across it only two weeks earlier while packing for the trip. Even then, I'd been tempted to toss it, but due to the rush of getting ready, had thrown it back in the closet, still in the same box it had been stored in since I first saw it as a child.

"If you can get it to Chinquapin's," I told him, "I'm sure Rob Tiger will ship it to me. Please tell him it's very important and ask him to send it overnight. I'll gladly pay him whatever it costs when I return. To save time, please send it directly to the Quilt in a Day store here in Paducah."

Hearing the urgency in my voice, Preacher Jake hastily replied, "Say no more. I've got it covered."

I gave him the store's address, an update on his favorite member and how she was faring in Paducah, and a big thanks. I would have promised him a special surprise, but I felt it a bit sacrilegious to bribe a "man of the cloth," which seemed ironic to me at the time, given I was standing in a cloth store.

I hung up the phone, barely able to wait until the next day to see my mother's quilt top with new eyes, ***or new appreciation***, and to show it off at the Quilt in a Day store. I was anxious to hear their comments and opinions about it, since they were the real specialists in the quilting department.

IT ARRIVED INTACT, for which I'd expected no less, because I was sure Preacher Jake had prayed over the box as he was shipping it. Women crowded around me as I slowly pulled back the tape and undid the flaps to reveal the contents. Carol, the expert demonstrating a long-arm quilting machine, helped me gently remove the "treasured heirloom" from the cardboard box. Although I was most appreciative of the complimentary comments from all the onlookers, hers was the opinion that mattered most. She was the professional and I trusted her to give me an accurate analysis of the "rag that should have been tossed years ago."

"You were right about one thing," she shared as she eyed it carefully. "It is from years ago, probably at least seventy-five. These are original feed sacks, not the reproduction fabric, and some of their Sunbonnet Sue dresses even have the writing of the feed sack company on them."

After a thorough evaluation, Carol gazed at me and said, “This is a treasured heirloom.”

Suddenly, I realized I was the owner of my own precious memories, ***or at least quilt top that was loaded with my mother’s precious memories***, as tears gently streamed down my face. I could not wait to tell my mother.

Wait! Don’t tell her. Have it finished for her.

I immediately looked at Carol and inquired as to whether she might know where I could find someone skilled in working with an antique piece such as this to finish it and quilt it.

The smile written in her eyes matched the smile on her face as she replied, “I’ll do it. It would be a treat for me to work on something this precious and valuable. This is something that should be passed down for generations.” She looked directly into my eyes. “But you must promise me that you’ll store it properly and keep the notes that I give you about its history with it.”

“I promise.” I didn’t dare tell her that I had no offspring for which to leave it, but I’d make sure it went to someone who could appreciate its value.

The moment was so touching that I didn’t even realize what had happened until it dawned on me that a man had just snatched the quilt top and was out the front door of the store and tearing down the street. I dropped the box and went chasing after him.

"Whose husband is that?" I heard someone ask behind me, as I flew out the door, with no one seeming to know.

The man opened the passenger door of a car which was parallel parked on the next block and the car pulled onto the street, the tires squealing as it went.

"Jump in," someone yelled beside me.

I looked up to see Southern Belle Susan sitting behind the steering wheel of a "souped-up" Candy-Apple Red Chevy. "Buckle up…,"

"I know the routine," I interrupted, slamming the door as we sped forward.

I wanted to close my eyes, but dared not, for I needed to help her keep a check on their trail. We were going so fast, however, that I couldn't even turn my head to look at her, or the speedometer, as we catapulted over railroad tracks and everything else in our path. ***Please Lord, don't let them go toward the river***, I prayed, having visions of jumping the Mississippi like the Duke boys had done over obstacles in the General Lee. The only thing missing from that scenario was a car horn blowing ***Dixie***.

This race was nothing like the one aboard the Delta Queen, but I surely hoped my luck of being on the winning vessel would continue.

My rambling thoughts halted when I heard sirens blaring behind us and was again reminded of Luke and Beau Duke. I wanted to ask if we were going to catch the "quilt-lifters," how she learned to drive like that, and whether the cops were chasing us or the car in front, or both. But I kept my mouth closed for fear of biting my tongue if I opened it.

I could tell we were gaining ground, but then the getaway car veered off the road and down a path, us right behind them. My ears kept listening for Waylon Jennings as my eyes kept looking for his hands on a guitar to appear from behind a tree.

"We're going to catch them, honey," Southern Belle Susan yelled over the engine and sirens. "Don't you worry. Couldn't nobody beat me back in the days of my powder-puff racing."

That answers two of the questions. Given those were the two most important ones, I let the other one ride. ***Or fly,*** as it seemed we were doing. I wished, though, that we had helmets like she'd had back in the days of her powder-puff racing.

A fork in the road lay ahead and I nearly shrieked as the getaway car went one way and Southern Belle Susan went the other. I was able to glance behind us just enough to see that the police cars split up and there was one behind each of us. ***Okay, Lord***, I said silently, turning the entire matter over to Him and knowing that this couldn't possibly be worse than some of the jams I'd been in with Miz Eudora and Mabel.

I wanted to tell myself that a jam usually meant you were sitting stuck in traffic somewhere and this was anything but that, but then I figured that would be like turning something over to the Lord and then telling Him how to handle it. Therefore, I sat back and tried to imagine myself back on the deck of the Delta Queen. ***Going at jet speed!***

"It's almost over, honey!" called Southern Belle Susan. "That tree on Pliney's Curve will catch them. It does it every time."

It seemed only seconds afterwards that I heard tires screaming and a loud crash of what I assumed to be the getaway car careening into the tree on Pliney's Curve.

"Yep, sounds like they scraped off whatever bark was left," she said, putting the pedal all the way to the floor and causing me to hope that we, too, didn't hit that same tree on Pliney's Curve.

I wasn't sure whether it was for old-time's sake, to impress me, or just plain fun, but she brought the Chevy to a screeching halt, including a 180-degree turn right before she got to the tree and the getaway car wrapped around it.

The quilt top was stuck between the passenger, which was the man who had grabbed it from me in the quilt store, and his deployed air bag. Now my prayers went from my safety to that of the quilt top.

"What could he have possibly wanted with an old quilt top?" I asked one of the policemen later, down at the station where he'd taken me for questioning while he filled out his report.

"A thief is a thief is a thief," he said sadly. "He was probably only a purse snatcher, hoping to grab the purse of one of the women who was honed in on finding fabric. The town's full of visitors ready to drop a lot of money this week, and those guys merely intended to help a few of them."

"When he heard Carol telling you about the value of your quilt top," explained Southern Belle Susan, "he probably thought he'd found something worth more than any wallet."

"That's hard to believe," I replied. "What about their checks and charge cards?"

"Those could be traced," the officer explained. "He had a captive audience of quilt collectors and enthusiasts this week and knew he could unload your quilt top easily. It's not like you've got a Picasso or something, so he figured it couldn't be identified."

"No disrespect," said a voice from behind me, "but that's where you're wrong, Officer."

I turned to see Carol, who was followed by Hattie, Theona, Mabel and Miz Eudora. Behind them came a young man whom I could tell, from his clothes, had to be the Purple Stallion.

"How'd you get here?" I asked "the Stallion," meaning how he'd caught up with the group.

"His red pimpmobile," answered Mabel. "He has a red Lincoln with suicide doors that he drives when he's wearing the purple suit and shoes."

Her answer caused every officer in the station to stop what he or she was doing and look up. Then they smiled, waved and went back to what they were doing. "It's only the Purple Stallion," one of the officers called back to the captain's desk.

"See?" asked Mabel. "I told you he was a pimp. He's been here so many times that they even know him by name."

"He's been here alright," said the officer filling out the report on my stolen quilt top, "but not in the way you think." His words were spoken directly to Mabel. "His grandmother is one of the best quilters in Paducah. When he comes to visit, he entertains all her friends down at the center for senior citizens. Seems all these Red Hatters have adopted him lately, though, because he likes to sing Elvis."

With that, the Purple Stallion slithered over next to Mabel and gave his best imitation of "the King's" hip and leg gyration, nearly knocking her in the police officer's lap. He then reached out, caught her and made sure she had her balance. "You okay, ma'am?"

"I certainly am," she answered, holding his hand. "Wait until I tell the ladies at Myers Park about the talent I found."

"***Who*** found?" Miz Eudora asked accusingly.

"Okay," Mabel conceded. "The talent you found. But I'm the one that got to 'bump-and-grind' with him."

"This is terrific!" exclaimed Hattie. "There's a whole busload of Miz Eudora's Sparklin' Shiners arriving here tomorrow. Would you possibly have time to sing an Elvis number or two for them?"

"I'm sorry," he answered with a sad smile, his charming eyes making me understand why Hattie had described him as such a nice-looking young man, "but I couldn't possibly do that."

I watched as the faces of all the woman in my group fell.

"How about I give them a whole private concert instead?" he asked playfully, giving Mabel a wink and bumping her again, this time first putting his arm around her to catch her.

"Ooh," she sighed, grabbing her hankie and fanning with it.

"There's only one stipulation," he added, seeing that he would be granted anything he asked. "I have to bring my grandmother along."

Heads nodded in agreement as he offered to take Miz Eudora, Hattie and Mabel back to the Ada's Bed & Breakfast, and Carol back to the store. "I've got to get back to my grandmother's house. We did a quilt together and it's hanging up in the exhibit. I have a date with her to visit the quilt show today."

"See, I told you he was a stripper," boasted Mabel.

"You got that right," he said, pulling back his jacket to reveal his "stripper shirt" that matched Miz Eudora's from the Quilt in a Day store. "Except that it was really my grandmother who taught me to strip!"

When I'd finished at the station, Southern Belle Susan took me back to the Quilt in a Day store, sharing many of the exciting stories from her powder-puff racing days. I learned she was as good a driver doing the speed limit as she was on the racetrack.

Carol and the gals at Quilt in a Day broke into a rollicking applause when we entered the store, quilt top in hand. I took it straight to Carol's workspace where she continued her appraisal of it, with my hands securely on it.

The faded peach-colored fabric that served as the strip between the squares had been terribly ugly to me before this day. Now I saw its unevenness and the not-perfectly-matched squares all as unique parts of a rare object of beauty. Each Sunbonnet Sue was made from a different flower sack. And, I was sure, the peach fabric had been all they had on hand back then.

"What adds to the beauty of this is the way the women who did each square stitched their names with a needle and thread." Carol looked up and down every inch of the quilt. "I'll have to find antique muslin to match what's already on here as this probably came from the late 20's or early 30's. I'm not sure I can match it, but I'll get as close as I can."

I didn't want to touch the quilt top any more than necessary, but I had to run my fingers across the names. Those were women who had shaped the life of my mother, and, in turn, me. Just as surely as the missionaries had shaped the life of Princess Fa Fa La Da and her granddaughter, Smiling Spirit, through her Sunbonnet Sue quilt, so had the hands that made these squares – which when put together formed this "treasured heirloom" – touched me.

Now I understood why my mother had kept the quilt top in its original box in the back of the closet all those years. It was a part of her. She had played with the children of the women who'd made it and given it to her mother. There were squares done by family members, close friends and neighbors. ***They were friends who had shared precious memories together.***

I watched as Carol carefully folded the quilt top and placed it back in the box. I knew that the next time I saw it, it would be as beautiful as one of the antique quilts on display at the quilt show. It would rival the Sunbonnet Sue quilt that belonged to Theona and had won an award.

I gave my contact information to Carol, who was to call me when the quilt was done. She was going to have it completed in time for my parents' 56th anniversary, which would be coming up in a couple of months. I was going to take the quilt, in person, to them so that I could see the look on my mother's face when she opened it, still in the original box.

"I'd like for you to have this," said Southern Belle Susan, handing me a purse as I left the store.

"This is exquisite! Did you make it?"

She nodded. I looked at the beautiful black fabric, covered in purse designs of bright neon-style colors, and the purple marabou trim that lined the top. I could hardly wait to show Miz Eudora. "Thought you might need something to remember this day."

We both laughed heartily at that joke. I loved this woman, who seemed to be everyone's soul sister, and her sense of humor. I knew this would not be the last time I would see her, as I looked forward to the next time.

"Hey!" she called behind me, "I have a cousin who lives in your neck of the woods. Check out her quilt that's hanging upstairs in the convention center. Her name's Dort Lee. Your friend, Miz Eudora, might like to visit her farm sometime and see all the original designs she's made. I think they'd get along very well. I'll be coming down to visit next fall. Maybe we can hook up."

I nodded and smiled, proudly carrying my new purse as I strode down the street.

Seems Mabel wasn't the only one who had no concept of the fine art of quilting. I thought of the "treasured heirloom." ***Or the value of antique quilt tops.***

TEN

Fat Quarters

"WOULD YOU LOOK at that?" Miz Eudora asked while reading the bronze plaque at the street's edge of the Museum of the American Quilters Society (MAQS). "This place was born on April 25th. That's the same day as our Red Hat birthday. Aren't Red Hat Nanny and all her friends going to be surprised? Oh, my, what a party they are going to have! Why, I'll bet they all become 'strippers' before it's over with."

My outburst of laughter was uncontrollable, to the point that Hattie joined me. Somehow, the vision of that was not something I wanted to imagine. I silently wondered if Paducah would ever be the same again. ***One thing's for certain***, I thought, still picturing that busload of Red Hatters, ***I surely won't be the same again***. My laughter turned to a smile of satisfaction at the realization that every day with Miz Eudora was a beautiful journey.

"Shall we go in now, or should we wait for our busload of friends to arrive?" Hattie asked.

"I don't think that's going to be a decision," I answered pointing to the bus rounding the curve in front of the museum.

There they were, all waving their hats out the window at Miz Eudora as the air became filled with red and purple flowers and feathers. Everyone remotely in proximity of the museum stopped and stared as Red Hat Nanny led the grand procession of her "sisters" off the bus and up the sidewalk that led to the museum's entrance.

"Wait!" called Miz Eudora as she hustled, as hard as she could, out to where they were. "Wait right there! I've got to show you something before you come in." She headed for the plaque that announced the birth of the MAQS. "Read this," she instructed. "You're just gonna love this."

"You read it," Red Hat Nanny said to Miss Bloomers, her second in command. "I don't have on my glasses."

"MAQS," Miss Bloomers began, "which is short for the Museum of the American Quilters Society opened on April 25, 1991. Meredith and Bill Schroeder dedicated this facility to promote, preserve, and perpetuate quilting. Paducah, Kentucky, home of the American Quilting Society, is visited by thousands of quilters annually. Mayor Gerry B. Montgomery has proclaimed this city Quilt City USA."

"April 25th?" repeated Red Hat Nanny. "Well, there you go, ladies. We're going to have two birthday parties instead of one."

"That's tomorrow," called Smokin' Barb. "We need to check around town and plan a big party, befitting of our Red Hat anniversary and the birthday of the MAQS."

"I've already decided where we're goin' to party," announced Miz Eudora. "We're taking the bus over to Sikeston, Missouri, to Lambert's Café. That's that place where they throw rolls at you, only we're gonna throw back."

"Food fight, food fight," chanted several of the ladies.

"And don't forget the reason we're all here, Miz Eudora Rumph," declared Miss Bloomers. "If it hadn't been for you winning the quilt contest, we wouldn't be here."

For some strange reason, I had a gut feeling that before the weekend was over, there were going to be way more than two reasons to party. I wasn't sure whether to look forward or be fearful.

"What would you ladies like to do first?" asked Miz Eudora. "You can see the museum or you can head on over to the Expo at the convention center to see most of the quilts. That's where mine is. Or," she added as an afterthought, "I can take you over to Quilt in a Day. It's just a few blocks." Her face lit up. "Or better than that, hop right back on that bus. We'll head over to Carson Park to see Eleanor Burns do her new ***USO Quilt Show***. She sure enough made a stripper out of me there yesterday, right on television."

I couldn't resist the urge to check all the bulging eyes of the Red Hatters.

"A stripper!" exclaimed the Sassy Grandma. "You, Miz Eudora?"

"Oh, honey, I've been a stripper for years," Miz Eudora said shyly. "It's just that Mrs. Burns, she's so good, that she finally got me to admit it yesterday while I was at her show. Why, it's my start in stripping that brought me here."

"Imagine that," I heard one of the women say, "she's had that stripping money socked up in a jar somewhere all this time. That's really what I call pinching pennies."

"Pinching quarters would be more like it," joked Miss Bloomers.

"Speaking of quarters," said Miz Eudora, "wait until you see all of Mrs. Burns' fat quarters." She reached deep into her purse and pulled out the sock change purse she had purchased at the show's tent the day before. "This is what I'll keep my quarters in now," she announced proudly holding the small change purse up for all to see, as she hopped onto the first step of the bus. "The jar is saved for other necessities," she concluded as she boarded the bus, the other women all following her like a flock of geese.

I was relieved that she saw no further need of explanation for that last comment. That was one tid-bit of information that I didn't feel the Red Hatters needed to know. ***At least not now,*** I deduced, with a strange feeling that there may indeed be a necessity for that jar before the trip had ended.

"I'm not sure I'm ready to go back to that show," Mabel said, despondently. "Not with this crowd."

"I'm not sure Eleanor Burns is ready for this crowd." replied Hattie. "Stay here if you want, but I'm getting on the bus. There's no way I'm going to miss this show. I have a feeling it's going to be one to remember."

Sure Hattie was right, I hopped on the bus right behind her. Mabel reluctantly followed me.

"How are we ever all going to fit on here?" asked the Queen of SASS.

"Oh, honey," answered Red Hat Nanny, "suck it in. You know we're a close knit group."

"Hey, Mabel, be sure to suck in your fat quarters," called Miz Eudora. "And Red Hat Nanny, this is a quilting group, not a knitting group. We're bees."

Laughter erupted all over the bus, spreading even to the driver, as the women shouted comments about what awaited them at the televised Eleanor Burns' ***USO Show*** at Carson Park.

Yes, I secretly thought to myself, ***there are definitely going to be more than two reasons to party this weekend. And one of them***, I reasoned with a quiet smile, ***is going to be the departure of Miz Eudora and her followers from Paducah.***

I watched a derby rider training his horse in the background at the stables, situated directly behind and beside the temporary quilting tents, at Carson Park. I wondered whether I should warn the derby jockey to put the horse away until the conclusion of this show.

Why bother? I then answered myself. ***A horse, a jockey and a stripper. That ought to add up to one heck of a show***, I concluded, imagining the horse breaking loose and tearing through the tent during the course of the show. ***Quilts and strips would be flying everywhere, not to mention all the quilters and strippers…and Mabel's fat quarters!***

Well, Eleanor announced this is a new show. It may even be unlike anything the quilters of America have seen before. I wonder what kind of blocks they'll come up with for this escapade!

I didn't bother to hide my outburst of laughter at that vision. Besides, the Red Hatters were all having such a good time, not to mention the quilters, that one more person's laughter was not going to add significantly to the cacophony of fun already being had on the grounds. There was shopping and Eleanor's show for the women, and horses and stables for the husbands who'd tagged along.

In that moment, I found myself thanking God for putting me in the path of this woman who had introduced me to flour sacks and whom I had introduced to paper towels. In that same moment, I also realized that I was thinking how good the world was and that, for the first time since Leon's death, my first impression of a place wasn't wishing he were with me to see it.

ELEVEN

She Made a Stripper Out of Me

"WELCOME TO THE store, ladies!" came the cheerful greeting as our "gang" descended upon the front door of the Quilt in a Day store. "The colors for today are creams and browns."

The greeting was extended by none other than Southern Belle Susan, along with three other clerks, all in turn.

"What does she mean, 'the colors for today are creams and browns?'" asked the Queen of SASS.

"They select two colors each day of the show. All their bolts of fabrics that are primarily either of those two colors are on sale for that day. That's how they keep people coming back daily," explained Hattie. "We learned that tidbit of information yesterday."

"That is," added Miz Eudora, "unless a body wants a quilt with only two colors."

"Well, that wouldn't be any fun," replied Miss

Bloomers.

"And it would be pretty boring, if you ask me," said the Sassy Grandma.

As I viewed the massive crowd inside the store, I saw that we were going to have to split up and do our rambling of the stores and the area in shifts. Red Hat Nanny came to the same conclusion and began dividing the Red Hatters into groups of six, assigning one lady of each sextet to be in charge of keeping her group together. Her action reminded me of young schoolchildren, but then, in this small town with nearly 35,000 other visitors from out-of-town, I had to admit Red Hat Nanny's rationale was a good one. Besides, she was the one most used to planning events with hundreds of women. This was a piece of cake for her.

Each group was assigned a place or area of the town to scope out for the rest of us. Then we'd meet back together to share the information and each group would head out again in search of a new adventure. Having a day's advantage, I suggested a few places they might want to visit.

"I'm hitting that ice cream shop with the big cow out front!" yelled one of the women.

"That place is delicious," offered a local. "There's a Homemade Pie Shoppe right beside it."

"Yummmmm…," the women of one group echoed in chorus as they headed toward the pies and ice cream.

"I'm hungry!" shouted several Pink Hatters in unison.

"Why don't you try Jeremiah's?" I suggested.

"Be sure they tell you all the history of that place," Hattie instructed. "Make sure to ask about the ghost that lives upstairs, too."

"And there's a great antique store at Jeremiah's," said Mabel. "I found several treasures there yesterday," she added, patting the new stole of fur critters around her neck.

"I also heard some of the quilters who'd gone to The Gold Rush for lunch yesterday say it was very good," I shared.

"With 35,000 women in this town, there's bound to be lots of good food," said Smokin' Barb. "If these women can quilt, chances are they can probably cook."

"Yeah, but all those cooking quilters are here at the show. I doubt their hubbies are barbecue kings, like yours!" replied Miss Bloomers.

"I need some peace and quiet," said another of the women, shading her eyes from the sun.

"There's a gazebo near the riverboat's landing where you can overlook the river, the floodwall mural, all the stores and shops and watch all the people," said Miz Eudora.

"Or you can just sit there and close your eyes," offered Hattie.

"I saw some benches on the lawn of the quilt

museum, too," stated one of the women. "Why doesn't our group find a place to get some sandwiches and have a picnic there?"

"We sat in that bus so long that my legs are screaming for some exercise," said another.

"There's plenty of ways to get that here and the weather's perfect. Why don't you take a walk along the river's edge and see the history of the town of Paducah on the floodwall? It's a mural that runs for two blocks and each painting has a historical plaque to give you information about it."

Within a matter of a few minutes, all the groups had trailed off in different directions, all in search of a new adventure. I knew there would be stories to be shared, and laughed at, when we all got back together for dinner that evening.

Red Hat Nanny's group stuck with Miz Eudora's "groupies" as we all made our way into the quilt shop. It didn't matter that cream and brown were the colors for the day as they trotted off for the reds and purples, where the best "stripper" of the group measured them for new outfits.

"How are we going to get all this fabric home?" asked Smokin' Barb.

"I'm taking mine home in my husband's transmission," a lovely lady, who had a lovely Australian accent, informed us as she waited to check out.

"Your husband's transmission?" asked Red Hat

Nanny.

"Yes, he's a racer you see," – ***not another one,*** I feared – "and the only way I could get him to let me come here was to fly into Chicago, pick up a new transmission for his race car, and then come here. I'm filling that transmission full of fabric before I take it home."

"Won't the fabric get dirty and oily?" asked the Sassy Grandma.

"I should hope not," replied the Australian lady. "It's brand new and cleaner than I was when I came into this world."

Her comment caused a round of snickers as we each thought of our own ingenious ways to get home with all the purchases we intended to make while in Paducah.

Not a single one of us left the store without an "Eleanor Burns Made a Stripper Out of Me" shirt, which we unanimously decided would be the dress of choice for the food fight. I secretly wondered how much food we'd be taking home with us for later.

TWELVE

Church: It's Good for What Ails You

LIVING ACROSS "THE road" from Miz Eudora was about "the best blessing the 'good Lord' could bestow on one of his servants." Although I'd not spent a lot of time in the faith, having this woman to brighten my days gave attending church a whole new meaning. Not only did you get a good sermon, you got a good laugh. You never knew when one of Miz Eudora's garters would pop loose, or when she'd decide to "take matters into her own hands." The one thing you could count on every Sunday though, since Horace's "celebration", was that Mabel would be sitting on the top row of the choir where she could keep a check on things.

"I don't know what's worse," Miz Eudora would sputter every Sunday on the way home, "Mabel clunking around in her high-heel shoes and that 'disgustin'-looking string of fur critters' she wears around her neck, or her perched up there in the top row of the choir loft checking out the roots of all the women, and men, seated in front of her. She looks like a confounded old hawk ready to light on some poor creature of prey."

It so happened that the words, "some poor creature of prey," were accompanied by a look of deep gratification in Miz Eudora's eyes. I knew that look. It was the same one she'd offered Mr. Grover Swicegood, Chair of the Church Council, on the Sunday when she warned him about "that blamed ole Kelvinator" and proceeded to announce that she was tired of being one of the "frozen chosen."

Oh, well, I told myself, ***at least he had fair warning that she was preparing to "take matters into her own hands."***

There were two things I could decipher about her expression on the way home on this particular day. One was that this "taking of matters" involved Mabel, and two, that Mabel was going to get no forewarning. As with that Sunday she pronounced that she would put an end to the "blamed old Kelvinator," I wasn't sure I wanted to experience the "matter" that involved Mabel, but on the other hand, I was more assured that I didn't want to miss it. I went home, after enjoying "Sunday dinner" with Miz Eudora, and circled next Sunday's date on the calendar, for it was sure to be a "red letter" day.

MIZ EUDORA HAD decided to walk to church the next Sunday. I'm sure it was because she wanted to take no chance of being late to see the reaction of whatever "matter" she had handled during the week. I saw nothing out of the ordinary on her that morning – at least "out of the ordinary" as far as Eudora Rumph was concerned. She did wear her colorful purple hat and quilted outfit that she'd donned for the quilt contest, which automatically told me she expected to be the center of attention before the morning was over. When she had any inkling that people were going to be looking at her, that outfit had become her trademark. Other than that, it seemed business – "the Good Lord's business" – as usual at First Church, Smackass.

That was until I heard the outrageous "ahhh-whoooop" coming from the choir room and all of the uproar that followed. The next thing I knew, I heard Mabel coming toward the sanctuary like a herd of elephants, yelling Miz Eudora's name with every step.

"She's the one responsible for this! I know she is!" blasted Mabel, nearing the sanctuary door.

I glanced in the direction of Miz Eudora's pew to see her sitting there, fanning calmly – as usual – with her fan from the Smiley Funeral Parlor. ***No doubt one left from the stash they provided her at Horace's passing.***

"Just you wait until I get my hands on her," Mabel ranted, heading the procession of Preacher Jake, the choir director, half the men in the choir, and Mr. Grover Swicegood bringing up the rear like the caboose of a train. And there they came, through the back door of the church and up the center aisle with Mabel "going off" like the train whistle of the engine, Preacher Jake taking on the role of the conductor and the men acting as train cars, with some as passengers merely along for the ride. I noticed there were no women aboard this "gospel train." I soon noticed the reason for that, for Mabel came "chuggin'" down the aisle, steam a-puffin' as she came and she was dragging her choir robe behind her. Not with her hand, mind you, but by her foot. The robe's hem had gotten "caught up" in her right heel. She had apparently thrown the robe on the floor in horror when she saw the added decoration of fur critters racin' 'round its neck that morning.

You'd think that would have been "most pleasin'" to Mabel, but there was a bit of an exception with these fur critters. They were little brown mice that Miz Eudora had, more than likely, scrounged up in one of the barns during the week and laced together to give her sister-in-law her very own fur-collar choir robe. And with every step Mabel took, their little brown heads were bobbing up and down on the wooden floorboards, their still-beaded eyes looking like they were giving the recipient of their graces the "ole once-over."

At the sight of this, every eye turned to see Miz

Eudora's reaction, which was nothing more than, "What's wrong with you, Mabel? What's all that hissy-fittin' about? You're the one who's always stirrin' a fuss 'bout needing to find a new fur wrap and complainin' that we have nothing to offer in the line of shopping in Clay County. I was just tryin' to help you out a spell."

"It's a spell, all right!" fumed Mabel. "You're an absolute witch and if Preacher Jake had any gumption about him, he'd put an end to your spells. He ought to have a good exorcism and rid this poor congregation of you once and for all."

I highly suspected that had a vote been taken, Mabel is the one who'd have won dibs on being "exorted" from the congregation. On second thought, I decided it was too bad this denomination wasn't into "excommunicating." The First Church of Smackass Gap might have been rid of Mabel Toast Jarvis long before this incident.

Mr. Grover Swicegood finally caught up with the "engine" of this "holy locomotive" and soothed her ruffled feathers. That is, after he got the robe loose from her heel and sent it outside with one of the "passengers" along with an order to "Get rid of these cussed varmints!" He looked at Miz Eudora, trying his best to find the "proper and right words," as Chair of the Church Council, to scold her. But try as he may, all he could do was purse his lips together in a larger effort to keep from bowling over in the floor, which is where much of the congregation was by that point.

To make matters worse, the choir's anthem for that morning was *This Train is Bound for Glory*, with Preacher Jake calling out "All aboard!" at just the precise moment when he was signaled by the choir's director, and the men giving a spoken accompaniment of "Chuga-chuga, Chuga-chuga, Chuga-chuga," underneath the women singing the upbeat spiritual. There's one thing about it. Thanks to Miz Eudora, the "spirit" was definitely in the air of the congregation that morning, so the choir's selection was nothing short of "shovelin' on a little more coal!" Mr. Grover Swicegood even blew a wooden train whistle at the end of the anthem, signifying the finale.

It was a fairly safe bet that not one person left the service that day with a care in the world, thanks to Miz Eudora Rumph's act of "handling matters." ***Nor will they have a care in the world for the rest of the* week**, I wagered, noting there would probably be a rise in attendance and the weekly offering on the following Sunday. There was no doubt that news would spread like wildfire "through the grapevine" about the "fascinatin' worship experience" to be had at First Church, Smackass. At this rate, I suspected we'd soon be competing in numbers with "Six Flags over Jesus." I couldn't help but wonder, though, how many other members went home raising the same prayer to the

"Good Lord" that I did – that Miz Eudora would never take up "handling snakes" instead of matters. I had a gut feeling that was the only way she could top the day's performance.

That's how it was that I came to learn that while Preacher Jake offered words of wisdom to live by for the week, it was guaranteed that either Miz Eudora or Mabel would provide a good laugh to heal anything else that could possibly ail you for the rest of the week.

THIRTEEN

If You Can't Beat 'Em, Join 'Em

IT WAS A lovely morning for planting the garden as I ventured across Highway 64 "bright and early" to offer Miz Eudora a hand with her gardening. Not that she needed it, mind you, for like everyone one else in Smackass Gap, she'd been gardening ever since she was old enough to walk. In fact, to hear her tell it, I'm not sure she wasn't picking up seeds and tossing them on the ground when her "Ma" was still carrying her, through the field in a sling pouch with the seeds, before her walking days. Leastways, I could easily envision that as I looked across her "garden" that would have easily been considered a whole farm where I came from.

The visits to her house were more for my benefit, for each one was a lesson. Not always a lesson in cooking, sewing or planting, either, but in the simple lessons of life – many of which taught me a lot about her perception of life, faith and the human race. I was hoping that this particular morning's lesson was all about planting seeds since I wanted a few plants of my own to make me feel like "I belonged" – not to mention that I was becoming accustomed to having fresh fruits and vegetables at my disposal. The idea of walking out my back door, grabbing a couple of tomatoes off the vine and having a tomato sandwich was one that fascinated me.

As I reached Miz Eudora's driveway, I sensed something in the air that told me this was going to be quite an intriguing day. By now, I should have learned that those "something in the air" sensations were accentuated warnings to get back across the road into my own house and bar the door as tightly as I could. But no, my feet kept treading up the Rumph driveway, with Clyde braying to welcome me and the songbirds warbling loudly, gleefully trying to outdo each other. Even the flowers seemed to raise their heads to wish me a "Good morning." Thinking back on that morning, I'm more convinced that they ***were*** raising their heads…to see me, once again, get "suckered in" by the winsome ways of Miz Eudora Rumph.

"Sadie," she called, beckoning me from the spare bedroom, which had been converted into her sewing room where she now turned out all of her "Smack from the Gap" items. "Come on back here and help me. I could have done this by myself, but since you're here, you can do it."

I had no idea what I could help with, but given my reputation with a needle and thread, I knew it had to be majorly minor. One step into the room made me want to turn and run back home as quickly as I'd come. ***No, make that faster!*** I was sure that Miz Eudora had either been nipping in Horace's jug or she'd had a stroke. Either way, I wanted no part of what I beheld. For there stood Miz Eudora in a ripped up white T-shirt with a red tank top underneath and a pair of Mabel's purple tights from her exercise class – the ones that I recognized from the day we all went to the fitness center together. They were impossible to forget, as that was the day Miz Eudora wound up inviting the class to her house to pull real weeds instead of the imaginary ones the coach used.

"Don't you pay no never mind to these britches," she said, making me further wish I stood ***any*** chance of forgetting them. "I'll take care of them in a little bit. I cannot believe that Mabel can rip the crotch out of a pair of these spandex things. Why, they stretch every way you do. I guess there was just too much of her to stretch. Reckon it's not natural for a body to stretch that way." She chuckled. "It's obviously not natural for these tights to stretch that way."

Try as I might, I couldn't help but notice the condition of the tights. Miz Eudora was right about one thing. It was hard to believe that a body could do that much damage to a pair of tights. More strange to me was that she didn't mention not to "pay no never mind" to the rest of her clothes, which were equally as mindboggling, given the fact they were on her.

Afraid of what her answer might be, but hoping beyond all reason there actually ***was*** a reason for this strange dress, I ventured forth. "Do you mind if I ask what you're doing in those tights…and the white t-shirt that appears to be falling to shreds?" I didn't mention the red tank top because I really didn't want to know.

"Didn't I tell you?" she responded cheerfully. "I'm going to join the new liturgical dance team over at Six Flags over Jesus.

"***Oh, yes. That's just a minor thing. Of course, you just forgot to mention it, I'm sure***," was running through my mind as I stood there, even more in shock. "You're what?" I gulped, sure that I was still in my own bed and having a bad dream.

"Those young'uns over there are having themselves such a good time that I went over to watch. At first I was flabbergasted…, and even a little bit embarrassed," she whispered, "at all that movin' around they were doing. But after a while, I saw how sincere they were in their praisin' and dancin' and glorifyin' the Almighty. You know, I never in my life saw anything like that before that church built there on the road in front of your house. I had half a mind to go over and give them a piece of my mind, but every time I got that notion, it seemed the Good Lord put a bigger notion in the other half of my mind not to."

Had I been listening to an answer from anyone besides Miz Eudora Rumph, I'd have been totally confused by that time, but as it was, I was right there - in that same zone - with her, making me unsure whether to be frightened or amused.

"I'd been traipsing down to the church every time I heard that loud music get to going, just so's I could keep an eye on things. You know," she added, as if this was the first thing she'd said that needed further explanation, "I finally decided they were having so much fun that maybe I ought to give it a try. Besides, it sure beats going off to that exercise class with Mabel. I get a lot more out of it, physically ***and spiritually***. You know, I feel like I'm getting a good feedin' of the Spirit every time I go over there and watch those young'uns.

"I got such a bellyful last week that I didn't even eat supper when I came home. Now that's what I call real dieting. That Mabel, and all the rest of them ladies, ought to get over to Six Flags over Jesus and work out with those teenagers. They could build up their muscles and minds all at the same time. Yes, sirree, and feel fed up by the Spirit all the while.

"And that's how I come to be dressed this way. I finally decided if I couldn't beat 'em, join 'em! That's my opinion." She paused only long enough to pick up a pair of scissors. "Now you take these and cut the back of the shirt up in strips just like I've done the front. I wanted to see what it looked like before I cut the whole thing. I think it works just fine. What do you think?"

My mind was still so boggled that I didn't think anything, but it didn't matter, for she went right on about her task.

"I've gotta sew up these tights where Mabel blew the seat out, though, or they'll think I'm doing the Moon Walk."

One thing I had to admit was that no matter what kind of lesson I was learning, laughter was involved. In her pure, simplistic comments, Miz Eudora kept me healthy with a good dose of laughter. That statement was, unequivocally, one of those doses of "the best medicine."

She continued with, "I saw where the congregation at Six Flags over Jesus sang ***Immoral, Invisible*** a couple of Sundays ago, but I don't think this 'get-up' is what Brother Terry had in mind."

"That's ***IMMORTAL, Invisible***," I corrected.

"No, ma'am, Sadie," she insisted. "The bulletin plainly said, '***Immoral, Invisible***.' Brother Terry must have known I was going to join their dance team. I think he had a vision of what I'd show up in and he wanted to make sure if I was going to be immoral, I'd also be invisible."

This was the second time we'd had such a conversation regarding this particular hymn. The first time had been while we were in Paducah on the morning we went to church with Mrs. Ada.

It's all your fault, Sadie. You have no one else to blame.

My conscience was right; I had no one else to blame. I'd been the one who, Sunday after Sunday, had tried to convince Miz Eudora that morning worship bulletins "were not merely a waste of trees, nor a sacred gossip column." About the time I resolved to give up, I noticed her reading the entire thing – ***cover to cover!*** – one Sunday.

She began to read the bulletins so thoroughly, in fact, that she had friends bring them to her from their various churches around the community. I suspected the local church secretaries ought to have hired her to proofread for them, for she caught every single blooper in short order. But then, had the secretaries done that, we in the congregation would have had nothing to laugh at when she pointed them all out on Sunday morning.

Such was the case on the Sunday morning in Paducah. We'd just sat down in the pew – ***close to the front, to be sure!*** – our bodies ***and*** our pocketbooks, patted the wrinkles out of our dresses, adjusted our hats, and done all those little trivial things that little old ladies do when they take their seats at church. That had given Miz Eudora precisely enough time to peruse the bulletin.

"Look at what the organist is playing for the postlude, Mrs. Sadie," Miz Eudora hastily informed me, wanting to make sure I knew she saw it first.

I looked to where she pointed in the bulletin and found myself already amused that this purebred mountain woman, who less than a year earlier despised church bulletins, was now a connoisseur of preludes and postludes.

"Toccata on ***Immoral, Invisible***," she read aloud, struggling with the first word of the title, which I was sure would be a part of her vocabulary before the day was over.

"I think that's supposed to say, '***Immortal, Invisible***,'" I corrected gingerly, not wishing to create a scene. After all, we were visitors and this was the congregations' first impression of us. ***It would be nice if we could remain invisible, like the hymn***, I noted to myself, aware that it would probably also be the congregation's last impression.

"I'm not too sure," she replied, still staring at the page. "Why would one want to be invisible if they were immortal? They'd have something to brag about in that case. But now, if they were ***immoral***, they would not want to be seen. They'd be trying to hide, so they would definitely be the ones what would want to be invisible. And not only that," she persisted, "but look at that fancy word in front of the title."

While Miz Eudora tried to make "heads or tails" out of the word "toccata," another elderly woman waddled her way down the aisle and sat on the pew in front of us, just in time to catch the end of the conversation.

"I'm miserable, too," I heard the woman turn and say to Miz Eudora.

"***Miserable?***" I asked myself. ***Where'd she get that? She must have thought she heard Miz Eudora say 'miserable' if she added the word 'too' to her sentence.*** "I'm miserable," I repeated to myself softly. ***Miserable? I'm miserable? I'm miserable…I'm miserable…INVISIBLE!*** I took a quick glance and, sure enough, the woman was wearing a hearing aid. ***It must not be turned up enough***, I surmised, wondering whether to advise her that she might wish to turn it up. ***Maybe that's the point, Sadie. You've not heard either this choir, organist or minister. Perhaps she's just fine the way she is.***

Agreeing with my conscience, I went back to listening to the pair.

"Who typed your bulletin this week?" Miz Eudora was quick to ask the "miserable" woman, as if she were a detective hot on a trail to solving a crime. Her question had nothing to do with the fact that she wanted to find out who made the mistake, but rather who the "immoral" one was.

"Why, the preacher did it," the woman answered with a nod. "He's mighty handy with all those computer gadgets."

"I see," Miz Eudora replied, more to me than to the woman. "Mighty ***handy***, huh?" she whispered in my direction. "Maybe that's why he wants to be invisible."

I pondered on her words, and her curious thought process, for a few seconds until she leaned toward me again. I knew she had a final word of wisdom on the subject, thus I was neither surprised, nor disappointed, when she added, "Oh well, at least he's not miserable about whatever he's doing immoral. I guess if he's okay with it, I don't have to worry about it. I'm not the one what'll be answering for his immoral sins when he reaches the Pearly Gate." With that conclusion, she was perfectly satisfied.

Seeing no point in explaining typographical errors at that moment, I let Miz Eudora sit there in peace. I was sure she'd be examining the minister closely to try to decipher what was immoral about him – ***and what he's trying to keep invisible***, I thought with a chuckle – during the sermon. Then it struck me, it wasn't the minister who was immoral at all. It was the organist. She was the one, after all, who was "playing around," – as my dearly departed Leon used to describe "toccatas," – on the immoral subject!

I sat there, trying to control the laughter inside me that hastily turned into another one of those "melting moments" – I had learned to call them – which I experienced when I was around Miz Eudora, as her simple childlike spirit took me back to a forgotten chapter in my memories. For here I was, in church, seeing myself as a child in a Sunday School classroom where a teacher, much like – ***No, exactly like!*** – Mrs. Theona Rouette was teaching us the evils of gossip. She'd used "the gossip game" where one child started with a phrase, given by the teacher, and we each took our turn in a long line of whispering that phrase into the ear of the person beside us. Naturally, the phrase we ended up with was nothing like the phrase the teacher had given at the beginning.

Here I was, fifty years later, playing the same game in church, only this time in the sanctuary. ***And for real. Ah, these lovely melting moments!*** Once again, in the presence of Miz Eudora, I felt my inner self melting away as it was replaced with a warmth that made me glow all over, but especially inside.

No wonder Miz Eudora had disproved of the bulletin so "doggedly" when she first thought of it as a "sacred gossip column." She was right. In her mind, the rumors it spread were definitely against the rules of "the Good Book."

Thanks to that day in Paducah, Miz Eudora was convinced the real title of the hymn was ***Immoral,***

Invisible. Thanks to that same day, she was also determined that was the same hymn that had been sung at Brother Terry's congregation of Six Flags over Jesus a couple of weeks before. Ready to let the matter rest, I decided to go home and plant the tomatoes, risking using only my own defenses.

That's when Miz Eudora asked, "You want to go to church me with tonight, Sadie? The prison quartet is playing."

"Prison quartet? I was unaware there was a prison near here." Any other time, I might have been shocked by a prison quartet set loose in Smackass Gap, but given the morning I'd shared with Miz Eudora, this seemed quite fitting for the day's activities. "Where are they from and how did Preacher Jake arrange to get them to your church? Has he started a new prison ministry?"

"Oh, no, ma'am. They're all four members of our congregation at First Church, Smackass. We just call them that because they're 'behind a few bars' most of the time and 'are always looking for the key.'"

Had Miz Eudora not been dead serious, that would have been the worst joke I'd ever heard. But there she stood, in that ridiculous get-up, smiling and inviting me to come to her church to hear some horrid quartet that evening.

My disinterest in the offer must have shown in the expression on my face, for she explained, "They are awful, but they mean well. They play their four hearts out and we always have a good time of fun and fellowship afterwards. There's cake and ice cream and tonight, I'm taking an apple pie. People come just to see each other and share in the Holy Spirit. Same thing I'm doing with those teenagers down at Six Flags over Jesus.

"Too many people want to go to church and bellyache just like they ate a pile of green apples. What you got to do is go and have yourself a good time "meetin' and greetin'" and you'll feel God there. Even if Preacher Jake's not on one of his best days, he says something I can sit there and chew on, instead of rushing out the back door to gripe and complain. If all these people what went to church spent as much time spreading love and laughter as they did gossiping and criticizing, why, land sakes, the church would be as full as that Georgia Mountain Fairgrounds always is over in Hiawassee."

You had to give the woman credit, she had a point. I wondered how many of the religion professors and ministers around the country had as much of an astute insight into "doing the Lord's work" as my simple mountain neighbor.

"I'm thinking of asking the "prison quartet" if they don't need a lead singer," Miz Eudora said. "I think I'll suggest Mabel and tell them about her experience in the strip joint."

"The strip joint?" I asked, seeing the moment of being "suckered in" on its way.

"Yes, the strip joint. You've heard her. She sounds like she's stripped a gear every time she opens her mouth to sing. And those knees of hers crackle and pop so loud that it sounds like her joints are playing percussion."

The precocious twinkle in her eye was worth the entire morning. ***And getting "suckered in,"*** I laughed to myself, hoping the flowers still had their heads raised to see it.

I walked home, after promising to hear the prison band that evening, realizing that I had indeed been given a "hands-on" lesson in planting seeds that morning, just not the kind I'd anticipated. However, Miz Eudora's "lesson of the day" did have a lot more value, I was sure, than tomato plants.

FOURTEEN

Miz Eudora's Sparklin' Shiners

"WHAT ARE WE going to call ourselves?" asked Smokin' Barb as "the entourage" sought to form a new chapter of Red and Pink Hatters while on an outing.

"Whatever it is, it must be ***befitting*** to all of Miz Eudora's 'groupies,' or loyal subjects," offered Red Hat Nanny.

"I know, the Smackass Strippers!" proclaimed Carly with a little too much gusto, judging from the gasps, blushing cheeks and shaking of heads from some of the women.

"That's creative," replied Miz Eudora. "After all, Smackass Gap got its name because they used to mine for corundum there and the miners stripped some of the mountains."

"I'm not sure my husband would let me participate in any of our activities if we called ourselves strippers," admitted the Queen of SASS.

"Now don't you worry about that," Miz Eudora assured her, "you wouldn't be stripping unless you took up quilting. But then we ***could*** all wear our shirts from Eleanor Burns' store." She gave a girlish giggle. "I just loved coming home and wearing that shirt. It made me the talk of the town."

Like she wasn't already, I wanted to add.

"It was so popular that every woman in Clay County begged Rob Tiger to carry those shirts at Chinquapin's. They even asked Clay to carry them at Clay's Corner over in Brasstown," she declared proudly at the thought of starting a new fad.

"That name might not be such a bad idea," responded The Sassy Grandma. "I remember hearing about a group of ladies who did a calendar as a fundraiser for some worthy cause. They bared themselves, but the clever ways in which they posed using various props kept anything from showing."

"I heard about that, too," replied the Spunky Georgia Peach. "From what I recall, they made a lot of money."

"Sounds like a good idea to me," offered another of Ila, Georgia's 'New Hattitudes.' "We could pay for all of our escapades with Miz Eudora."

"I'm not sure those could be considered a worthy cause," warned Miss Bloomers.

"Of course they could!" announced the Queen of SASS. "Being on a trip with Miz Eudora is a trip in itself. I've laughed so hard in the last two days that I'm sure I've taken ten years off my life."

"You got that right," seconded the eldest hatter in the group. "If we keep this up on the other trips, I'll be a kid again by the time we get to next Christmas' trip."

"And Santa can bring you a doll down the chimney again," Miss Bloomers responded with a laugh.

"There's nothing wrong with that," replied the Sassy Grandma. "I play dolls with my granddaughter and her favorite part is dressing up in my red hats and purple clothes while she's dressing the dolls."

"Who needs granddaughters?" asked Miss Bloomers. "My favorite part of any day is getting dressed up like this to do anything."

"That's right! We all love any excuse to dress up," added the Spunky GA Peach, getting caught up in the red-and-purple avalanche of hormonal adrenalin. "Otherwise the lot of us wouldn't be standing here now, dressed like this and trying to decide on a name for ourselves!"

"BRAVO!" I exclaimed, clapping wildly before abruptly stopping, realizing that I had just unknowingly inducted myself into "whatever-this-group-was-going-to-be-called" and that I was now "one of them."

"Think about it," challenged Red Hat Nanny, "when we were young, we used to dress paper dolls. Now we have too much fun dressing ourselves. For some of us, we really are nothing more than human dolls. I actually love that thought. It makes me feel…younger!"

"You got that right!" agreed Carly. "My husband says I'm a more fun doll now than when he married me since I got into wearing all this bling and glitz."

I hoped she'd stop with that comment for I was afraid of receiving a little too much information. In my naïve state, I wasn't quite sure I was ***that*** into being "one of them" yet. Besides, Leon would never get the opportunity to experience me being a "past-middle-age doll," so why bother? Not to mention that I knew Miz Eudora wouldn't go for considering herself a doll, and there was no way I could picture anyone giving a child they loved a doll that looked like Mabel.

To my relief, or so I'd thought, Miss Bloomers quickly interjected, "Personally I like The Rosy Red Smackassers."

The Queen of SASS wheeled around and snapped, "I can't believe you said that!"

"Well, it was a sight better than the alternative," defended the Sassy Grandma. "She could have said 'Rosy Red…, well you know, the reverse of that other word."

It took some of the women a tad longer than others to catch what she meant, but as they made the connection, trickles of laughter dribbled throughout the group.

"What's wrong with Rosy Red Smackers?" asked Mabel. "Then we could have something that tied us to Smackass Gap and Rosy Red is the color of my favorite shade of lipstick."

Why did I know that would start a ruckus? I asked myself when I saw Miz Eudora turn to face her sister-in-law.

"Mabel, I've wanted to smack you many times over the years, but on the lips wasn't one of those places. I don't think I could bear thinking of your 'Rosy Red lips' every time I talked to one of my sister Red Hatters."

Somehow I was prepared for more of a comeback, but Smokin' Barb took care of that when she suggested, "I think we should call ourselves Miz Eudora's Sparklin' Shiners."

"Sparklin' Shiners," repeated Miz Eudora, her mind instantly forgetting Mabel's recommendation. "I believe I like that." She was silent for a moment as she apparently said the name over a few times in her mind. "Yes, I do like that. 'Miz Eudora's Sparklin' Shiners.' It has a nice ring to it. Why, if we had Brother Tidwell here to play the washtub and Old Man Simms here to blow the jug, I do believe we could make ourselves a little song out of that name."

A washtub and a jug, I thought, my mind drifting as I stood visualizing the pair of instruments ***and*** their players. ***Sounds more like* moon *"shiners" than***

glitzy "shiners." I smiled at the play on words. ***Well, she did say "Sparklin' Shiners." It could have a double meaning.***

My inside joke quickly came to a halt as I noticed that Miz Eudora had her coat off, her shirtsleeve rolled up, and was threatening to give Mabel "a real shiner if you say something like that again." I had no idea what Mabel had said, but it didn't matter. I had to find a way to stop this developing altercation.

"I ***really*** like the name 'Miz Eudora's Sparklin' Shiners.' May I be the first member?" I hastily asked, loudly enough to capture Miz Eudora's attention and interrupt the chase that was off to a good start.

Miz Eudora stopped, turned and offered me a gratifying smile as if she suddenly remembered that she was a queen and should behave as such. "I'd be honored if you'd be one of my Sparklin' Shiners, Sadie," she said, rolling her shirtsleeve back down and replacing her purple fopher coat. "How would you like to be my Vice-Queen Mother?"

I glanced at the three women – Mabel, Hattie and Miz Eudora – now all staring at me in anticipation of a response. Not one of us had children of our own; not one of us had ever given birth. This was my first chance to be a mother, ***vice or otherwise***, of anything. I felt a wave of guilt overtake me as I looked at these women who had become my family. I couldn't be a mother without them.

"I'd dearly love that, Miz Eudora, and am deeply honored that you asked," I answered, choosing my words carefully, "but I think it would be more appropriate if you named Smokin' Barb and Red Hat Nanny your Vice-Queen Mothers. They're more familiar with the 'goings-on' of chapters and have more experience in what to do. I do think it would be nice, though, if we three, Hattie, Mabel and myself, were your special loyal subjects so that we could help with any of the royal details which you might wish to hand off to us." I wasn't sure I'd sold her on allowing Mabel to be a part of that honor, but I was saying a prayer as well as crossing the fingers of my right hand behind my back. I also wasn't sure about the legitimacy of the crossed fingers, but just in case, I was sure a combined dose of luck and prayer couldn't hurt.

"I guess that's alright," she said slowly, summing up Mabel with a hard glance. "There's got to be something Mabel can do." A big smile broke across her face. "I know. She can be in charge of our Halloween event. She's the closest thing to a witch I know." Her smile turned into a full-fledged laugh. "Why, if we give her a broom, I'll bet she can even fly."

"I'll show you a broom," replied Mabel, angrily, stomping back toward Miz Eudora. She stopped in her tracks, realizing that she'd just been donned the closest thing to royalty she'd ever see. Looking at me, she asked, "Does this mean I get to wear the crown sometimes?"

"Maybe," I answered, "if Miz Eudora can't be at one of the meetings." I feared that was the wrong choice of words for I was certain that Mabel would find something to keep "the queen" from appearing at one of the meetings, even if it meant pouring arsenic over her breakfast.

Deep inside, I knew that even Mabel wouldn't go that far. Although she would never admit it, she had no one besides Miz Eudora and she wasn't about to lose that companionship, no matter how loudly she protested. As bad as it seemed at times, she had more attention and friendship in Smackass Gap than she'd had at home with Melba and Milton T. She had buttered her "Toast" on the wrong side of them long before.

"I think that's an excellent idea," I agreed, causing Mabel to glare begrudgingly at me. "Miss Hattie can be in charge of an Easter Parade and Mabel can do the Halloween Haunt. I'll plan our bus trips and you…well, you can just be the Queen and tell us what you need done. That and entertain everyone with your stories."

"I second that," chimed in Hattie. "I think we've got a plan. Now all we need to do is decide who we want to invite to be a part of our chapter."

"Well, I'll tell you one thing," replied Miz

Eudora, "whoever we invite, they'd better be able to sparkle and shine as much as we do. I surely don't want any dull or tarnished members in my group."

"I don't think there's much chance of that, Miz Eudora," I assured her, thinking how "dull" and "tarnished" were the last two words that came to mind when I was in her presence. "Not as long as you're the Queen Mother."

"Does that role also include officiating at weddings and funerals like Preacher Jake?" asked Miz Eudora, causing me to wonder what was coming next and knowing it must concern Mabel.

"All I can say," concluded The Sassy Grandma, "is that when I die, I want Miz Eudora at my funeral. What a celebration!"

"P'SHAA!" exclaimed Miz Eudora, blushing from all the attention. "I've got you ladies all beat. You'll be coming to my celebration, and you'd everyone better be there 'sparklin' ***and*** 'shinin.'"

"Here, here," called out Smokin' Barb. "Let's hear it for Miz Eudora's Sparklin' Shiners."

I watched in awe, raising my imaginary Mason jar of Horace's special blend with "the rest of them" as Smokin' Barb and Red Hat Nanny led the entire group in a hearty toast to being one of Miz Eudora's Sparklin' Shiners.

FIFTEEN

Smack from the Gap

"WOULD YOU LOOK at this?" asked one of the Red Hatters. She, like scores of others walked through admiring all of the original creations laid out or hung in Miz Eudora's living room, where she'd set up a temporary gallery for the initial showing of her new line of items from her "Smack from the Gap" Collection. Word had spread and on the morning she "officially" opened her doors for business, cars were lined up both sides of Downings Creek Road. I, personally, wasn't sure whether they had come to buy or simply sample her pies, a treat that came with the shopping experience.

"Every single one of these are different," stated a Pink Hatter.

"I can't believe this," said another. "She must have attended a fashion institute to pull all of this off. There must be at least a hundred of these jackets and shirts and they are all different. Some have openings in the front, some pull over the head. Not a repeat of a single design."

"Where did you find the patterns?" asked the queen of a Georgia chapter.

I loved that question for I foresaw that its answer would seal Miz Eudora's success in her new business venture as a fashion designer of her own "Smack from the Gap" original label.

"What patterns?"

"Don't tell me you didn't have a pattern for any of these," asked one of the Pink Hatters.

"Nobody in these parts had money for patterns," Miz Eudora explained. "You simply held the fabric up to the child who was fortunate enough to be getting a new set of duds and went to cutting."

"You mean to tell me that every single one of these is a different design and you had not one pattern?" asked another queen.

"Well, I did have a vision for each one in my head, if that counts," answered Miz Eudora.

"I simply cannot believe it," noted yet another queen. "Wait until I go home in my original 'Smack from the Gap' shirt. I'll be the envy of the chapter. Every single one of our members will want one. I'm not even sure I want to tell them where I found this. It may be a secret I want to keep to myself."

"You'll not be keeping it to yourself long," said

the third woman. “Look at this.” She held up a catalogue that I’d created that showed several of the designs of shirts, jackets, totes and bags. “Once these get out, every Red Hatter I know is going to be rushing to get an original made by Miz Eudora.”

That one statement was enough to cause every woman there to start grabbling to get her own original. They all wanted to be the first person on their block, or in their chapter, to possess this new fashion trend.

“Look at the velvet bags!” exclaimed another. “They’re reversible, with red on one side and purple on the other. What’s the embroidered oval for, Miz Eudora?”

“That’s where you pin your favorite piece of bling to match each particular outfit. It’s the same with my capes and satin jackets. I call them my ‘Bling It Your Way’ Line. You purchase it basic, and then each one becomes an original by the bling you add to make it fit your mood and personality.”

“How clever!” noted one of the women as hands started flying through the air to grab a bag and start blinging.

“My favorites are those reversible capes. You can dress them up or down for a day outing or an evening at the theater,” observed one of the women. “Ooh, I like the style with the point hanging down in the back. Pass me one of those,” she requested.

"Please," added her queen "mother."

"I wish I knew her secret," admitted one of the Red Hatters. "I can't believe she did every single one of these from scratch with nothing in her head."

"Oh, I had something in my head, alright," Miz Eudora assured her. "The real reason for me coming up with a different design for each one is simple. Who in their right mind would want to be walking down the street and find themselves dressed in the exact same thing as Mabel Toast Jarvis? Land sakes, that'd be enough to give a body heart failure.

"Besides, all I have to use are the scraps from the quilts I make, so I use what I have. You know, we don't have the money to be wasteful here."

"Miz Eudora, that's a great lesson for all of us. Look at the beauty that you've made from your left-overs."

"Speaking of which," asked one of the women, "I'll bet you eat leftovers, too, don't you, Miz Eudora?"

"Leftovers?" repeated Hattie. "Obviously, honey, you've never tasted a bite of Miz Eudora's cooking. I'll bet there's never been a leftover on her table."

"You cook as well as you sew?" asked the uppity queen. "Why don't you cater one of our events?"

"We've been trying to talk her into that," said Theona. "But Mabel keeps insisting that people won't drive this far to eat hog jowls."

"Hog jowls! You really eat those things?" asked one of the Pink Hatters in astonishment.

"Hey, I'll bet if she can cook hog jowls, she can make killer chicken and dumplings."

"Oh, no, ma'am," replied Miz Eudora. "I don't want my food to be giving anybody food poisoning. But I ***can*** throw together a pretty decent batch of chicken'n'dumplin's."

"A pretty decent batch?" repeated Hattie, beginning to sound like a parrot. "That's one of her specialties," she announced to the crowd.

"She can whip up anything you'd want to eat," said Theona.

"And desserts! My gracious," I added, "you haven't lived until you've had one of Miz Eudora's cakes or pies, not to mention the banana pudding."

"How long did you say it would take you to throw up a batch of chicken'n'dumplin's?" asked one of the vice-queens.

"Not as long as it would take you to ring the chicken's neck, I'll bet," answered Miz Eudora. "One of you go out and get me a chicken and I'll start the apple pie."

The looks on the faces of the Red Hatters were as priceless as Miz Eudora's creative ability to craft all the items that were quickly being renowned as her "Smack from the Gap" Collection of Miz Eudora Originals.

SIXTEEN

No Bull

THERE WAS AN event in Denton, North Carolina, where Leon had always wanted to go. It was called the Threshers' Reunion. I have to admit that I had no idea ***why*** Leon wanted to go, having never heard him mention anyone surnamed Thresher in his family. But the thought of going, if nothing except to honor his memory, was one of those notions that kept gnawing at me for some unknown reason.

Some unknown reason, that was, ***until one morning's front porch visit with Miz Eudora***.

"Sadie," she began, right off the bat, in a way most uncommon for her, "you're such a dear and you always haul us around like you were running Bud's Taxi Service up here on the mountain. I have a place I've always wanted to go because I heard Pa talk about it. Don't know how he even heard about it, because I don't rightly know exactly where the place is located, but he talked about going the last couple of years before he died, back when it first started."

She looked down at her feet and shook her head. "Poor thing, he never did go. Guess he 'figgered' his tractor wouldn't make it that far.

"I always felt bad because if baby brother John G. hadn't died so early, he might have taken Pa in his fancy automobile. But there was no way we'd ask Mabel. She was out-of-sight, out-of-mind – the same place she should be now. I'd have taken him, and Horace mentioned going every year, too, but we'd have been lucky if that old truck of his would have made it past Franklin. It was like that old thing had a mind of its own and knew when we hit the Macon County line. That's when it would 'come uncranked' every time we'd head down the mountain."

She took a sip of her coffee, which was always strong enough to make the spoon stand up and take notice. It seemed especially robust today, maybe because she'd made chocolate gravy to go with biscuits as a special treat. That, in itself, was a sure sign that this morning would be different.

"I know you said if there was ***anywhere*** I wanted to go that you'd be glad to take me," she continued. "I've been in a terrible quandary about asking you this, but while I was talking to the Good Lord this morning, he told me that you're a big girl and can answer for yourself, so now I'm a-asking. I hope you won't take no offense."

"Of course, I won't take offense," I answered, pleasantly pleased that she'd allowed me an opportunity to give her back a bit of the happiness she'd bestowed on me. What I didn't consider, at the moment, was what people say about "payback." I won't use either of the words I've heard to describe "payback," but it's too bad my mind didn't remind me of that at the time. As it was, I was too busy being excited about this occasion to have the blessing of doing something in return for my kind neighbor.

"Where exactly, and when, would you like to go, Miz Eudora?" I proceeded blindly, already sure of what my answer would be.

"It's in a place named Denton, North Carolina, and it's called the Threshers' Reunion."

Her answer caused my rocking chair - that kept the same slow, relaxing pace each morning during our front porch chats – to come to a complete halt. "Did you say the Threshers' Reunion…in Denton?" I repeated, from sheer shock at her words instead of a desire to acquire more information. I couldn't conceive that her desire was the same one which Leon had carried to the grave, and the same one which nudged me from time to time. ***Like now.***

"Why, yes, Sadie, I did. But you look like that's the Devil's Playground, like you had a horrible experience there or something. We don't have to go. I shouldn't have asked."

"No…no, Miz Eudora, it's not that at all. It's just that…well, Leon mentioned several times during our years together that he'd like to go there. I had no idea why because I'd never heard him mention anyone in his family named...,"

"Yoo-hoo!" I heard from down the driveway.

"I declare, here comes Theona Rouette," announced Miz Eudora. "Wonder what brings her out this morning? She doesn't usually pay visits lessin' it's to tell you that somebody on the other side of the mountain passed. She's sort of like the Paul Revere of Clay County, except she's always announcin' when somebody's goin' instead of comin.'"

She got up from her rocker and stepped to the edge of the porch. "What brings you here this morning, Theona? Come on up and sit a spell. I'll go to the kitchen and get you a cup of coffee. You had breakfast yet?"

The last question struck me as odd, for I'd learned long ago that I was the only person in Smackass Gap who didn't jump out of bed and have my egg frying within the same minute that my feet hit the floor. I'd grown accustomed, in my years with Leon, of getting up, reading the paper over a cup of coffee and then having breakfast after I'd had time to get fully awake. That wasn't the way of life in Smackass Gap. People here were not only awake, but running to take care of the first chore the minute their breakfast was down. They sipped the last drop of coffee going out the door so they wouldn't miss "a minute's daylight." Their newspaper reading came at night after "supper," if, during daylight, they hadn't already learned everything through the grapevine – the grapevine in Clay County known rather as visits by people like Theona Rouette.

Anyway, the question about breakfast was an inborn part of Miz Eudora's hospitable "upraising." It didn't need an answer, really, but served to make one feel welcome and know that if they were in need, they would be fed. It amazed me that in the exact time it took Miz Eudora to get to the kitchen, take a stoneware mug from the cupboard and pour hot coffee from the enamel coffee pot on the pot-bellied stove, Theona had climbed the front steps and was taking her seat in the white, wooden-slatted porch swing which I was sure Horace had made.

"Just felt an urge to come visit. The Lord told me to get on over here this morning because there was something brewin' besides your strong coffee."

I stared at her for a moment, as she took the mug from Miz Eudora and gave a cautious sip, wondering whether she was serious about her premonition from the Lord or if that was a common statement for the "mountainfolk." Besides which, I was still wondering why Miz Eudora would have business at the Threshers' Reunion. ***Surely Leon and the Jarvis family weren't both connected to the Thresher family. Wouldn't that be the biggest "WHOO-HA" of all? To find out that I'm kin to Miz Eudora Rumph. Even if it were only by marriage, that would be "some more" coincidence.***

"Well, I wouldn't rightly say that something's brewin', but we do have a mess of chocolate gravy and a big pan of biscuits, if I could interest you in a bite."

I took Theona's face lighting up as an affirmative answer as I headed for the kitchen to retrieve the biscuits and gravy. Over my shoulder, I heard Miz Eudora continue with, "And I was just asking Sadie about possibly taking me somewhere. You see, I've always wanted to go to the Threshers' Reunion."

"You mean the one in Denton?" asked Theona.

"Yes, that's exactly the one," answered Miz Eudora. "You ever been there?"

"No, but I've heard about it and all that goes on there plenty of times. People say it's something else. I wouldn't mind going myself sometime."

Don't tell me she's kin to the Threshers, too? I was so intent on listening to these two women that I completely missed Hattie drive up.

"Are you ladies having a party and somebody forgot to invite me?" she asked from the open driver's window of her "reclaimed Hattie-mobile" before even getting out of the car, just as I came out the front door.

"No," I called, beating the other two to the draw, "we're planning a road trip and you might as well throw in your two-cents' worth." The one thing I'd learned about Hattie Crow was that if there was a trip going anywhere, Hattie would be a passenger when the bus left town. ***No matter if that bus is my car***. And she'd have plenty of games to keep us busy once we got there. ***Besides, I could count on her to be the peacemaker between Miz Eudora and Mabel***, I resolved.

Speaking of which, I reminded myself as I headed back to the kitchen for another plate, ***Mabel isn't here. Could we be that lucky?*** I breathed a sigh of relief. ***There's no way Mabel Toast Jarvis could be kin to the Threshers, too. It wouldn't matter anyway,*** I told myself, ***she wouldn't claim it if she were. There's no way she's going to put herself in the same category with Miz Eudora Rumph.***

"***Don't be so sure,***" announced that voice of warning. "***After all, she is Miz Eudora's sister-in-law.***" I looked around, half expecting to see Leon staring down at me with a big smile on his face.

Hattie took a seat on the swing beside Theona while Miz Eudora took off for another mug of coffee. "Hail, hail, the gang's all here," Hattie began to sing.

I didn't dare mention that Mabel wasn't there, but then, there were two good reasons. One, she ***wasn't*** actually part of the gang – even though she always magically appeared for anything of significance which they did – and two, I saw no reason to stir up the ire of these dear women. ***Especially this early in the morning***, I cautioned myself.

"You ever heard tell of a place called Denton?" Miz Eudora asked.

Why did I know the answer before Hattie spoke?

"Isn't that the place where they have that big Threshers' Reunion every year at the Fourth of July?"

"It sure is," answered Miz Eudora. "You ever been there?"

"Nope, and I don't know where Denton is or a thing about it except that people say it's the place to be on July 4th."

"The Dam Fireworks Show is a great place to be every Fourth," heralded Miz Eudora. "I really have a hankerin' to go to that reunion, but I'd hate to miss the fireworks."

"They have fireworks at Denton," Hattie assured her.

"How do you know?" asked Theona. "I thought you said you'd never been."

"I haven't ever been," reiterated Hattie. "But anything that big held on the birthday of our country has to have fireworks. That's a given."

Theona nodded, accepting the answer.

"I've had friends from Hickory go," admitted

Hattie. "They go every year. They say it lasts for five days and some of them just stay there and visit with the people that come in from all over the country."

My eyes grew in astonishment. ***A pretty large family. Maybe Leon* was *related to Miz Eudora. Oh well,*** I told myself, ***they say that we're all related if we go far enough back***. I had a guilty thought, which I was sure had been instigated by Miz Eudora and Hattie, that I didn't want to dig far enough back in my family tree to find out that I was related to Mabel.

"What brings you here this morning, Hattie?" asked Miz Eudora. "Not that you need a reason to come over, but you generally have a plan in mind when you come a-callin.'"

"Well, I have been thinking," answered Hattie. "Mabel's birthday is coming up this fall and I thought it might be nice if you made her a quilt for her birthday. We could all help," she suggested.

"I think that would be a lovely idea," agreed Theona. "Each of us could make three or four squares."

"That's just dandy," said Miz Eudora, sarcasm apparent in her voice. "We could call it 'One-Ring Circus' in honor of Mabel. You know, Pa always did used to say that she could screw up a one-wagon funeral. I'd hate to see what she'd do with a circus." She gave an evil snicker. "'Course she wouldn't need a circus 'cause she takes her own everywhere she goes."

"Miz Eudora?" I asked calmly. "Don't you think

that's being a little drastic?"

"No, I don't. Have you ever seen that woman in action when she gets on a roll? Now there's a good act for a circus. Maybe I ought to put up a circus tent on the back side of the mountain and charge admission for people to watch. Besides, she ought to be pullin' her weight, and I don't mean physically, around here. There's got to be some way she can give back to the community, and I think this is just the ticket."

Miz Eudora chuckled louder this time at her own pun. "Ticket! See there? We could be selling tickets in no time." She paused just long enough for me to see the wheels, the ones that spelled D-A-N-G-E-R, spinning in her head. "On second thought, pullin' her weight might be interesting, too. It'd be more fun than a tractor pull."

"A tractor pull?" I asked.

"Yes." She saw the puzzled look on my face. "Haven't you ever been to one before?" I guess my expression answered her question because she didn't wait for words. "Sadie, I thought you'd been everywhere and seen everything. Why, I declare. I've found something new that I can introduce you to. How exciting!"

A huge grin broke out on her face. "This is going to be fun. I can give you something back for all them things you been introducing me to. Pack your bags because we're going to Denton." She stopped in mid-sentence and suddenly looked as if she might retreat from her offer. "It is July 4th week and we would have to miss the Dam Firework Show, but I guess this is worth it. Although I've never been, I hear it's the best tractor pull and threshing show anywhere around."

Miz Eudora gave a wicked giggle. "And here we were talking about Mabel giving back to the community and look what we've come up with. Cancel that idea about the circus tent. We'll haul Mabel off to Denton with us. I've heard they have a Parade of Power there, too." She gave a belly laugh this time. "It'll be interesting to see which one of them old coots' tractors can pull Mabel the farthest."

I still had no clue where Denton was on the map, but I suspected it was nearly as far off the beaten path as Smackass Gap. I also had no clue what a threshing show was, but I decided to wait and see. It was going to be enough just to hear and see Mabel's response when she learned that she was going to be "hauled off" to the Threshers Reunion.

To see how far she could be pulled. I mused, thinking how she'd just gone from being the star of her own one-ring-circus to being the star of the Mabel Pull. ***She isn't even here and she gets herself in trouble***.

"When is Mabel's birthday?" asked Theona.

"It's on October 31st," answered Hattie. "I remember that from grade school. That those three Toasts "popped out" of the toaster on Halloween Day."

"Well, at least we don't have to wonder whether their mother got the 'trick' or the 'treat,'" blasted Miz Eudora, still greatly amused at all her one-liners. "Hey, that gives me a great idea. Not only is she a circus with her own tent, she's a haunted house with her own horrors. We can sell tickets in the spring for the circus and the fall for the haunted house. We'll get ***double*** duty out of her."

"Or you could invite Melba and Milton T. and get triple duty," expressed Hattie.

"Wrong! Mabel's already double duty. If that pair joined her, we'd get quadruple duty."

It must be our lucky day, I told myself as I finished my coffee, feeling a little sorry for the fact that Mabel wasn't here to defend herself.

A cloud of dust coming up the driveway told me that our luck had run out. ***She must have smelled the chocolate gravy***, I said to myself as I headed for a refill, and another plate and coffee mug, to save Miz Eudora the trouble. ***"The trouble is driving up the driveway, Sadie."***

"Right! Thanks for the warning." I twirled around to see whom I had answered. ***Lord, have mercy***, I thought, sounding more like Miz Eudora every day, ***these women are enough to make a body start hearing voices.*** As I reached the front door, I realized the only real voices I heard were Mabel and her infamous sister-in-law.

"Threshers' Reunion? ***I'm*** not going to any Thresher Reunion," stormed Mabel. "I've never heard of the Thresher family and I'm sure if they'd been anywhere in my family tree, someone would have mentioned them." She stopped her ranting for a moment as a speck of reality set in. "That is, unless they were the black sheep of the family."

She flung her body into a squared-off position with Miz Eudora's. "That's it! You've somehow dug up some dirt on my family and now you're trying to rub my nose in it. Let me tell you, Eudora Rumph, I'm not going to have any part of it."

"No, Mabel," Miz Eudora assured her in a calming voice, "settle down. Nobody's trying to ruffle your feathers." She turned back toward me and whispered, "It's a shame, though. I'm not sure I could have done this good a job if I ***had*** been trying!" That "mule-eatin'-briars" grin, which was becoming a trademark, was smeared on her face. "What a waste! This would have been a good one."

Miz Eudora turned back to Mabel. "For your information, Threshers isn't a family name. Threshers are farmers. You know, they're the ones who threshed the wheat that made the flour that made the bread that made you fat," she said, exactly as if she were reciting the children's story of ***The House that Jack Built***. "This is a reunion of lots of old farmers and landowners and people who simply enjoy being around the simple ways of life for a few days."

"Who in the world would want to go to something like that?" Mabel retaliated, thoroughly bored and disgusted by the thought.

"Sixty-five thousand people, from what I understand," replied Theona.

"You're kidding?" Hattie asked. "What on earth do they do in a place that tiny for that many days?"

"Mostly the men get together to shoot the bull," answered Miz Eudora.

"Then what do the women do?" I questioned.

"I can tell you what they don't do," insisted Mabel. "They don't 'shoot the bull' since it isn't proper for ladies to 'shoot the bull.'"

"Well, there you go, Mabel," replied Miz Eudora. "After all this time, you've just admitted that you're not a lady because you shoot more bull than anybody I've ever seen."

"I do no such thing! You wouldn't know bull if it hit you upside the head."

"At least I know which one ***is*** the bull. I'm not the one who tried to milk it, like that time you did after John G. and you got married, remember? Land sakes, I thought we'uz gonna have to bury Pa right there and then.

"And you were mistaken about having no relatives there," Miz Eudora contradicted. "They don't have bulls at the Threshers' reunion. They have horses and mules. I'll bet half your family is there. I just pray my Clyde doesn't ever discover he's kin to your side of the family."

I was proven wrong in my choice of the peacemaker for it was Theona who stepped into the ring. "Sadie, dear, the threshers really are like one big family. People come from miles around to reunite with each other, so it really is a lot more involved than just coming to see tractors and farm equipment. And there are lots of vendors there who have old parts for the machinery."

"People get together for five days just to look at tractors and farm equipment?" I asked, astonished as to why so many people would find that so inviting.

"Five days!" exclaimed Mabel. "I'm with you, Sadie. There's no way I'm going to spend an entire week of my life looking at a lot of old junk farm equipment."

"That old junk farm equipment, Mabel," scolded Miz Eudora, "is considered very valuable. In fact, all of those restored tractors are worth way more than all those antiques in your house!"

"And there's sure to be fireworks!" chimed Hattie, in an attempt to head off another argument.

I found her choice of words most interesting, for it appeared to me that we were having our own fireworks show on Miz Eudora's front porch.

"It's an educational experience for the children as they enter a world of days gone by," Theona continued, in her best teacher style.

"Sort of like we did in Paducah," noted Hattie, expressing the same thing I was thinking. "Sounds like a good thing for the entire family. Count me in. I'll bet the food is outstanding."

"That's for sure. There's a church from the area that cooks breakfast and lunch every day right beside the concert stage, and you can find yourself any kind of food or beverage you could possibly want. But there is one rule. No alcohol on the grounds," she stated in her best Sunday School teacher voice of authority. "It's definitely a laid-back, family-oriented event. There's even a Threshers' Beauty Queen for all the different ages of girls. Reminds me of how things were when I was a girl," she added, taking a long breath as she reminisced of her own past. "Of course, most of those tractors and I ***are*** the same age."

"If that many people converge on such a tiny place all at one time, where do they stay? Surely there aren't enough motels to house all of them," observed Hattie.

"No, there aren't. Whole families come from everywhere and set up camp," replied Theona, so energetically I thought she was ready to "hightail it" to Denton right there and then.

"Oh, no, you don't!" shouted Mabel.

The circus is coming to town, I thought. ***I can hear the fanfare starting.***

"This is where I put my foot down. I am ***not*** going anywhere in a tent," she continued.

"You take your own tent with you, remember*?*" I started to ask, catching myself just in time. "Mabel," I interjected. "There are some fine camping accommodations nowadays. Leon and I rented an RV a few years back and took a road trip to Arizona. It was quite comfortable and we had the peace of being in our own home while being on the road. Why don't you let me take you to see the kind of luxury they have in those new motor homes?"

I had heard the words come from my mouth, but I couldn't believe I had just made that offer. This was one of those times that I had that "sixth sense" feeling that Leon had just spoken, through me, from the grave. Before I had time to reconsider or retract my words, Mabel jumped right on the offer "like a duck on a June bug," as Miz Eudora would have said.

"You know, that might be kind of fun. A few of my friends from the Myers Park Country Club talk about how their doctor and lawyer husbands want to pretend they are hunters and fishers every once in a while to get away from the usual golf routine. They own those motor homes and only take them out of storage for a couple of times each year. It would be nice to tell them of my experience of playing farmer to get away from the high society scene."

I could see Miz Eudora's eyes rolling, but I quickly shot her a "whatever it takes" glance so that she wouldn't say something to change Mabel's mind. We had Mabel in "Go" mode and I saw no reason to rock the boat. ***Or motor home, as it might be!*** I told myself.

That was until I had a reality check. I looked at the foursome – ***make that a threesome and a "circus"*** – now seated with me on the porch and wondered whether I'd ever given Miz Eudora an answer to her original question of whether I'd be willing to drive them to Denton. ***If so, I wonder if it's bad manners to renege!*** Leon or no Leon, this venture was sounding more frightful all the time. ***Given the "circus" doubles as a "haunted house!"***

"You actually thought the Threshers were a family?" Hattie finally asked of Mabel, the suspense killing her.

"And the Threshers' Reunion was a real family get-together, like with ham, potato salad, deviled eggs and lemonade?" quizzed Theona. "And people pitching horseshoes?"

"Scratch the horseshoes, Theona!" warned Miz Eudora. "Nobody wants to pitch horseshoes with Mabel. Let's have them playing badminton instead. No one minds serving the little birdie to Mabel."

Good thing they're plastic birdies, I chuckled

to myself. ***With Mabel's luck, there would be mess all over her.***

I still knew little more about Denton than I had when I first arrived that morning, only that now, I was thankfully not kin to Mabel. ***Nor the rest of them***, which, I thought at the moment, was a good thing.

"Let's put it this way. The reunion is when all the old geezers get together with all the young wannabes, and all the ones in between," explained Miz Eudora. "At least that's the way I've heard tell. Since I've never been, I can't really tell you for sure."

"But they have tractor pulls, and lots and lots of old tractors," added Theona.

I'm not sure what's worse, I chuckled to myself, now that I fully understood the Threshers' Reunion, ***spending the week with a bull or a tractor***.

The real outcome of that morning's front porch chat – complete with biscuits and chocolate gravy – was that come July 1st, I would be carting the five of us to Denton and the Threshers' Reunion for five days. ***No bull!***

SEVENTEEN

Every Beautiful Flower

I'D ORDERED RED bandanas for all five of us, monogrammed with the initials of Miz Eudora's Sparklin' Shiners, in commemoration of our trip to the Threshers' Reunion. I didn't think about the fact that those initials spelled out the word 'MESS' until I opened the package when they arrived.

Well, well, that ought to give the sister-in-laws something to "chat" about on the way there, I thought, laughing aloud. I stared at the purple embroidered letters standing out against the red background. ***It certainly is appropriate, considering that every time we do something, we get ourselves into one big mess. The only thing that could have been any better***, I mused comically, ***is if the initials had been PICKLE, for we stay in one of those!*** Ironically, I had no idea how prophetic those bandanas would prove to be.

The trip hadn't even begun and it was already off to a good start, at least as far as I was concerned. We had a great conversation piece with the bandanas, so I decided not to pass them out until we were in the car and on the way out of Clay County. With those four passengers, that should keep them busy all the way to Denton.

In order to get the full effect of the Threshers' Reunion, we did decide to rent an RV. The game plan was that I'd pick it up on the way through Charlotte and Hattie would drive my car behind the camper the rest of the way to Denton, which was only another hour or so. That seemed to be "a stupendous idea" to everyone. Everyone except, you guessed it, Mabel.

"Stupendous idea, my foot! ***Stupid***, just plain stupid, is more like it." She'd fussed and fumed so much that I really thought she might not go. But then, I should have remembered that this was Mabel Toast Jarvis we were talking about. She was determined to go, if for no other reason than to gripe and complain the entire time about what a huge mistake renting the RV instead of the expensive motor home had been. If she'd had her way, we'd have actually been staying at a motel in one of the next towns over, since there were no lodgings in Denton. I even offered to let her take my car back and forth to a motel in Lexington or Asheboro, should she rather not stay in the camper with the rest of us. It became quickly apparent that either "hell could freeze over," or it would be "a cold day in July" before that happened.

Someone met us at our campsite within five

minutes of our arrival at the Denton Farm Park. In no time flat, the groundskeeper, who had ridden his golf cart over, had us in the right spot and leveled, all ready to go. "You ladies need anything else?" he asked. "I'll be glad to help you with all the hook-ups."

"We've got it," I informed him.

"Surely between the five of us, we can take care of everything," seconded Hattie.

"You ladies knock yourselves out," stated Mabel. "I have no intention of taking a shower, or relieving myself, in that tiny contraption. Where's the nearest bathhouse?" she asked the groundskeeper.

"Across that field, through the entrance and about two roads over. You'll see it on the left there about 200 yards down," he answered.

"And where's our golf cart to get there?" she inquired, looking around.

"There are no golf carts. You have to walk."

"All the way over there?" she screeched.

The rest of us went about setting up our "house" for the next five days in an effort to ignore her. We'd barely gotten parked good before we were in our first "MESS." I should have known that Mabel would be our biggest, and first, MESS.

"I'm going back in that direction," said the groundskeeper. "I'll be glad to ride you over, if you'd like."

"Yes, I would like," she replied, no gratitude in

her voice. "And who's going to bring me back here?" she stormed.

"You're on your own there," he answered, showing no intimidation, which to me, scored big time.

"You can't just leave me there," she demanded.

"Maybe we can rent you your own personal portable toilet," suggested Miz Eudora, way past being fed up with the embarrassing tirade.

"Nonsense, I'd rather go to the woods first."

Miz Eudora looked around. "That's a good thing because there's plenty of them here."

"HMMPH!" huffed Mabel.

It was a good thing she was such a loud "huffer." Otherwise, she'd have probably beaten Hattie, Theona and I at our outburst. The vision of Mabel "going to the woods" was too good to pass up. ***I'll bet she doesn't know the difference between poison oak and poison ivy, either. That ought to prove to be a really good MESS.***

She finally opted to ride to the bathhouse which, when she got there, she liked little more than the idea of sharing that "tiny closet of a bathroom" with the rest of us. "Besides, you don't know who's been in there last," she'd complained.

"You don't know that at the motel, either," Hattie reminded her, but to no avail. Her comment was a waste of breath.

It's going to be a long five days at this rate, I

decided, determined to make the best of it. ***Besides we have our monogrammed MESS bandanas. We have a precedence to live up to.*** What I'd meant to be a token of personal inspiration with the bandanas had backfired. ***That precedence is off to a good start. So's the customer relations department here at Denton. You'll be lucky if you lay eyes on that groundskeeper again after he's had to haul Mabel around.***

I turned on the water to make sure everything was hooked up properly. ***Wonder if he's for rent? They could make a mint on golf car rentals here***, I assessed, before recognizing that they'd only get in the way of all the foot traffic, tractors and lawn mowers during the week. I decided to put off testing the toilet so that I wouldn't waste water or room in the "holding tank."

Although I wouldn't admit it, I'd already chosen to make my stops in the bath house, too. That "tiny closet" for five women wasn't my idea of luxury. ***It was your idea to rough it, Sadie. Cool it!***

Other than that, the camper was adorable. Small, ***very*** small, but well laid out with bed space and closet space for everyone. ***Think of it this way, Sadie. When their eyes are closed and they're asleep, they'll never notice that you're all packed in here like sardines.*** Naturally, I got the bunk over the top of the driver's seat. I didn't want to take a chance of one of the other four falling on top of the kitchen table and squashing all the cakes and pies Miz Eudora had brought. Not to mention the coconut cake that Hattie had made. You'd have thought, from that spread, that we were the only ones bringing desserts to the Threshers' Reunion.

What no one had shared with Mabel was that Miz Eudora's two now-distinguished quilts were to be on display at the reunion. She had her own booth with tables and chairs where she could sell her "Smack from the Gap" items, and the biggest fan I'd ever "laid eyes on" nearby – which, I concluded, was a good thing because with 65,000 people on July Fourth, it looked to be a hot one. We other four had planned to take turns being in the booth with her so that we could help customers while she "talked shop" with people who came to meet her. Personally, I think we all figured Mabel would take up too much space in the booth. My own thoughts were that we didn't have to listen to her "carryin' on so" if she was elsewhere.

Little did I know how very wrong I was in that assumption.

"While the four of you work today," boasted Mabel on the first morning, "I'm going to learn how to make my flower garden grow."

"You ought not to have any trouble in that department," replied Miz Eudora. "You're ever' bit as contrary as that 'Mary, Mary' who had the silver bells, cockle shells, marigolds and daisies."

I saw no point in informing Miz Eudora that

"Mary, Mary, quite contrary" was believed to be a portrayal of Queen Mary, although sources differed in their opinion of which one. I was quite sure, however, that it was not based on Mabel Toast Jarvis.

"And I'll have you know that your own brother, John. G., called me "the fairest flower of them all."

"That's because Ma taught him that every beautiful flower has to go through some manure. Guess he didn't forget that tidbit about gardening."

"For your information, Miss Smarty, a visiting instructor at my Queen City Garden Club informed us that fertilizer plays an important role in the successful growth of plants and flowers. I do not believe that is what John G. had in mind when he referred to me as 'the fairest flower of them all.' I believe he meant that I was his beautiful rosebud."

After that lovely analysis, we went our separate ways, Mabel to learn the "ins" and "outs" of gardening, and the rest of us to mingle with the crowd and show off Miz Eudora's award-winning quilts and original designs. Little did we know that when we crossed paths again at the RV for dinner, Mabel would be wearing the most original design of all.

"LAND SAKES, MABEL," declared Miz Eudora when we neared the RV after the day's activities, "where have you been? You're covered in...,"

Hattie, seeing the mess Mabel was in, hastily interrupted. "What in the world happened to you?" She squinted her eyes as she shook her head in disbelief and held her nose.

I stood frozen, dumbfounded, staring at the despicable sight sitting on the steps leading into the RV, as Mabel sat there sobbing.

"I had to leave the gardening class this morning before it even got off the ground well. Something I ate, which I'm sure Eudora cooked, must not have agreed with me because…well…it upset my stomach…and…I've spent most of the day…disposed." She sniffed a few times and added, "Then a few minutes ago, I…I…felt this horribly strange movement in my…my lower bowel…and rushed to the toilet again."

She paused as she wiped her face with a wadded-up piece of toilet tissue. "When…I…flushed...it," she stammered, beginning to wail instead of sob, "it went the wrong way." Without warning, the gentle wailing stopped as she looked up. "Eudora Rumph," she then bellowed, ire in her eyes, "this is all your fault. You probably didn't hook something up right."

"I'm the one who took care of all the hook-ups," I defended. "I did exactly what the man at the rental store told me to do."

"Looks to me like he left out a step," observed Theona, gazing in total astonishment at the woman in front of her. "Mabel, dear, I'm not sure the woman who instructed your gardening club meant for you to use it as facial cream, even if you do consider yourself a budding rosebud."

"I'm ***NOT*** using it as facial cream," whined Mabel. "I'm not ***using*** it as anything."

"Obviously, she got the leftovers of what somebody else's already used," responded Miz Eudora, roaring in laughter and creating a tidal wave of laughter from the rest of us.

"Why didn't you shower it off?" Hattie asked, fighting to get the words out between laughs.

"Because it's all over the shower, too," Mabel answered, getting madder by each minute that we saw more humor in the situation. "I pushed the handle to flush the toilet and the next thing I know, there was this...explosion...and I was covered in this...this...this mess."

I did at least pull off my MESS bandana and offer it to her. That's what I meant about the bandanas being prophetic. I didn't know we would actually need them, for literal reasons.

"It went flying everywhere," Mabel continued while wiping the mess off her face with the MESS bandana, which did nothing but smear it.

Guess the bandanas were meant for accessorizing, not sanitizing! I deduced, laughing harder.

"It got on the wall, in the shower, on the floor. I couldn't even wipe off with the towels because it was all over them, too."

"I don't know how it could have gotten all over that stuff. Looks to me like it got all over you!" observed Miz Eudora, still howling. Then as spontaneously as Mabel's wails had stopped, so did her laughter as her face took on a philosophical expression. "And you were worried about hitchin' a ride on the Porta-John truck to get here," said Miz Eudora, taking great pleasure in the distastefully awkward predicament.

"I'm not sure about you ladies," she said to Hattie, Theona and me, "but I'm ready for some lemonade. I've had enough lemons for one day."

"Last one to the frozen lemonade stand is a rotten…," started Hattie.

"I think Mabel wins the rotten award for this day," I said, trying to be sympathetic, but making matters worse. "Why don't we just go and leave you to…clean up?" I offered. "There are some clean towels in my storage bin." My eyes looked again at the sight before me. "On second thought, I'll go inside and get them for you." ***Thank goodness, the bathroom is at the back of the RV***, I decided, grateful that my sleeping quarters were at the far end of the RV.

"You mean you're not all going to stay and help me clean up this mess?" Mabel asked, incredulously.

"The one that makes it, cleans it," replied Miz Eudora. "Didn't your gardening instructor teach you that, too?"

I must admit that I felt horribly for Mabel, yet it was all I could do not to also feel she'd brought the mess on herself. "I'll tell you what. You get yourself all cleaned up and I'll take us out to dinner in the car."

"Maybe you'd better let Mabel ride in the trunk," offered Theona in her sweet well-meaning voice.

"I hope we eat somewhere there's an outdoor patio," Hattie added.

We all stood there, taking one last glimpse at Mabel. It suddenly dawned on me that, for once, Mabel had beaten out Miz Eudora at something. For while the rest of us had been showing off the quilts and original creations from Miz Eudora's "Smack from the Gap" collection, Mabel had come up with the most original design of all. There was no way she'd see someone else walking around Denton in that get-up.

"It may work for roses," Miz Eudora said to me blandly, as we turned to walk back toward the main entrance of the park, "but it doesn't do a thing for Mabel." She look one last look over her shoulder and gave a big huff. "And she had the nerve to bad mouth my outhouse. At least it's never sprayed fertilizer on anybody. P'SHAA! A flying fertilizer contraption, I reckon."

EIGHTEEN

The Great Train Robbery

THE FIRST COUPLE of days, except for Mabel's unfortunate incident, were a time of relaxation making lots of new acquaintances. Except for a few locals and people who wanted to avoid the large holiday weekend crowds – being that July 4th fell on a Saturday – most of the people there were the ones with campers. Hattie and Theona had been right in their explanation. It really was like a big family. People spread out their food like a giant picnic and after dark, they'd gather at two or three of the campers where some of them sat around "pickin' and grinnin.'" ***Mostly "grinnin.'"*** And yes, there really were people pitching horseshoes, although I saw no badminton games. People had their laundry hanging out, and they had everything on display, and for sell, from antique bottles to rusted tractor parts to the largest-sized underwear I've ever seen. Nothing was kept private, including one conversation that I wish had been.

"You know," shared one of the wives one night after hours, "you have different categories of friends. I have friends at home who've been close friends of mine ever since my husband was transferred to Richmond. If I need something, I call them. If I go out for an evening, I call them. But Vivian, here," she continued, pointing to the woman from the next camper over, "she's more than just a friend. She's family. We've folded each others' underwear. You know you're family when you've folded each others' underwear."

"Oh, thank you, Lord!" Miz Eudora cried into the heavens with an unexpected proclamation, disrupting both the "pickin'" and the 'grinnin.'" "I knew that old Mabel wasn't kin to me." She gave an energetic "Whew!" as she looked at me and then glanced around at everyone else who'd joined the nightly entertainment, her eyes totally passing by Mabel. "I wouldn't touch Mabel's drawers with a ten-foot shotgun. Why, I'll bet she's got fur critters around the edges of them, too. I knew we wasn't kin to each other. I just knew it!"

Her eyes fell dead on Mabel. "So don't you b telling nobody you're my sister-in-law anymore, y hear me? I don't want them a-thinkin' that we've d our hands on each others' drawers."

Miz Eudora stood and headed toward our "ome for the week." "I believe the thought of that ha done made me right puny. I think I better go sit a spell."

With that, she turned back and directed her final statement to me. "And don't worry, Sadie. I don't mean in the bathroom. I'll save that pleasure for the woman I'm not kin to."

BY THE TIME it rolled around to the third day, Miz Eudora was ready for adventure – which meant the rest of us were in for an adventure, too. "I don't know about you four," she announced that third morning, "but I'm headin' for the Handy Dandy Railroad this afternoon. I've always wanted to ride the train. There was one in Dillsboro that went to Bryson City every fall. I never got there to ride on it, though."

My daily agenda had mentioned nothing about a ride on a steam locomotive, but I was sure if Miz Eudora was going to be on it, I'd get my money's worth. I was right in that prediction, for not one passenger was about to ask for a ticket refund after the ride with her.

The event program listed a Special Ride once each hour, on the hour, from noon until five each afternoon. The train ran between those times, as well, but I knew Miz Eudora had ideas of being on the Special Ride. I was right, for she announced at 2:30, on that third afternoon, that she was closing the booth and taking the 3:00 train. A kind lady, who had a booth across the aisle from ours, offered to watch Miz Eudora's long enough for "the adventure."

We had to stop to see every baby in a stroller, try out the ice cream – with the promise of getting lemonade on the way back to the booth – and look at every exhibit all the way to the Handy Dandy Railroad Station. We bought our tickets and went out the back to wait beside the tracks for the next departure.

While the rest of us sat on a bench with all the other waiting passengers, anxious to see what was included in the Special Ride, Miz Eudora marched herself by every single bench, speaking to every single person and telling them how excited she was to be taking her first train ride. As if her purple fopher coat and red hat weren't enough to draw attention to herself, she was known by everyone at the station by the time the train pulled in to pick up the next load for the "Special Ride."

What I found to be most interesting was that there was also another notable passenger aboard this train. It happened to be a man who was running as governor in the upcoming election. He was doing the same thing as Miz Eudora, only he didn't have the purple coat and the red hat. He should have, for she was getting more attention, it seemed.

"Would you look at that?" asked Hattie. "She's just like the politician. Standing on the corner and crowing like a rooster."

"She looks like the rooster, too," noted Theona, "with that red hat looking like a red comb."

I was glad to hear the train's whistle, announcing its arrival. People lined up to board the various cars while the arriving passengers debarked.

Miz Eudora was like a little kid, she was so excited. All she needed to complete the picture was an all-day sucker, which I would have gladly bought for her had they had one at Denton. She held onto her purse like she was afraid it might go flying out the open window when the train rolled out. Her smile was so contagious that I felt rather giddy myself as I sat taking note of the other passengers. I noticed that the gubernatorial candidate sat two cars back from us.

Guess he couldn't handle the competition, I mused.

The conductor came through the car and punched each ticket, followed by "the sheriff," who was strong enough to handle what might come.

Ah, me thinks there might be a Wild West show, I observed.

The engineer blew the whistle and the narrator of the Special Ride instructed us to give a big "Howdy" to all the people watching the train pull out of the station.

"Sure are a neighborly bunch of people, aren't they?" asked Miz Eudora, who was seated next to me, with Theona and Hattie across the aisle from us. She bobbed her head back and forth, taking in all the surrounding scenery, which was quite picturesque, until the narrator came back over the intercom with an announcement that "it looks like trouble ahead."

They must have sighted Mabel.

"You don't need to worry, Sadie. That nice strong sheriff will take care of us. Did you see that nice smile he had? You can tell he's a good guy." She sat for a second and then added, "That's more than I can say about that 'crowing rooster' back at the station!"

I didn't bother to inform her that the 'crowing rooster,' to which she'd been compared, was sitting two cars back. Nor that Hattie had thought the two of them had a lot in common.

"Ladies and gentlemen, it looks like there's a gang of train robbers up ahead. This is not looking good because we're carrying the payroll on this train."

"Train robbers? Oh, dear me!" exclaimed Miz Eudora. "Where's that sheriff?"

The train bumped its way to a grinding halt as Miz Eudora jumped up to get a good look at the outlaws. "Sadie, look, they're shooting at the sheriff." She watched intently as the outlaws of the Sage Brush Six Guns and Rawhide played "shoot 'em up" in real-live western style. They were most impressive.

"Oh, no, Sadie. They've got the sheriff's gun. Somebody needs to do something." She looked back through the other train cars. "Where's that crowing politician? Here's his chance to get himself a lot of votes. He needs to go into action and take control of this situation."

About that time, I heard one of the outlaws yelling that they were going to take a hostage from on board the train. Miz Eudora must have heard it, too, for she sat down in her seat, lowered her head and held her "new, used red leather pocketbook" close to her body and became as quiet as a church mouse. I was most amused. I'd never known her to be such a theatrical person, and thought how it was too bad that Six Flags over Jesus didn't also have a drama team for her to join.

I watched as one of the outlaws boarded the train in the car behind us. He looked up and down the aisle at the passengers and then proceeded forward to our car. When he had stepped past us about three rows, he stopped and turned around. ***He must have noticed how melodramatic Miz Eudora is, too***, I thought, as he reached out, grabbed her arm and pulled her past me from the seat.

"You can't be taking me hostage!" she screamed, playing her role to the hilt. "I'm just a poor old, defenseless lady. Who's going to take care of my farm and my mule if you take me?"

Like all the other passengers, including the "crowing rooster" two cars back, I kept my eyes and ears on her. If I hadn't known better, I'd have thought she was one of the acting crew for the Special Show. She was so into what was happening that she had us all on the edge of our seats waiting to see what would occur next.

The outlaw pulled her out into the clearing, which was a huge open semi-circle following the curve of the track, so that the entire train could watch the show. When he'd gotten far enough from the train car for everyone to see her, one of the outlaws jumped out from behind a tree, identifying himself as a federal marshal. He demanded they let the sheriff and Miz Eudora go, to which all the other outlaws laughed. A shoot-out began, with a couple of the outlaws falling to the ground. Miz Eudora broke loose from the one who had a hold of her and began beating him for all she was worth with her red pocketbook.

What is she doing? I wondered. ***He must have given her some stage directions on their way off the train.***

She beat even harder and when she'd knocked him silly, she took off after another one. By the time she finished him off, the other outlaws screamed for the federal marshal to please come and get her and take her back on the train, saying she was "a wild woman!"

I was getting a huge kick out of watching Miz Eudora take care of things "Smackass style" when I saw her look down at the ground. ***What's she looking at?*** I stood up to get a better view. There, on the ground, lay a bullwhip that had been dropped by one of the outlaws who'd been shot.

Don't tell me..., My thought was too late. Before I could finish it, she had the bullwhip up and was slinging it around her head. ***I do hope she knows what she's doing with that thing. She could mess around and hang herself if she isn't careful.***

The outlaws all promised to surrender if she'd put that thing down. No time was lost as the sheriff gathered all the bad guys and the federal marshal went over to Miz Eudora and helped her back to the train. She looked terribly sweet as she pulled a hankie from her pocketbook and wiped her brow like the poor, little defenseless person she had been chosen to depict. I heard her tell the marshal she didn't need him to help her up the steps, that "I'm fully capable of gettin' up by myself." She hiked her dress tail up and up the steps she came as the passengers of the train clapped and cheered. She bowed her head in thanks in both directions, being the polite soul she was, and came back to her seat, with me moving over to the window to give her breathing room.

"Where's that special blend when I need it?" she asked me, so softly that no one else heard her.

She really* is *a great actress. She doesn't lose character until the fat lady sings. I chuckled lightly, enjoying the entertainment of this Special Ride immensely. ***Oh, I forgot. The fat lady can't sing; she isn't on this train.***

The rest of the ride was uneventful as a cool breeze came in through the windows and the engineer took us on a ride of the entire Farm Park, giving us a birds-eye view of the entire acreage. It was a thrill from start to finish, with the experienced engineer literally playing music, it seemed, on the whistle. I'd never realized the importance of all the different sounds until then.

We pulled back into the station and got off the train, with people shaking hands with Miz Eudora and telling her how much they enjoyed her "performance." One young woman even stuffed a baby in her arms and began snapping pictures. Cameras began to go off from every direction as we started through the crowd.

"That was quite a performance!" called the engineer as we passed the engine.

"Thank you kindly," acknowledged Miz Eudora. "I never rode on a train before. I can't believe there was a train robbery on my very first ride." Her comment brought a huge laugh from both the engineer and the coalman.

"You're welcome to come back and ride in the engine with us," he invited.

"I'm not sure I trust riding on this train again,"

she replied, causing me to wonder whether she realized the entire thing had been an act.

"Miz Eudora, you do realize…,"

The outlaws and lawmen came walking up right then and made a point to find her. "You did a great job out there, young lady," the guy who played the marshal said, congratulating her.

"I hope I didn't rough you up too much," said the guy who'd pulled her off the train.

"Hey," she said to one of the other outlaws, "I thought they shot you."

"We only use blanks," stated the sheriff. "Can't take any chances on anybody getting hurt."

"Blanks?" she repeated, confusion written on her face. "You mean you didn't really shoot those trifling bad guys." She took a head count and saw that all the outlaws were "present and accounted for." "Why, if'n I had a-known that, I'd have hung 'em from the nearest tree."

I yanked Miz Eudora aside before she "commenced to hanging" and explained that the entire robbery had been pretend and that all the guys, the good guys and the bad guys, were hired actors.

"You mean…," she began looking disappointed. Then, as if a light bulb went off, she beamed. "You mean I got to be on stage with real live actors?"

"Well, yes, kind of, if you can call the grass of that clearing a stage," I affirmed.

"I do declare. That's the biggest news to hit the ***Clay County Progress*** in a long time. I sure do wish you'd have got a picture for me to take back to the editor."

"I wish I had, too, Miz Eudora. You did a 'bang-up' job of banging up the outlaws. I don't think they knew what hit them at first." In fact, I was sure they didn't know they'd been beaten by a red pocketbook.

"How'd you like to come back tomorrow and be a part of our Special Ride again?" asked the guy who'd played the marshal. "That way you can get a photo for your newspaper editor."

"You mean you'd take me hostage again and I could beat you guys up again?"

"That's what we mean," answered the outlaw who'd taken her from the train.

"That's what I call a ***real*** Special Ride. I think I'd like that a lot. What time do you want me here?"

"How about 3:00? We'll make that a really special performance. And go ahead and plan to do it on the next day, too, if you're still around. That was a real hit."

I'd never seen Miz Eudora look so proud. "Just wait 'til I tell Mabel," she said. "She'll be so jealous she won't know what to do."

"I don't know, Miz Eudora. She had a pretty good performance of her own yesterday. It would be hard to beat that one."

"You got a point there, Sadie. She was still rank this morning, even after going to the bathhouse with a can of tomato juice. That's what we always use to wash off skunk back in Smackass Gap. But I don't know what they use to wash off a mess like that. I've never seen anyone else get sprayed by an outhouse before."

Hattie and Theona had rushed back to take care of the booth. I knew they'd be as proud of Miz Eudora as I had been, and would probably have something special planned for her upon our return.

"We'd better get back," I reminded her, hating to burst her bubble, "but Hattie and Theona may start to worry."

"You're right," she said, waving to "the guys." "Hey," she yelled, "what about that crowing rooster? Was he make believe, too?"

"Oh, no ma'am," answered one of the "bad guys" who'd been shot. "He was the real thing."

"Hmmm," she groaned, "we really did have a live skunk in our midst. If I'd have known that, I might have made better use of that bullwhip."

I bit my lip, glad he'd not been around to hear that comment. ***But then,*** I reconciled, ***I'm sure he's heard much worse. It must go with the territory, whether you're a rooster or a skunk.***

NINETEEN

Hittin' and Missin'

"HOW' DO?" MIZ Eudora asked a young woman, in the same manner she'd been greeting everyone since her arrival in Denton. It was also the same way she greeted folks in Smackass Gap. Shortly after my move there, I finally figured out that she was asking, "How do you do?" but was saving syllables since she greeted everyone with whom she came in contact. She'd done it in Paducah, at the beach and was now off to a good start of doing it here.

Her responses ranged from people ignoring her, to people snapping her photo, to people who considered her a "deranged old woman." Personally, I hoped most of them would choose to accept the last option. It meant we'd worm ourselves through the crowd much quicker and with far less attention.

By the fourth day, however, people had come to see that she was for real and had every bit as much sense as they did, if not more. One old gent, in fact, made a habit of catching her each morning as we entered the gate. I wasn't sure whether it was because he actually liked her, or whether she was the only person that bothered to ask him "How do?" and acted like she cared how he did.

Each morning, his answer to Miz Eudora's question was the same. "I'm blessed," he'd reply, taking her hand in his and nodding his head with a huge grin. She'd been "rightly impressed" with that answer the first three days, saying how more people in the world needed to share that opinion and outlook on life.

That was until Cheryl, the sweet teenage daughter of the groundskeeper, "bent her ear."

It's important to understand here that Miz Eudora had fallen in love with Cheryl the minute she met her. "If I'd have ever had grandyoung'uns," she said, "I'd have liked for them to have turned out just like that sweet little Cheryl. She's the nicest young lady I ever did meet. If it wasn't so far from Denton, I'd ask if she'd like to come join the liturgical dance team at Six Flags over Jesus."

I'm sure her mother would love that! I said to myself, knowing it was a good thing for Cheryl's mother that Smackass Gap was such a long drive. ***Miz Eudora would have offered to come and pick her up every week in the motorized outhouse!*** I was surprised she didn't offer Mabel's service as a chauffeur to come and get the endearing teen each week for practice. And she probably would have, had she not liked the "sweet young thing" so much. That was the only thing that saved her from Mabel.

There was another fine quality which I came to appreciate about Cheryl. "The sweet young thing" was keenly astute, far beyond her youthful years, in her perception of people and their thoughts. What she wasn't perceptive in was how to make Miz Eudora keenly astute of certain people's, or rather one old man's – desires. Had she accomplished that, I do believe Miz Eudora would have described them as "comin' ons" instead of "goin' ons." As it was, Cheryl's efforts turned into the point of no return.

"Miz Eudora," Cheryl, oozing with innocent charm, warned, "You'd better watch out for that man. He's trying to hit on you."

"Hit on me?" Miz Eudora gave a little chuckle. "He's not hittin' on me, Miss Cheryl. He's too nice a fellow to be hittin' old ladies. All that man is doing is sharing his blessing. He hasn't laid a hand, nor his cane, on me..., much less hit me," Miz Eudora assured her. "Besides, he'd better be careful. If he goes to hittin' on me, I'll go to hittin' back."

"No, Miz Eudora," Cheryl shrieked, "don't do that! Whatever you do, don't hit back. That would give him the impression you like him."

"But I do like him. He's near 'bout the only

person in Denton what's talked to me without looking at me funny."

"That's the whole point. He ***does*** look at your funny."

"Does that mean everybody else here has been looking at me normal?" Miz Eudora asked. "In that case, you surely got some funny looking people wandering around this Farm Park. That's all I can say."

"Look, I know you like him. You're that kind of person. You like everybody..., well, almost everybody," she corrected, thinking of Mabel. "But you don't want him to get the impression that you "***like***" him," she said, leaning into the word "like." "'Hitting on' means he likes you and wants you to go out with him," Cheryl tried to explain.

"Oh, no, honey," replied Miz Eudora. "He doesn't want to go out with me. He sees me when I come in each morning and he's not ready to be leaving already. Why, there's still a full day of fun ahead each day. He couldn't want to be a-leavin' at nine in the morning."

Trying another strategy, Cheryl stated, "He's trying to pick you up."

"He couldn't possibly try to pick me up. He can barely pick himself up. From the looks of him, I'm surprised he can still put one foot in front of the other. Surely he's got better sense than to try to pick someone up. Remember, he's blessed. He wouldn't be too blessed if he was sportin' a broken back from pickin' someone up."

"No, ma'am," Cheryl continued desperately, "that's not what I mean." She heaved a long sigh, trying to find a way to make sense between the generational gap. "What I'm trying to tell you is that you give the impression you're a lot of fun, and he'd like to cash in on that."

"Cash in on it? You mean he can sell me if I'm fun?"

This conversation is moving about as fast as all those "hit and miss" engines around here, I thought, analyzing the situation. ***Poor Cheryl is hitting and Miz Eudora is missing.***

I feared that poor sweet dear was going to dig herself into a bottomless pit before she educated Miz Eudora on the present-day terminology for flirtatious synonyms. Plus, I was rather apprehensive about how far she would delve into the subject of "selling fun." ***That might send our dear little 'Smackass gem' into a real tailspin!***

"That man speaks to everyone who walks in that gate. He doesn't miss a soul," defended Miz Eudora.

"Yes, he does," conceded Cheryl, "but he doesn't hold onto their hands, or look into their eyes dreamily, the way he does with you. That's what I mean by him looking at you funny."

"Do you really think so?" asked Miz Eudora,

who looked as if she could have been knocked over with a feather. She wobbled back and forth unsteadily on her feet as she grasped that possibly there were some subliminal messages in this man's approach. "What on earth does an old crow like him want to do with an old woman like me?" she asked, visibly struggling to allow Cheryl's words of wisdom to "take root."

"I can't answer that."

Nor could I, I mused, ***nor would I attempt to,*** wanting no part of imagining that state of affairs. However, it was comical to imagine what an affair it would be if he ever did have the misfortune of tangling – ***or should that have been "fandangling?"*** – with Miz Eudora Rumph.

"All I'm trying to say to you, Miz Eudora, is that you'd better beware. That man thinks you are one hot chick."

"Hot chick! Land sakes, he must be blind as a bat if he thinks I'm a chick. I've been called a wet hen before, and in my prime, I was quite a 'spring chicken.' But to think I'm a chick. He must be crazier than he looks. And to think I'm hot? Well, of course I'm hot. What kind of fool couldn't see that I'm hot? Who ***wouldn't*** be hot in this fopher coat on the Fourth of July? P'SHAA! A hot chick, I reckon!"

Miz Eudora started to walk away and leave Cheryl with her worries when she suddenly stopped dead in her tracks. "Wait a minute!" she exclaimed.

"Sadie!"

Her yelp made me wonder if I should call 911.

"I've got it!"

What's she got? A gall stone? A kidney stone? A broken bone? A chest pain?

"That cute Purple Stallion in the red pin-striped suit," she blurted excitedly, "he wasn't going to eat fried chicken after all. I thought he was having his pet hen, Sarah, for lunch that day on the way to New Orleans when the car broke down. He told us he was going see a 'hot chick' named Sarah after that Red Hatter thing he was doing in Birmingham. I thought that was some new-fangled way of saying he was going to have fried chicken. That wasn't what he meant at all. Sarah wasn't his pet hen. She was some sweet young thing, just like Cheryl here, and he'd taken a special likin' to her and was going to see her after his 'gig.'

"Now I understand what you were tryin' to tell me, Cheryl! Why didn't you just say the old, blessed buzzard had a crush on me?"

"Because you'd have probably asked, 'Orange or grape?'" I wanted to answer, but decided against it.

She stopped raving, took a breath and appeared tremendously satisfied by her hypothesis, which to me had more angles than a geometric progression. ***As pompous as a peacock, she is,*** I noted, ***speaking of***

fowl.

"I surely do hope that things worked out well between that nice Purple Stallion and that sweet young filly, Miss Sarah," Miz Eudora added, her face full of concern. "Do you think maybe we could call him one day, Sadie, and find out? I know I've got his number still somewhere at home. She might even like to be a Pink Hatter in my Sparklin' Shiners."

I nodded and offered her a big smile.

"Do you think he'll remember me?" she asked, a worried look in her brow, as she looked at me.

"I'm sure there's no chance of him forgetting, Miz Eudora," answered Cheryl with a wink. "A hot chick like you, how could he forget?"

Miz Eudora cackled. "Maybe I'll ask that blessed "buzzard" if he likes his hot chicks baked, broiled or grilled when I see him tomorrow."

The nod of a moment earlier turned into a shaking of my head as I listened in amusement at the character in front of me. There was one thing that came out of the afternoon's conversation. It was my determination to watch Miz Eudora when she entered the gate the following day. I couldn't wait to see how she reacted to "the old buzzard." Her choices of words were most interesting, considering the old gent had gone from a crow to a bat to a buzzard. ***Whatever he is, he's quite a bird! At least in Miz Eudora's way of thinking. And whatever happens, he's going to be***

"eatin' crow" when she's finished with him.

Speaking of "Crows," I mused, I wasn't about to let on to Hattie that there was another "Crow" in our midst. He might start "hittin' on" her.

"HOW' DO?" MIZ Eudora greeted everyone as usual the next morning, including the man in question. I suspected she wanted to examine the situation for herself. ***Or maybe she simply wanted to teach him a lesson.*** Either way, I knew it was worth getting up with "the chickens" – ***wet, spring or hot!*** – when I saw the curious sparkle in his eyes.

He immediately grabbed her hand and answered, "I'm blessed. How are you?"

"I was blessed," she replied, "until I saw you."

Whoa, Nellie! I exclaimed to myself. ***This old gray mare is definitely still what she used to be, and a little more, if you ask me!***

"That's what I love in a woman with age," he replied, his eyes sparkling, "gumption. I can look at you and tell you're full of...***spunk!***"

"And I can look at you and tell you're full of...,"

I had no idea of what was coming next, but I was taking no chances as I jerked Miz Eudora toward the Craft Barn where her ***Precious Memories*** quilt and the Sunbonnet Sue quilt were displayed.

What I had suspected would take care of him

for a while did nothing but fan the flame. ***Or pilot light, as it is.***

Everything went on as usual for the rest of the day. I'd alerted Hattie to play scout and was prepared to call on Theona and Mabel, if necessary, to act as bouncers. ***At least one of them fits the bill***. There were so many visitors to the Farm Park that day that no one gave "Mr. Blessed" another thought. It seemed our problem had vanished.

At 2:30, right on cue, I reminded Miz Eudora that it was time for her to make her way to the train station. It had taken her ten minutes to walk it the day before. That was without the stop for ice cream, lemonade and to speak to at least a hundred passersby. The "sheriff" had asked her to come early and greet people, hoping her "electrifying" presence would drum up a good crowd. There was no doubt that he was right as we neared the station and saw the crowd that had gathered for the "Special Ride" featuring Miz Eudora.

Only now there was a different problem. The "blessed" man caught sight of the purple coat from across the park and marched himself straight toward us as fast as his legs, and cane, would carry him. I tried to dodge him as I led Miz Eudora toward the Handy Dandy Railroad for the 3:00 show. But thanks to her "How' do?" to everybody, and her stellar stage presence during the train hold-up the day before, she had too many fans for that.

"Are you going to be on the train again today?"

"That was a great show you put on yesterday."

"Miz Eudora, that was quite a fight you put up on the train," called another admirer as he asked for an autograph. "The way you handled those bank robbers was quite a sight."

"You fought off the bank robbers?" the old crow, who had now caught up with us, asked.

"She sure did. You should have seen her," bragged a spectator from the day before. "If I hadn't known better, I'd have thought she'd been taking lessons from Chuck Norris."

"Oh, my dear lady, you're my kind of woman," replied the old gent, fascination growing in his eyes.

"I'm their kind of woman, too," Miz Eudora was quick to reply, pointing toward the members of Sage Brush Six Guns and Rawhide. So quickly, in fact, that I knew she had finally grasped the meaning of "gettin' picked up." "I gotta be gettin' out of here. All those guys are waiting to rob the payroll again."

When the program said Special Ride at 3, it meant it, I speculated, seeing the old man rush to the ticket office.

I grabbed the train engineer as he boarded the engine. "Excuse me, sir, but our hostage has a stalker and he just bought a ticket. Is there any way I can get on this train? I couldn't stand it if something happened to her. I'd feel responsible."

"You hop on up here with us. It's loud and it's dirty, but you're welcome to keep a watch from here."

I barely got on when the conductor yelled, "All aboard!" and the train gave a forward jolt. It was so much fun watching the engineer and the coalman that I nearly forgot that I, too, had a job.

The bank robbers stopped the train and took Miz Eudora hostage. From the look on her face, she was enjoying her role a little too much. She really got into the scene of "beatin' up the bad guys." I wasn't sure whether she was taking out her frustrations over "Mr. Blessed" or Mabel, but somebody was surely "gettin' theirs."

Other than the fact that we were on a steam engine in the middle of nowhere, bad guys robbed the train and took a little old lady – dressed in a purple fur coat and red hat – hostage, dragged her off the train, where she proceeded to beat the tar out of them, there was nothing out of the ordinary about the ride. The minute the train stopped, I jumped from the engine and rushed to retrieve Miz Eudora. I wasn't fast enough, it seemed, for she'd found the cowboys and was having her picture made with them. Everyone else was, in turn, making pictures of all of them.

The old gent was staring, bug-eyed, at her as if he could lap her up with a spoon. I started to suggest he go get some ice cream, ***my treat***, but I'd left my wallet in the booth.

He waited patiently until Miz Eudora told the "train gang" good-bye. She'd apparently decided it was time to take this bull by the horns and end his infatuation, given the look of determination in her eyes.

"I'm sorry," she said to him, "but I have to get back now. My friends are back at the craft exhibit waiting for me."

"You mean there's more like you?" he asked, either ignoring or missing the hint. "Oh, I must go with you. I do believe I've found 'the mother lode.'"

"Well, you see, sir, the only one of us big enough to be called 'the mother lode' is my sister-in-law, Mabel Toast Jar…,"

I could tell by the glimmer in her eye that Miz Eudora's gears were turning and I knew what was coming next.

"On second thought, why don't you come on right along with me? I think you just might enjoy meeting 'the mother lode' in person."

She started to walk toward the Craft Building, but suddenly stopped. "Hey, guys," she yelled back at the members of Sage Brush Six Guns and Rawhide, "I really enjoyed 'hittin' on' you this afternoon. You can 'pick me up' anytime."

The guys all laughed and waved. "Why don't you come on over to the campfire tonight and have dinner with us?" invited the leader of the group. "We're havin' chili beans."

"Now that's what I call a real date," she said to me, finally bridging the generational gap. "Chili beans cooked over an open fire, eating out of enamel plates, sitting around the campfire singing cowboy songs and lots of hunks to look at. As long as you don't smell too closely, it can't get better than that."

Miz Eudora hooked her arm inside that of the old man, who'd already forgotten about her as a prospect in anticipation of "the mother lode." She looked back at me, gave a foxy wink and whispered, "'Motherlode,' now there's a new name for Mabel." Before she had time to finish her comment with, "This ought to be real in'trestin'," I'd already had the same notion.

"Now where did you say you're from?" the man asked.

Surely she's not going to fall for that. That's the oldest trick in the book. He knows good and well she didn't mention where she's from.

"I'm from Smacka..., I'm from near Franklin," she noted with pride. "Ever been there?"

The old gray mare wasn't born yesterday and she doesn't have her head buried in the sand. That's my Miz Eudora!

"My friend, the mother lode, though, she's from a place called Smackass Gap over in Clay County. Do you know how they greet people from there? I'll bet you do," she stated, a mischievous glimmer in her eye.

"Why don't you surprise her after I introduce you and give her a little smack on the back side. I'm sure that'll get her attention."

I could hardly wait to see how Mabel handled this one. At least, if a wedding grew out of it, there was a lovely little church on the premises. We didn't have a riverboat captain handy to perform the ceremony, but we did have the Handy Dandy Railroad engineer. I was sure he'd know what to do with Mabel, and his coalman would certainly know how to give the "old buzzard" a little more steam.

Speaking of, I'd have never guessed that "hit and miss" engines, Parades of Power and "old-timers" could provide so much fun. My only regret was that Leon had not been there to 'hit on' me. Although, I did have to admit that, even from the grave, there were many times when he was still able to "pick me up."

TWENTY

Broadening Your Horizons

I HAD FELT more than a bit uncomfortable allowing the four of them to go to Atlantic Beach on North Carolina's faraway coast without me. Call it self-proclaimed, but I had taken the role of being their guardian, not simply their driver. ***Why did I have to be called for jury duty on this exact week?*** I asked myself, knowing there would be no answer to come back to me. Suggesting the beach trip were moved to another week would have been to no avail, for all of Miz Eudora's friends she had met on that "fateful" bus trip to "Hotlanta" had planned this trip over a year before. They had rented a gorgeous beach house, complete with spiral stairs and large enough for all of us, as well as them. Given its proximity to the shore and the fact that it was rented for the third week in August, there would have been no chance of finding another week when it would be vacant. Not to mention the fact that all of the women signed up to go would be unable to find another clear week on their combined calendars.

So there I stood, holding the letter from the Clerk of Court and tapping my fingers on the railing of my front porch, as they drove away singing ***On the Road Again***. They had surprised me by coming over to tell me good-bye. Mabel honking the horn all the way down my driveway had been a surprise all right. At four in the morning, I wondered how many others along Highway 64 she had also surprised with that stunt. However, given it was going to take them over nine hours to get there, it was alright. I had to admit I was glad to at least see them "off."

"Off their rockers" might have been a better way to describe them that morning. The spark inside that silver Buick was enough to easily ignite a fire that would engulf all of Smackass Gap, plus half of Chunky Gal Mountain. That silver Buick had actually been the deciding factor of why I said nothing of them going on without me. I knew that if Miz Eudora Rumph was willing to get in a car with Mabel Toast "Mrs. John G." Jarvis and ride that many hours, ten there and then back not counting stops, it was of dire necessity.

Watching them scurry around the car like a bunch of field mice, while each told me what all they were going to do when they got there, took me back to the morning after I got "the letter." Hattie and Theona had joined Miz Eudora to come over and help me plant some flowers for the next season.

"Ladies, I hate to be the bearer of bad news," I had admitted as we dug our hands into the rich fertile soil of the mountains. "I have jury duty on the same week as our beach trip. Try as I might, I can't come up with one good reason of why I'm unable to do my civic duty."

"We'll have to cancel the trip," said Theona, who had the least of any of them invested in the trip. She'd only heard of the "beach crew" and had not yet met them.

"Nonsense," replied Hattie. "Two of those women are my sisters and I don't get to see them except on special occasions like this."

"Besides," offered Miz Eudora, "they've already gone to the trouble and expense of renting that fine house for us. Did you see the pictures of it, Sadie? They took what I'd call an old one-story fishing barn and made it into a fine dwelling fit for a prince.

"I been looking forward to sitting on that upstairs deck and watching the ocean for a whole year now," said Miz Eudora in a voice that nearly broke my heart.

She's never seen the ocean's waves. She's never heard the ocean's roar. She's never reached down to pick up a seashell. Sadie, you've got to come

up with a way to make sure these women get there without you, I'd thought at the time.

The "Hattie-mobile" came to mind, but I dared not suggest that. I was afraid it wouldn't make it to the South Carolina line, if it got that far, even though it was only forty miles or so. There was no way it could travel the nearly five hundred miles, much less the same number back. Not considering that they had to cross through both Georgia and South Carolina to get back to the coast of North Carolina, much of it on back roads. ***Which further proves my point that you can't get there from here!*** I concluded. I'd been so busy exhausting all my resources trying to find a solution that I'd failed to hear Miz Eudora speaking. I had no idea what she'd said, but when the two others chimed in with great enthusiasm, my ears returned to the conversation, fearing I'd missed something important.

"That's a great idea!" chirped Theona.

"At least it would be a comfortable ride. Buicks are known for comfort, you know. That's why I bought the Century in the first place," stated Hattie.

Surely they don't think they're actually going to take that Hattie-mobile.

"They'd be room for all of us," Miz Eudora ventured. "Two in the front seat and two in the back seat. I wouldn't even have to sit in the front with her. One of you could do that. I could take some sewing or one of Sadie's books to read, and I wouldn't have to lay eyes on her the entire trip."

"Here she comes now," alerted Theona. "Let's ask her."

Miz Eudora suggested that* Mabel *take them? That had to be it, I answered myself. ***She'd have had no problem with sitting in the front seat with Hattie or "laying eyes" on her during the trip.***

The three of them lurched out the front door like a cat ready to pounce on scurrying field mice. I wondered which one would ask her. Miz Eudora might have suggested it, but I knew there was no way she'd bring herself to directly ask that of Mabel. Not after all the times Mabel had offered to drive and Miz Eudora emphatically put her foot down in refusal. The other two women must have known that as well for Hattie took "the bull by the horn" and walked out to the car.

"Good morning, Mabel. It's nice to see you."

"It surely is," Theona added.

Miz Eudora said nothing but watched with anxious eyes.

"We're all going to the beach the third week in August to see my sisters and their friends from the coast," explained Hattie. "We wondered if you might like to go with us."

"We wondered if you might like to drive," blurted Theona, who typically did not blurt.

A look of suspicion came into Mabel's eyes. "Isn't Sadie going?"

The heads of the other three women turned in my direction where I stood on the porch. "I had planned to go," I answered, not telling a lie. "There would be five of us, and…,"

I was relieved that Mabel took the bait for I had no clue as to what to say next. "You're right. My Buick would be much more comfortable than that old rattletrap of yours, my dear. I'm glad you ladies finally realized that."

"Now don't go thinking you're going to be driving us all over town all the time," started Miz Eudora.

Afraid that the cat was about to slip out of the bag, Hattie jumped in. "It is going to be a long ride and I'm so looking forward to seeing my two sisters. And," she looked back at Miz Eudora with her "Don't say a word!" eyes, "since you grew up in Hickory with us, we thought you might like to be a part of our group."

As badly as I wanted to see Mabel's face for her answer, my eyes drifted to Miz Eudora. I was certain that her tongue must be bleeding from the effort with which she was surely biting it. But she stood there, her face in a soured expression, as she waited for a response.

"I'd have to stop in Charlotte to pick up my swimsuit," Mabel said, swirling the idea of playing chauffeur around in her head. "I haven't had it on in years, and I didn't bother to bring it here since there are no beaches nearby."

"You're going to wear a...," began Miz Eudora.

Hattie squinted at her.

"...seatbelt, I hope. We'd all have to wear seatbelts for such a long haul." Miz Eudora stood pondering. "And you didn't realize Lake Chatuge had such a nice ...,"

Theona squinted at her.

"... view, I'll bet, when you moved here from Myers Park. I can't wait to see the view at the beach."

I couldn't help but think that morning that I'd probably need to send a gag along, in my stead, for Miz Eudora. At this rate, she would not have a tongue left by the time they reached the coast. She'd have bitten it off, bit by bit.

And now, watching the dust settle as they pulled onto the highway on the morning of Miz Eudora's first beach trip, I hated even more that I wouldn't be along to watch the festivities. I was sure their adventure would be far more interesting than the juicy novel I'd sent along with Miz Eudora.

Oh, no! I forgot the gag!

My fingers tapped harder and faster on the railing as I plotted my defense against being on the jury. ***I could tell them I moved here from Atlanta. They'd throw me out for sure. No one would want to have***

some "citified broad" on the jury. That's when I came up with an even better one. ***I'll tell them that I was married to a college professor who was also a counselor. Then they'll not only throw me out, they'll kick me right out the front door and slam it behind me. No one here in their right mind would want an intelligent citified broad who was the wife of a college professor/counselor seated in their jury box. That would be a worse curse than Mabel driving the four of them to the beach.***

Why didn't I think of this before? I asked, rushing to get dressed and out of my civic duty. Yet, before I'd zipped my skirt, I knew the answer to that question. There was a purpose in those four women going to the beach alone. I wasn't sure what it was, but there had to be a good one.

They're all older than you are, Sadie. Why are you worried?

I put the matter to rest and entered the courtroom, my head held high and ready to serve my civic duty.

"HOW'S THE ROAD trip, Eudora?" I asked the next morning, determined not to reveal that they'd selected all twelve of the jurors they'd need for their case the morning before and dismissed the rest of us to go home. I was convinced that this was one trip

Miz Eudora and her entourage were destined to "go it alone."

"Well, it's just fine," she said, mimicking the response she'd heard every time someone called for one of the others. "I got out of bed this morning bright and early and I've already farkled while I was having my coffee."

"You did ***what***?" I asked, holding the phone out and shaking it, glad I wasn't having my own coffee at that exact moment.

"I farkled. Not once, but twice. It's not just anybody who can farkle on the first try, but I've done it every time." Miz Eudora gave a little laugh. "So did Hattie and Theona. I guess you could say we're down here having ourselves a farkling good time."

I listened as boisterous laughter erupted from the other end of the phone line, coming from what sounded to be at least a dozen women.

"But Mabel hasn't farkled yet today," Miz Eudora went on. "You know how she is, stuffed up and everything. Rita said we ought to give her a peppermint pattie to loosen her up a bit, but all that does is make me think of that horrendous obituary she wrote about poor John. G."

I was contemplating whether I was brave enough to ask for a further explanation on farkling, but I missed my chance. For at that instant, Miz Eudora ordered, "You hurry on up with your jury duty and get down here, Sadie, so you can farkle, too." Then she promptly hung up the phone with, "I have to go now. It's my turn. I have to see whether I'm gonna farkle again."

I stared at my phone, wondering whether or not they had all fallen prey to Horace's "special blend," but then determined that Miz Eudora would have never stood for that. ***She'd have never let those ladies loose in that stuff. Mabel? Yes. But Hattie and sweet, little Theona? Never!***

That's it, I decided, throwing the last of my things into the suitcase. In less than five minutes, I was singing ***On the Road Again*** myself, but not sure I was having as much fun as the others. I wasn't entirely sure I wanted to have as much fun as it sounded like they were having, but I definitely wanted to find out what they were doing. Not to mention that I needed to make sure things hadn't gotten out of hand without me there to watch out for them in their naive, innocent frame of minds.

Sadie, I heard from within. ***You're sounding more and more like Mabel, thinking you have to be there to supervise***. I smiled. ***Besides***, I convinced myself, ***since when have you seen Miz Eudora Rumph unable to handle anything that comes flying at her?***

My foot pressed harder on the accelerator. ***On second thought***, I snickered. ***perhaps I'd better hurry***

and make sure all those around Miz Eudora are okay.

"They're fine," I could imagine Leon assuring me. ***"After all, you heard her yourself. They're all down there having a 'farkling good time.'***

The numbers on the speedometer increased by a few as I made an attempt to hurry and see if I could farkle myself on the first try.

LAUGHTER WAS POURING out the doors and windows so loudly that I heard them before I even reached the beach cottage. There was no question that I was in the right place, for I recognized the cars of Peggy, Marlene and Vickie, from the year before, parked along the front of the house. The only thing that surprised me was that there was no police car or "paddy wagon" there to arrest them all for disturbing the peace. All I could imagine was the story Miz Eudora had told about Horace and his buddies all riding tricycles in the basement of the local Smackass Gap Hardware one Christmas Eve after they'd gotten into a batch of the "special blend."

Lord,* please *don't let me find those women in a drunken state when I walk through that door*.** As I added the ***Amen, I figured that God had added a couple of stars to Miz Eudora's crown for she had surely turned me into a religious person. I'd never prayed so much in my life as I had since I'd met her, and those prayers generally concerned her.

"Sadie Calloway, what on earth did you think we were doing?" Hattie asked when I told them how glad I was to see them all sober and having so much innocent fun, just by rolling six small dice.

I hated to admit that I wasn't quite sure, and had, in fact, been a bit fearful of being quite sure.

"Well, you have to agree," Peggy commented in my defense, "that it is a rather strange sounding word. I'm not sure what I'd have thought if one of my children had come home and told me that they'd been farkling all afternoon."

"Where do you think the name came from?" Vickie asked.

"Maybe it's the last name of the person who came up with the game," suggested Marlene.

"I don't know, but I think one of us should Google Farkle," said Rita.

"Google Farkle?" repeated Mary Beth. "That sounds like a curse."

"A curse?" Miz Eudora scrunched up her nose as she turned and looked accusingly at Mabel. "Google Farkle," she repeated, seemingly lost in thought. "I wonder if maybe that's what came over my brother when he decided to marry Mabel Toast. He could have been suffering from the curse of the Google Farkle, placed on him by the Wicked Witch of Carolina or some such thing when he went off to that high-fallutin' university to study proctology."

I should have never let her see "The Wizard of Oz," I deduced, blaming myself for her logic.

"Why, it could have even been performed on him by one of those boys in the fraternity with him. You know you always hear tell of them doing strange things."

As far-fetched as those ideas sounded, it made perfect sense to Miz Eudora. She was still trying, after all these years, to make up some plausible excuse for "why come my baby brother got stuck with her."

"It could have been something horrible like a voodoo doll or something. Except instead of them sticking him, he's the one what got stuck with the voodoo doll."

"Eudora Rumph," Mabel scoffed, "sometimes I'd like to have a voodoo doll of you."

"Why, isn't it good enough that you're one yourself?"

"I am not, and your brother was not cursed when he married me. I'll have you know that was the best thing that ever happened to him. Why, if it hadn't been for me, he'd still be living in Smackass Gap."

"If it hadn't been for you, he might still be living. As it is, he's gone and you're the one still living in Smackass Gap." Miz Eudora gave such a huge gasp of exasperation that everyone in the room jumped. "That's it! He's dead and gone and the hex got passed on to us. Now we've all got to suffer with putting up with you."

Seeing that things were about to get too far out of hand, I quickly interrupted. "Miz Eudora, I haven't had a chance to farkle yet. Can you please show me how?"

"Oh, Sadie," she apologized, "I'm so sorry. I forgot. Here I was going on about Mabel and you've missed all the fun."

Peggy, Rita, Marlene, Mary Beth and Vickie all gave me thankful glances as Miz Eudora and Hattie quickly gave me a run-down of how to earn points, explaining how you had to roll a one or a five on one of the dice in order to stay in the game. Soon I had scored five hundred points and was "on the board," all without farkling.

I wasn't sure how much of the beautiful view of the beach Miz Eudora would see, but she was surely having a great time with her beach cronies, and was getting not a "birds-eye," but a "seagull's-eye" view of little black dots. At first, I wondered whether farkling would become a part of our morning front porch chats back home, but then I quickly realized the game would mean nothing to her without Hattie's two sisters and all their friends. ***She's broadened her horizons***, I realized, ***those horizons having nothing to do with the one on the beach.***

Now I understood why I was selected for jury

duty, I concluded, smiling broadly. I watched Miz Eudora's eyes beam with enthusiasm as she rolled the six dice and yelled, "FARKLE! I farkled!" It didn't matter to her that the point of the game was not to farkle. It only mattered that she was having way more fun than the normal beach blast. "Here, Mabel," she said encouragingly while passing her the dice, "see if you can farkle, too."

TWENTY-ONE

The Red Hatters Are a-Comin'

"SADIE...SADIE," MIZ Eudora called, trotting toward my house as fast as her red orthopedic shoes would carry her. I knew good news was on the rise for I could hear and see the excitement in her voice and in her stride. "Sadie, they're a-comin'!" she proclaimed, as boldly and proudly as if she had been Paul Revere making his revered Midnight Ride, as she leapt up the front steps of my house, where I greeted her with a mug of coffee. ***She's been around Theona Rouette one too many times. She's supposed to be the "town crier" around here.***

"Whose a-comin'?" I asked, wondering what had her "goin' on" so.

"All my friends who wear the red hats," she answered boldly.

I was right, I mused, ***only Paul Revere was warning about the red coats, not the red hats!***

"They're all a-comin' right here to Smackass Gap," she continued, "just to see me. Can you believe it? We'd better start getting ready. You know what they say about making people welcome, we're going to roll out the Red Carpet for the Red Hatters."

I ventured that singing ***Roll out the Barrel*** might be more appropriate, especially if Mabel showed up during the visit, but I decided it best to keep that thought to myself – at least for the moment. I did, however, make a mental note to keep a jug handy in case of emergencies.

"When are they coming?" I asked, finding myself both thoroughly enthused and amused that I would finally get to spend some time with them. I had recently even thought of getting a red hat if it meant having as much fun as Miz Eudora.

"They're going to be here in two weeks. They'll arrive on the Friday afternoon of September 19th and leave after lunch on Saturday, September 20th. Do you think we can get everything ready in time?"

I looked around at the beauty and serenity of the mountains and wondered what there was to get ready. "Miz Eudora, they're coming to Smackass Gap, not New York's Tavern on the Green. I don't think we have to worry about 'Puttin' on the Ritz.'"

"No, we surely don't," she replied, almost indignantly. "I have no intention of serving my guests crackers. 'Puttin' on the Ritz,' I reckon! I'm going to put on some good old chicken'n' dumplin's and fix them every kind of vegetable I can think of. They're going to get some real mountain cooking. If they're here long enough, I'll even take them over to The Fam for some of Tommy's good chicken livers. That boy can throw a spread just like his grandma did!"

That lone comment told me that my dear friend had not only finally entered the 20th century, but that she had gotten past the "kickin' and screamin'" stage. When I first met her, there was no way she would have ever considered taking a guest anywhere besides her own kitchen and now she was talking about taking them to The Fam.

I'll have to share that tidbit with Tommy Hooper. He'll think he's finally arrived! I chuckled to myself as I watched her glow like a Christmas tree. ***Heaven forbid she ever be introduced to the 21st century, though! I don't think any of us could stand her.***

Then, in that same instant, the eyes that had been twinkling like the Christmas lights at Tavern on the Green turned into eyes of horror. "Dear me," she fretted, "what on earth are we going to do with Mabel?"

At a loss for an answer, I suggested, "Why don't you speak to Preacher Jake about her?"

"I can't ask him to keep her for the weekend. He'd never speak to me again, not even if I bribed him with ***two*** fried chickens. Besides, she's enough to make a preacher cuss and that wouldn't fare well for him in the community, especially after those last two preachers Hattie had. We don't want him getting any unnecessary attention."

That statement caused me to laugh, for Miz Eudora had brought Preacher Jake plenty of attention by her own doings. As the laughter subsided, I tried to come up a suitable option. I knew I couldn't offer to get Mabel out of town because it would mean that I'd miss all the fun, and I had no intention of letting that happen. "Why don't we suggest she go back to Charlotte and visit her friends at the Myers Park Country Club?" I finally asked.

"That might work. Why don't you or Hattie ask her? If I ask her, she'll know something's cookin' and that we don't want her in the recipe."

"Anybody home?" called a voice, which I immediately recognized at Theona's, from the front door.

"That's it," I suggested. "Why don't we ask Theona what to do? She's a reasonable thinker. Maybe she'll have an idea."

Miz Eudora rushed to the door and came back with Theona in tow. From the look of deep thought on the visitor's face, I knew the question had already been popped. "There is a choir workshop that weekend over in Blairsville, Georgia," she said. "Some of us in the choir have been thinking of going. It's called 'You Can Sing, Too.'"

"Land sakes, they haven't heard Mabel yet,"

Miz Eudora blurted. "But I'll tell you what. If they can work that miracle, I'll pay her way. I'd even put an extra ten dollars in the collection plate on the Sunday of the cantata. I used up that much of Horace's 'special blend' getting her past ***O Holy Night*** at last year's cantata. She'd be saving me money." Now it was her face that was deep in thought as I fought hard to hold back an escaping snicker.

"Do you think I could really get her to go?" asked Theona.

"P'SHAA!" exclaimed Miz Eudora. "She'll be the first one in the car. If you're not careful, she'll be trying to take over and before you know it, won't nobody in the room be able to sing. They'd have to give everybody a refund."

My snicker slipped out, thankfully unnoticed.

"Besides," she concluded, "at the very least it'll give her a whole new view of heads to check out the roots on when she perches herself on the top row. You know, every time she plops herself up there on Sunday mornings, I keep praying she don't topple over in them high-heel clunkers of hers. We'd have our own game of dominoes right there in the front of the church." She snickered herself at that thought. "Hey, that might not be such a bad idea. Brother Terry and Six Flags over Jesus might hire her to come in and teach their youngun's on the skateboards some new tricks."

"What about Theona?" I asked. "If she has to babysit…I mean, create a diversion for Mabel, she'll miss all of your friends."

"Land sakes, Sadie! Once she gets Mabel over to Blairsville, she can come right back. Mabel will be so busy struttin' and bossin' everybody around, she'll never miss Theona. Besides, Theona's so tiny, she'd get lost in the crowd. Mabel wouldn't know where she was even if'n she was there."

Theona smiled. "Well, there you go. I guess there are some things in life that are better when you're short."

"Yes," agreed Miz Eudora. "I'll bet you can still play on all those cool toys they have over at Six Flags over Jesus. I'm half a mind to go over and ask Brother Terry if we could all come over and play one afternoon. I've never seen youngun's have so much fun in all my life. If we'd had all those things to do when John G. was coming along, he might not have trekked off to college and hitched up with that Mabel. Then we wouldn't be having this problem at all right now."

I had to admit that I absolutely loved Miz Eudora's thought process. You never knew where it was going, but it was surely a fun ride on the way to the end of the journey.

Miz Eudora proceeded to inform Theona about the upcoming visit while I went home to call Hattie and invite her over for "a planning luncheon" of what all would be included when the ladies arrived. Miz Eudora was determined that nothing would be undone. Suddenly Smackass Gap had become just like Atlanta with all of its charity and civic planning groups of which I had once been a part. As I grabbed a pen and paper, I realized that I had not made a single note of anything on paper since my list of moving from downtown "Hotlanta" to downtown Smackass.

***Perhaps Miz Eudora* is *getting a little too close to the 21st century*,** I mused as I walked back across the street with my pen, pad and, of course, my Ritz crackers.

TWENTY-TWO

Smackass Gap or Bust!

THOSE WERE THE fastest two weeks of my life. I helped Miz Eudora weed her flower beds, sweep out barns, knock down spider webs and everything else that she saw necessary to "roll out the Red Carpet." I even made sure I found Horace's "special blend" in the cellar, just in case. However, I did draw the line at spreading manure all over her yard and fields, which she had also sent out an instruction to her friends and neighbors to do to their own yards and fields, since she wanted everything "all pretty and fresh and green upon the arrival of my Red Hatter friends to Clay County."

The workload tripled when Miz Eudora "got word" that all her friends from the Hotlanta excursion from Chinquapin's, where she was first introduced to her Red Hatter friends, had apparently shared word of her to their friends and neighbors, who now also wanted to come. The final tally was seventy-eight ladies, donned in red and purple or pink and lavender, from five states filling up two buses to "come a-callin'" on Miz Eudora.

Word also spread around Clay County and before long, the entire town was anxiously awaiting the largest crowd of visitors they'd ever had at Smackass Gap at one time. I suspected Guinness' Book of World Records could proclaim it as the largest crowd they'd ever had all total in Smackass Gap and I was "half a mind" to call and inform them of the visit.

The Friday afternoon arrived and everything was on course. All of the preparations had been completed, and the aromas coming from Miz Eudora's kitchen were nearly more than I could bear while waiting for the ladies to descend on "downtown Smackass" and the square of Hayesville. Photographers from the newspaper were on call to transform into "the paparazzi" the minute the buses rolled into town. People were roaming the streets with their cameras in anticipation of the "approaching scene," not only of people, but the hats they'd heard about from Miz Eudora.

The only thing missing was Mabel, who was on her way to Blairsville in the church van. As it turned out, Theona got to stay home. She was "down in her back," which she really had been the day before, after helping Miz Eudora peel apples and chop pecans for the twenty-two pies for her "company."

Miz Eudora even sent a large box filled with pecan pies, apple pies and banana pudding with Mabel for safekeeping. "It's safe for keeping her in Blairsville," she admitted. "Once they hear her sing, they're liable to send her home. At least this way, they'll keep her just so's they can have all those desserts."

She had a point, for I'd sampled all those desserts in the making. They were the same ones she planned to serve the ladies that evening at a dessert party, which she was calling a Moonshine Mash. "I want them to think they're getting the special treatment, and they are. Just not the special blend," she said with a playful wink. "Without Horace here to make it anymore, I'm saving what's left to take care of Mabel, when necessary. I did put a little in the filling for the pecan pie, though. It wouldn't be my famous Sourmash Pecan Pie without Horace's special blend." With that, she gave me the biggest grin I'd ever seen.

I couldn't help but wonder if this wasn't the biggest shindig she'd ever put on. I was sure it was more exciting to her than her own wedding day had been. ***Which probably also consisted of a little moonshine from Horace's family recipe, truth be known***, I wagered.

"I decided to use Cheerwine soda, ginger ale and pineapple juice to make them punch to go along with all the desserts," she explained. "Since I don't have a punch bowl, I'm going to serve it in my big tin tub and pour it into those little dainty cups Hattie found at Ingle's with the gourd dipper my daddy used from the well. Do you think anyone will mind?"

"There's no doubt in my mind that those who might shrivel up at the thought of a community dipper will forget all about their whims once they get a taste of your pies and pudding," I answered truthfully. "As good as they are, they'll probably be licking their plates when they're done."

"I hope not. I wrote 'Join in the Celebration' on the bottom of all those little white paper plates with a red pen. Since it was because of Horace's 'celebration' that I first met some of them, I wanted them all to feel like they were partakin' of the celebratin' experience. You know, kind of like communion on Sunday mornings. It's for everybody. I wanted those plates to be a little souvenir from me to them and if they lick off the red writing, there won't be anything special about the plates."

"I have a feeling that those ladies are going to enjoy anything you give them, Miz Eudora. I'll bet they're as enamored with you as you are with them. After all, you even said there's one coming all the way from Jacksonville, Florida to see you."

"That's right! And she drove all the way to Charlotte first to ride here with her mother. I don't think

I've ever ridden that far in my life, even in all my years on the tractor and in the truck with Horace."

As hard as that was to imagine, I suspected she spoke the truth. It would take a lot of rides on her acreage to total that many miles.

"Smokin' Barb said in her letter that there's women from all over North Carolina comin' here. Some of them are ridin' all the way from the east coast to here, and we're about as far west as they can get without going into Tennessee or Georgia. There are also women from all over South Carolina, even as far as Myrtle Beach, and Georgia and Alabama coming here. I'm so excited that I could nearly sprout wings. In fact," she laughed, "I just believe I would except that then I'd fly away and miss all of them."

Her eyes showed she was contemplating their arrival. "Oh, Sadie," she said dreamily, "this is the most exciting thing that's ever happened to me in my whole eighty-six years. Can you believe all those women are coming here just to see me?"

Actually, I found it very hard to believe that all those women were riding that far. But then, knowing Miz Eudora as I did, I knew they were in for a real treat, long ride or not. I didn't offer her an answer, but then, she didn't seem to expect one. She was clearly caught up in her own thoughts as she sat in the swing, going back and forth, back and forth. Watching her, I wondered how many times she'd swung back and forth from that very spot. ***Probably more times that all those miles those women are traveling put together***, I concluded.

We sat in silence for a spell, her swinging and me rocking, looking over the mountain view as the waiting became longer and longer. "Wonder why they're not here yet?" she asked, at least once every three minutes after the proposed arrival time.

After nearly thirty minutes, I got a call from Smokin' Barb on my cell phone. "Sorry I'm just now calling," she apologized. "I didn't realize there was no phone reception for much of the way."

"Welcome to Western North Carolina," I laughed. "That lack of reception ***is*** a part of our tranquil reception here in Clay County."

"I'm seeing that," she agreed, "as we go around each of the curves and see another more scenic view with each one. I wanted to let Miz Eudora know that we're about ninety minutes behind schedule. One of our drivers left the original destination almost two hours early without any passengers. They had to load into one of the gals' vans and 'haul buggy' over to where he was waiting for the rest of us. Then it seems he took a wrong turn and, well, I won't go into the rest of it."

There was no need. I would have feared that the ladies were in a foul mood had I not heard all the bouts of laughter in the background, mixed with the "oohs" and "aahs" at the view they were enjoying on the way. It sounded as if they'd taken all the mishaps and made them into a part of the adventure that went with "touring Smackass Gap."

Sounds like their driver has already "rolled out the barrel!" I decided after hearing Smokin' Barb's news and the hilarity of the bus passengers.

"I hope you saved room for dessert," said Miz Eudora, taking the phone from me. "I've got enough food here to serve a small army."

Which is exactly what she has coming here, I laughed to myself. ***I'd hate to get on the wrong side of all those hormones at one time. I'll bet they could fight off anything that got in their way!*** With that thought, I found myself as anxious about their arrival as Miz Eudora was.

"We're just leaving Macon County," answered Smokin' Barb when asked where they were.

"Good," replied Miz Eudora. "That means you're in Clay County. Watch for Shootin' Creek and Burnt Schoolhouse Road. You'll know you're getting close. Once you see the sign for Chunky Gal Stables on your right, be on the lookout for Lake Chatuge. You can't miss it. It's the big swimmin' hole on your left. Keep on coming until you get to Downings Creek Road. Take a right and you'll see me sitting on the front porch with my friend, Sadie. We'll call Hattie and Theona right now and have them here waiting for you, too."

If I'd thought Miz Eudora looked like Christmas lights the day she'd first informed me of this visit, she now looked like Christmas from space, complete with an orchestra playing carols to accompany a magnificent light show. I'd never known a person could glow so vividly. She walked the porch for the next thirty-five minutes until she saw the buses coming down the hill on Highway 64. Because of her anxiety, I hadn't bothered to tell her that Smokin' Barb had also shared with me that one of the drivers had never driven on a mountain before. ***Oh well,*** I'd commiserated at hearing that fact, ***nothing like a crash course on your first try***.

"They're here!" she finally screamed, in such a loud voice that I had trouble realizing all that sound came from one single person.

"Careful there, Miz Eudora!" I warned. "You keep that up and Mabel will hear you all the way over in Blairsville. She'll be getting herself back here to see who's coming."

"You're right," she replied, wringing her hands to keep calm.

"Besides, you don't want to 'strip your gears' before they even get here. I've an idea that you're going to be doing a lot of talking in the next couple of days."

She nodded her head as an effort to save her

voice. Then suddenly, a panicked look came over her face. "Do you think those buses can get in the driveway?"

"I think you've got plenty of acreage for them to park those buses anywhere they want. Besides, those drivers are used to maneuvering in any kind of space."

As long as they know how to get there, I reminded myself, thinking of the unusually long time it had taken them to get here. That was when I looked down and realized that my own knuckles were ghost-white from grasping the rocker's handles so hard while praying for the safety of her guests.

When they turned from Highway 64 onto Downings Creek Road, huge banners on each bus became visible as they announced "Smackass Gap or Bust." Women were now hanging out the windows and waving as the entire mountainside exploded with red and purple.

"Isn't that the most beautiful sight you've ever seen?" Miz Eudora asked, her voice quivering from finally letting go of the excitement that had been shut up inside her for the past two weeks.

As odd as it seemed, I had to admit that she was right. It ***was*** the most beautiful sight I'd ever seen. Not simply the vision of red and purple flowers, plumes and feathers, but the love that bounced back and forth from the women on the buses to this woman on the porch. I'm sure had Miz Eudora known that

Horace's passing would have brought about such camaraderie, she'd have prayed for him to cross the Jordan long before he did.

TWENTY-THREE

Welcome to Smackass

I DON'T BELIEVE a single step met Miz Eudora's feet as she jumped off the porch and went flying toward the buses. ***I'm not too sure she didn't sprout those wings!*** I observed. She ran up and down the aisle of each bus, greeting everyone with "Welcome to Smackass," introducing herself to all those she didn't know and hugging every single person, including the bus drivers twice for getting "the ladies here safely."

"I've been 'about to bust a gut,'" she said, "waiting for ya'll to get here. Hop off and stretch your legs a mite and I'll introduce you to Clyde. I've even got a red hat with a purple flower on his head just so's he'd feel like he was a part of the welcomin' committee."

She passed out little brown lunch bags filled with treats to each lady. "There's even a peppermint patty in each one in memory of my baby brother, John

G.," she added. "You'd have all loved him." She stopped and thought for a minute. "Even if he did have the misfortune of being married to Mabel. When you stop to think about it, dying is the best thing that ever did happen to that poor boy."

She stopped her gushing for a moment as she stared at one of the women. "I do declare, ma'am," she observed, "that is the strangest hat I do believe I ever did see."

I turned to see that "the hat" was actually a red undergarment that had been strategically decorated.

"These are my ear warmers," the woman explained.

Miz Eudora leaned to me to offer unnecessary words, for I knew what was coming. "Do you think I should tell her that her ear warmers are supposed to keep another part of her body warm?"

Giggles erupted throughout the crowd as the ladies' cameras flashed, taking in the ear warmers and Miz Eudora's shocked expression. I indicated that I thought it would be best if she let the matter rest, while I fought the urge to laugh at the vision of Mabel in a set of ear warmers.

Taking my advice, she continued her carefully-rehearsed instructions. "Ya'll's all goin' to have to stay over in Hiawassee this evening at the Holiday Inn Express 'cause our lovely little Deerfield Inn, right in the heart of Smackass, didn't have enough beds for all of you. Which is a real shame, 'cause you'd have had such a lovely view of Lake Chatuge." She barely took a breath before she went on with, "Did you all see it as you passed by?" and then turned around and answered her own question with, "Why, of course, you did. Ya'll don't wear blinders like Clyde.

"But the Holiday Inn Express is a nice place and you'll have a good time there. Sadie is goin' to take me over there this evening so that Hattie, Theona and me can show ya'll a real good time. I've got lots of games planned for you. Even Sadie doesn't know about them so they're gonna be a big surprise."

There was no doubt in my mind that they'd be a big surprise. The only surprise was just how big it would be.

"The manager of the Holiday Inn is giving us free reign of the conference rooms this evening so we can do anything we want to do."

Even before she uttered the last word of that statement, I could have told her that was a catastrophic announcement. From the looks of some of the ladies on those two chartered buses, there was no telling what they might want to do. A tad of relief swept through me as I saw Red Hat Nanny and Smokin' Barb. ***Surely they can keep this crowd under control***. But then, I should have realized they were only human. Especially when I saw Miss Bloomers and the Sassy Grandma amidst the ladies.

Poor Miz Eudora! She'd planned for weeks to make these two days the perfect "Smackass Experience" for all her Sparklin' Shiners and their friends. But as luck would have it, namely in a city-slicker driver who'd never driven on a mountain, many of her plans went down the outhouse.

Which, by the way, she did offer each of them a ride in her motorized outhouse before she led them all over Smackass Gap on a tour of all the notable places and distinguishable characters. ***All except for Mabel,*** I noted, thinking how the most notable character was in absentia.

By the time the New York City driver, who'd spent his career driving on the same few city blocks, figured out how to maneuver the bus on the mountainous curves, not to mention the time they'd lost on the way to those mountainous curves, it was too late for the Dam Picnic which Miz Eudora had planned. Bless her heart, she'd planned for the picnic to end right at dusk so they could see the spectacular colors of the sun as it set behind the hundred-plus mountain peaks you could see from the dam. And to end the celebration, she'd gotten sparklers so that her Sparklin' Shiners could have their own Dam Fireworks Show. As it was, there was ***no*** dam situation, period, for the bus driver couldn't get the bus on the dam road, much less the dam bridge.

What happened instead is that they shuffled

tables around in the conference room of the hotel, put out the picnic spread and chowed down. The Moonshine Mash – which was actually only going to be Cheerwine punch – that was planned for bedtime desserts, happened in conjunction with the makeshift picnic. That way, the ladies were able to enjoy the homemade banana pudding, complete with real meringue, apple pie and pecan pie that she'd spent three days making so that every lady could have a serving of each variety. "Sweets for my Sparklin' Shiners," she'd said as we were making them. I didn't bother telling her that the saying was, "Sweets for the Sweet," for she'd have declared it was the same difference.

As for the sunset, there was a good view of it from the conference area of the hotel, which Miz Eudora pointed out. However, the sunset overlooked the pool, so all the young guys there working on some electrical project thought all the ladies were staring at them and then came in to flirt back with us. That's when the Sassy Grandma got a case of the hot flashes so badly that she went out to the pool and jumped in, clothes and all.

"Now that's what I call a ***real*** 'wet hen!'" exclaimed Hattie.

The young guys loved that and flirted even more. I, personally, was grateful when some "younger chicks" checked in and stole the guys' attention. It's a good thing, too, for about that time, I heard this Mid-

Eastern music begin and turned to see one of the Red Hatters belly-dancing across the hotel's lobby. She'd traded the red hat for some red "outfit," but I think there had actually been more material in the red hat.

Here's the part where I said Miz Eudora's invitation to do "anything you want to" was catastrophic. The belly dancer must have inspired one of the other ladies, for she got up from the sofa and began to move the middle of her body in some strange gyrations.

"What is she trying to do to that pole?" Miz Eudora asked. "I don't believe I've ever seen anyone move in that way before."

"Oh, she's just one of ours," answered the Spunky Georgia Peach. "Don't mind her. She can't move her feet, but she can sure move her body. Whenever she hears music, she loves to get her exercise."

I didn't have to look at that red hatter's name badge for I was sure she was one of the New Hattitudes from Ila, Georgia. I'd already learned that those ladies had a great attitude and they didn't mind sharing it. It's important here that you note that the one with the "ear warmers" was also a New Hattitude!

What I'd really wished I didn't have to look at was Miz Eudora rushing over to join her.

"This looks like way more fun than that 'pulling weeds' stuff Mabel does over at her gym. I think I could get into this," she stated, imitating the woman's every move.

I finally decided I could deal with that, just as long as she didn't buy herself an outfit like the belly dancer's.

The real fun began after the "picnic" and "moonshine mash" when the games started. There wasn't much room for two busloads of women to be moving around in the lobby and conference area, so most of the games, too, were preempted. By the way, just so you know, those are the same games that were supposed to have been played on the shore of Lake Chatuge at the Dam Picnic.

They had games to guess the number of pinto beans in the quart jar; they had games to see how many words they could make out of "Lake Chatuge" and "Miz Eudora Rumph," they had coin tosses, and even a race to see who could blow up a red balloon first.

But the one game that took the cake – or actually a plunger and a roll of toilet paper – was "the Outhouse Trot," as Miz Eudora called it. She assigned teams, each consisting of eight ladies, and divided them into two rows. Four ladies from each team lined up behind each other on one row and the other four lined up the same way on the other row. She then gave the front person on one row a plunger and every person on the other side a roll of toilet tissue.

After handing out the supplies, which already had the women in a dither of laughter, she instructed those with plungers to place them between their knees, and informed all the ladies with toilet tissue to place the rolls between their knees. She then proceeded to demonstrate, with a plunger between her own knees, how to waddle across to the other side, retrieve the roll of toilet tissue from your team member and waddle back to where you started, where you were to drop the roll of toilet tissue into a laundry basket. Did I mention that the ladies couldn't use their hands?

And I thought the gyrations with her New Hattitudes' friend were bad! That was the moment I learned a very important lesson. If you think things are rough when you're around Miz Eudora Rumph, let it go. They can always get worse, especially when Mabel Toast Jarvis is also in the picture! Watching the women in front of me gave me cause to utter several prayers of "Thanks" that the singing retreat had fallen on this exact same weekend.

Miz Eudora had introduced the game as an "ice breaker," explaining that ladies were placed on teams with people from towns besides their own. I don't know how much ice was broken, but a couple of the women fell down in the process, and one of them was quoted to have said she broke something that sounded remotely similar to 'ice.'

Those ladies howled so long and so hard that I was surprised the dog catcher from Clay County's Animal Control didn't come out to rescue all of them.

Once they settled down from that, the ones who

still had any steam left went outside to set off the sparklers. Those Sparklin' Shiners were doing just that as they twirled them around, wrote their names in the darkness, and "oohed" and "aahed" like a bunch of youngsters. I had to admit that I, too, felt like a child at play, running footloose and carefree – well, almost, I did have my sneakers on – as I took my place among them under the stars, my own soul and spirit shining just as brightly as any of those in the heavens, as I lit sparklers from those of my new neighbors.

I was sure that God was looking down, seeing many glorious constellations shaped by the light of our "glowing sticks," but viewing ones even more beauteous and magnificent by the lights that shone from within each of these women. ***Including me***, I realized while understanding, for the first time in my life, my place in the universe and among the stars. ***And Sparklin' Shiners.*** I was grateful it was dark, for it kept anyone from noticing the joyful tears that I felt moistening my eyes and cheeks.

Just so you know, I did learn, after the fact, that the buses and one of the drivers that had originally been reserved for the ladies Tour Smackass trip had been reassigned to take buses to Houston and help with the transporting of Hurricane Ike evacuees. Needless to say, Miz Eudora had a comment to make on that, too.

"You do know why the hurricane hit Galveston

and Houston instead of Corpus Christi, as expected, don't you?" she asked when I explained to her about what happened.

"No." I really didn't know, but even if I had, I'd have answered the same way. There was no question that her explanation would be more amusingly noteworthy than the real reason.

"Well, he ***was*** named Ike, and like any other man, he refused to stop for directions. That's why he took a wrong turn and landed up in Galveston and Houston instead of Corpus Christi."

Like I said, there was no predicting her thought process, but it usually led to a good laugh. Which meant that, in spite of all the "foiled" plans, there was not one Red Hatter who left Smackass Gap without a belly full of laughter and countless stories to share once they got home.

That, in reality, is exactly what I love about Smackass Gap. You deal with whatever mess is thrown at you and keep on "a-kickin!'" Given that, I'd say those two chartered busloads of Red Hatters had the perfect welcome to Smackass Gap.

TWENTY-FOUR

Saturday on the Square

THE MORNING BEGAN with a surprise stop at a yard sale. “I doubt you’ll find any urns of ashes today,” noted Miz Eudora, “but I’m sure there will be a lot of other good bargains.” Oh, that was after the real surprise of one of the buses not moving for thirty minutes from the hotel in Hiawassee. That was actually the first surprise.

From there, they went to a small shopping area. That was the second surprise. The shops, which were supposed to open at nine, didn’t open until ten. However, one shopkeeper did rush in to open up early for all the anxious customers. That was fortuitous, for there was a couple of statues in the store that looked exactly like Mabel and John G., where most of the ladies posed for keepsake photos. One lady even snapped Miz Eudora giving the one resembling her baby brother a kiss on the cheek “for old times’ sake.”

Then came the real fun of the morning. The buses headed back to the town square of Hayesville for the Saturday morning Farmer's Market. "This is how my pa, and his pa before him, fed their families for decades," Miz Eudora shared, pointing to the tables and trucks' tailgates and reminiscing about the past. "And ya'll be sure to go in Chinquapin's and say hello. The Tiger family that owns it has been a help for people in Clay County ever since I know about."

Heads popped up when vendors, shopkeepers and townspeople spied two chartered buses pulling to a stop on the square. ***I'll bet this is the first time they've seen the customers coming in by the busloads***, I ventured, glancing at the faces of the farmers as we passed by. The ladies hopped off the bus and scattered, "flying" in all directions, their feathers and plumes leading the way. I was reminded of the scene from ***Sister Act*** when the nuns spread out in the casino. Except this was the town square and the habits had been replaced by red hats. It was much better than any movie I'd seen. I would have paid a hundred dollars to watch this on screen, and two hundred to have watched the satisfaction on Miz Eudora's face at being surrounded by so many loving friends.

One man waved his hand close to one of the pink hats in a shooing motion. "I think I just saw a bird fly out of that," he said, reaching for his camera with the other hand.

Several of the ladies put their heads together for what looked like the biggest showgirl hat I'd ever seen. ***These women could make the Vegas girls blush***, I thought with a grin. ***I'll give them one thing. They all know how to pose for the camera. The "paparazzi" and townspeople ought to have a field day with these ladies.***

They crowded Chinquapin's for the longest ice cream line I'm sure Rob Tiger had ever had, they browsed the shelves of the Phillips and Lloyd Book Shop and sampled the desserts, they asked shopkeepers questions about Cutworm, a historic figure of the town, and they visited all the booths set up along the Farmer's Market. Some of them danced in the courtyard in front of the bandstand where a country band was performing. Others simply sat on the benches of the courtyard and enjoyed the gentle breeze and scenic view while doing absolutely nothing.

Once everyone had finished shopping, Miz Eudora told the buses to follow her. She trekked down the hill to the Hayesville Family Restaurant and gathered everyone at the front door. "Now listen up, ladies! Tommy's put on the biggest spread you've ever seen. Wait until you get a load of all the things he's fixed to make you ladies feel special today. And Mabel," she added to the unexpected guest who'd shown up, "you get at the back of the line 'cause if you go first, you'll load up on everything before the ladies even get a chance to get a load of all the food."

I'm glad she made that perfectly clear, I mused, thinking how this woman, amidst all her varied faults and virtues, had the power to amuse me in any setting, even as serious as Mabel's appearance.

Once "dinner" was over, there was an awards ceremony to give out all the prizes from the previous night's games. Miss Bloomers guessed the closest to the number of pinto beans in the jar, so she was awarded the beans and a pound of cornmeal. "Ain't nothin' like a big ole pot of pintos and cornbread," said Miz Eudora as she made the presentation. "Funny you won this, honey. You'd better make sure you check those bloomers on Monday to make sure there are no surprises."

There was the "I'm Still Hot" award that went to the Sassy Grandma for jumping in the pool with all her clothes on the night before. ***Guess there's something to be said for those hot flashes!*** I deduced. There was the "Biggest Penny Pincher in Smackass Gap" that went to the Red Hat Nanny for winning the penny toss. There was the "Biggest Bag of Hot Air in Smackass Gap" award that went to the Queen of SASS. Miz Eudora had gotten a red-leather dictionary for the winners of the three word games, but it seemed one woman won all three. "I was gonna give you a dictionary, but it would seem you already got one in your head," announced Miz Eudora, "so I'll give them to

Theona, Hattie and Sadie."

The final award went to the sweet little pink hatter from the winning team of the game with the toilet tissue and plungers the evening before. I would like to have been a fly on the wall to hear the comments on Monday when she returned to her office with the framed award that read, "Let it be hereby proclaimed that I had the Outhouse Trots in Smackass Gap, NC."

The ceremony ended with one of the Red Hatters, a palm reader, giving Miz Eudora her own private "reading" in front of all the women. I learned many things about my neighbor that I didn't know, but the two that stuck in my mind were that she had, and would, always lead a life of service, and that there was another man in her life.

That's when she jerked her hand away and said she "didn't need to hear no more." After that pronouncement, I thought the visit had come to an end, but it appeared Miz Eudora had one last trick up her sleeve.

"For all you Elvis fans, which I know is most of you," she announced, going over to the piano in the corner of the restaurant, "I have a special treat. Everybody always knew when Elvis had left the building because of the music they played. I wanted you to be the same way with Smackass Gap, so I've got a special song for you. And you don't have to worry about Mabel butcherin' it 'cause she don't know the words." With that Miz Eudora sat down at the piano, took her right hand on the upper end of the keys and after two long, descending glissandos, lit into a rip-roaring rendition of ***I'll Fly Away***. I guess the glissandos served to rev up the engine, like on a jet, or else get her fingers to "boogieing" because that piece surely did fly the rest of the way. She had those women so stirred up that they were clapping and stomping "to beat the band."

All of them except for Mabel, that is. She was scrounging the place to find a hymnbook with the words to ***I'll Fly Away.*** Right as she finally found them and took a deep breath to cut loose, Miz Eudora brought the soaring piano solo to a smooth landing with one last glissando that glided all the way down the keyboard, which was a good thing because if Mabel had opened her mouth, the musical airplane would have surely had a crash landing.

The Red Hatters went wild with their standing ovation. I felt the only thing missing was, "Miz Eudora has left the building." However, in this case, it was the Red Hatters who left the building to get on the buses and go back to their points of destination. I knew this visit would long be remembered in the annals of Clay County history, and would never be forgotten in the mind of Miz Eudora Rumph.

Nor Sadie Calloway, I realized as I wiped away

a bittersweet tear at seeing them leave. ***Whoever decided "Hotlanta" was the place to go for a good time never visited Smackass Gap.***

TWENTY-FIVE

There's Within My Heart a Melody

HOME. A WORD that means quiet afternoons spent on the front porch seated in the swing or a rocker. A word that means listening to the gentle breezes, the babbling brooks or the mockingbird's song. A word that calls you from the "filled-with-wonder" road trips with Miz Eudora's crew to a rejuvenation of peace and tranquility. And to make sure home is all those pleasant things, you drop Mabel off first when returning from one of their adventures.

Home, I sighed heavily, already tasting the freshly-brewed sweet tea that would be ready in the time I got from my front door until I unpacked my bag and was ready to sit in that rocker on the front porch. It mattered not that "Six Flags over Jesus" would be having their choir rehearsal that evening, with sounds of pounding drums and blaring electric guitars echoing up the hillside in the direction of my porch. I would be on my turf with no one, nor thing, to interrupt that blessed solitude.

That was before Mabel checked her answering machine as I toted the last of her bags inside her front door and sat them in the foyer. The foyer should have been my first indication that there would be trouble, for folks who are born-and-bred in Smackass Gap don't have foyers – which, of course, Mabel pronounced with a mock French accent. They have front doors that open directly into the living room or either a hallway that leads straight to the living room on one side and the kitchen on the other. That's to make you feel welcome from the moment you step inside the house. And they definitely don't have answering machines. Anyone who has any need to call you knows where you are and when you'll be home.

But, after all, this was Mabel Toast "Mrs. John G." Jarvis, who – to hear her tell it - was "the social bumblebee of the Myers Park Country Club." I guess she thought that distinction reached all the way into Clay County for she screamed at the top of her lungs for Miz Eudora and Hattie to get out of the car and come running to hear the news.

"Would you listen to this?" she asked haughtily, pushing the replay button on her telephone answering machine. "I've been asked to be the song leader for the next United Methodist Women's Spiritual Renewal Retreat at Lake Junaluska. It's about time someone stood up and took notice of my vocal talents. I can't wait to share this news with Preacher Jake and the choir."

"Well, I guess that means my chance of getting my spirit renewed just washed right back out into Lake Junaluska," responded Miz Eudora.

"What do you mean?" asked Hattie.

I wished she'd have kept that question to herself because I feared the answer was not going to be pretty. My imaginary shield went up to protect myself from the approaching blows.

"You certainly don't think ***I'm*** going to sit through Mabel Toast Jarvis being a song leader. Shoot fire, if I'd wanted to look at, much less listen to, a turkey buzzard squawkin', I'd have signed up to go to the annual Turkey Buzzard Sunday in Hinckley, Ohio. ***Not*** a peaceful, quiet annual weekend of spiritual renewal at Lake Junaluska."

I saw an expression of relief appear on Hattie's face that the answer had concluded this peaceably, but I knew that Miz Eudora was merely getting wound up to go again.

"Song leader, I reckon! Especially at Lake Junaluska. I've heard stories of how glorious it is to sit in that big, old round auditorium looking out over the lake and listening to the strains of music echoing across the waters. Land's sakes, with her bellowing up there like an old freight train, they'd think there was a hurricane blowing in. It'd take Jesus, himself, to appear and say, "Peace, be still," to calm the waters. Not to mention those poor ducks. They wouldn't know what hit them and they'd be running for cover.

"Besides, the only thing that Mabel's ever led her entire life was my baby brother, John G., straight to the grave. Land sakes! They'd have so many funerals from the shock of her singing that every preacher in Western North Carolina would all have to get paid overtime!"

I sensed that it was time to play referee, but I greatly feared putting down my shield. Besides, watching the two of them "go at it" was always good free entertainment. My conscience, however, won out and told me to resolve the issue. I was grateful that the ringing of the telephone pre-empted the use of my reconciliation skills, learned from years of marriage with Leon, just in time.

"Hello," said Mabel, excitement over the message still present in her voice.

"Who in their right mind would want her to lead the singing?" whispered Miz Eudora in my direction. "P'SHAA! She can't even stay awake during the sermons. I've half a notion to stick her with my hat pin one of these Sundays when Preacher Jake gets to going. There's no telling how many times he's stepped on her toes and she snoozed right through it."

I placed a finger over my lips in hopes that she'd

take the hint, which she did, but not without a coda to her tirade.

"Land sakes, there's some Sundays I'm surprised she's even able to walk home from all the toe stompin,'" she concluded, looking quite pleased that she'd gotten in all she wanted to say. I was sure that had the phone not rung, we'd still be listening to her.

But once she delivered that last statement, we all stood silent as Mabel listened intently to the voice on the other end of the line. I prayed that I'd received my reprieve and would now be able to escape the role of referee.

"No, I'm sorry. This is Mabel, Mrs. John G., Jarvis," she said slowly, glaring at Miz Eudora. "You must have the wrong number."

I saw repulsion writhing in Miz Eudora's eyes and was glad she had the decency not to say anything else until Mabel got off the phone. Maybe the lapse of time would soften the blow.

"Yes, I did get that message and I'm looking greatly forward to being this year's song leader."

I caught Miz Eudora rolling her eyes. She crossed her arms as her expression turned to one of total disgust as she listened to the remainder of our side of the conversation.

"What…? What do you mean, there's been a mistake?"

That apparently was all Miz Eudora could stand.

She stepped right up beside Mabel in an effort to eavesdrop, leaning her head as closely as possible to the phone's receiver. Mabel turned and lowered her head, trying to cover the receiver with her hand, as her responses became more of a whisper.

"That couldn't be possible. Wouldn't the committee like to reconsider? I'm a faithful member of the church choir and I did the most wonderful job on ***O Holy Night*** during last year's Christmas cantata that the congregation had ever heard."

"Mabel," interrupted Miz Eudora, making no attempt to keep the listener from hearing, "there's not enough of Horace's special blend left to make you sound good for a whole weekend. The Good Lord, with a little help from Horace's special blend, truly worked a miracle in our little church last Christmas and that's the only reason you managed to soar through ***O Holy Night.***"

"What…? What do you mean?" This time Mabel's questions were directed toward Miz Eudora.

My imaginary shield was repositioned as I readied my defenses while Miz Eudora relayed the entire story of how she'd pretended to be sick in order to go home and "fetch some of Horace's special blend. While you were busy knocking wrinkles out of your choir robe and trying to screech up to the high notes in practice, I snuck a few drops of 'courage' into your water bottle. Land sakes, the Good Lord sure did use that powerful stuff to work a mighty miracle that night! First time in my life I ever thought something good could come out of Horace's 'hobby.'"

She paused for a moment to turn and grin at Hattie and me as she uttered that last statement, and then turned her attention back to a serious mode as she finished explaining to Mabel about that night. "And if it hadn't have been for the fact that Christmas Eve was known for being a night of miracles, I'm not sure the Good Lord would have granted that one. Besides, he wouldn't have wanted something as bad as your solo desecrating the birth of His precious Son anyway."

"You don't mean…?" Mabel started and then stood silent in shocked disbelief. Her eyes darted toward me and then over to Miss Hattie to seek the truth in our eyes. She watched in disdain as we nodded our heads to affirm Miz Eudora's words. "Oh…oh, whatever am I going to do? How shall I ever explain this?"

"Hello…hello…are you still there?" The woman on the phone was yelling so loudly by this time that we could all hear her.

Mabel appeared startled as she stared at the receiver. She slowly raised it back to her ear. "Yes, I'm here. After considering your offer, I'm afraid I'll have to relinquish the task of being your song leader to someone who has more…more…more time to do it. I'm afraid it takes all my time to care for my elderly, ailing sister-in-law these days."

"Why you...you...," began Miz Eudora. "Mabel Toast Jarvis, the only thing ailin' about me is my eyes ever' time I have to look at you, and my ears ever' time I have to listen to you. In fact, you're right! I'm ailin' pretty powerfully right now."

Much more and I believe I could have detected smoke coming from Miz Eudora's ears. Had Mabel not been on the phone, I'm sure her next words would have been "fightin' words." While Miz Eudora took a moment to compose herself, only because Mabel still had listening ears on the other end of the phone line, the conversation continued.

"Yes. Yes, I'm afraid she is." There was a brief pause as Mabel listened intently to the voice on the other end. "Well, as a matter of fact, she's here with me right now."

Hattie, Miz Eudora and I exchanged glances as we wondered which of us was now the topic of conversation. I didn't wonder too hard, for I was pretty sure which one it was. From Hattie's expression, it was evident she shared my opinion.

"Do what?" Mabel fairly shouted into the phone. "You want Eudora Rumph to do what? Surely you jest!"

Hattie and I each beamed in recognition of our right answers as Miz Eudora's eyes shot straight toward Mabel.

"You can't possibly mean you want Eudora Rumph to serve communion wine at the Spiritual Renewal service. Why, there's no telling what she might pour in that chalice!"

Miz Eudora reached over and grabbed the phone so quickly that I was sure the woman on the other end missed that last word, which I was also sure was a good thing. "Hello, this is Eudora Rumph. Can I help you?"

I lowered my head to hide the snicker at my dear neighbor's phone manners. As forceful as she still sounded in her greeting, she had come a long way since the first day I had invited her over to my house to return a call to Smiley's Funeral Parlor regarding Horace's "celebration."

"I'd be delighted to do that. It's mighty neighborly of you to ask me. Thank you kindly. You know, I had just about decided against coming to your retreat," she added, glaring at Mabel, "but in light of today's phone call, I believe I'll be able to make the trip. I'm sure my friend, Mrs. Hattie Crow, could come with me and I'll bet my sweet neighbor, Mrs. Sadie, might even bring us." Miz Eudora glanced at me for a sign of either approval or disapproval. Seeing the nod she'd hoped for, her eyes softened a bit as they moved back in Mabel's direction. "And if you need a helping hand, I'm sure Mabel Toast Jarvis might be free to do something. Just put her on the other side of that big auditorium from me. If there's any overflow seating outside, you might want to consider putting her there. That way, if she goes to fuming while everyone else is retreating, they won't feel the heat coming off of her. I've heard it can get rather hot inside that place when you put lots of warm bodies in it. And I'm sure the Spirit of the Lord will certainly be moving while everybody's retreating, so they'll already be good and warm."

The snicker that came from the other end of the phone was, thankfully, loud enough to cover mine. I could tell that Mabel was "itchin'" to give Miz Eudora a snappy reply, but her desire to "look all important" in front of all the ladies won out as she pursed her lips together and gave a big huff.

There was one thing for certain. Miz Eudora, in her infinite mountain wisdom, had ensured that Mabel would be far away from her at the conference, but by getting her an invitation to be involved, she'd made sure there would be no backtalk once the phone conversation ended. In fact, I was willing to bet that Mabel wouldn't mention this "little episode" again until after the conference for fear that Miz Eudora would pull another stunt like hitching a ride on the Porta-john truck to keep her from joining the party. Given the expression on her face, I would have also wagered that Mabel would have even taken a seat ***in*** one of the Porta-johns to be a part of the weekend in question.

As I took the other two ladies home and left them with their own devices for a quiet evening, I found myself looking forward to my first Spiritual Renewal retreat. From what I had heard and learned, no one was better with "spirits" than Horace Rumph, and Miz Eudora would surely have a thimbleful handy in case Mabel got out of hand. My neighbor had made going to church so much fun, I found myself counting down the weeks until the event as I imagined harmonious strains of music floating across the lake.

Within minutes of my arrival at "home," I was seated in the rocker with my glass of sweet tea and my conscience softly humming ***There's Within My Heart a Melody***.

TWENTY-SIX

What Goes Up Must Come Down

LAKE JUNALUSKA, NORTH Carolina proved to be more beautiful than I'd imagined. The Rose Walk was in full bloom as what seemed like thousands of blossoms greeted all the "retreating ladies" – as Miz Eudora continued to call them – and the air with rare beauty and aroma that could only come from one Source.

"A thorn among the roses," Mabel mumbled repeatedly as Miz Eudora stopped to pose for pictures with adoring fans who'd heard of her quilting abilities and Smack from the Gap Collection. Even those who had no inkling of who she was wanted a photo of the big hat and joyous dress to share "back home."

I left the pair to stroll along the Rose Walk and enjoy making lots of acquaintances while Hattie and I struggled to find a parking place among all the church vans and buses. Once that was accomplished, we made a mad dash to get settled into our rooms at the Lambuth Inn, the stately, majestic jewel of all the accommodations at Lake Junaluska. Before I'd taken ten steps inside the lovely dwelling, I felt a longing for Leon's presence to be able to share all of this with me. It was the first time, thanks to Miz Eudora and all her antics, in which I'd been struck by such a powerful yearning for him.

Relax, Sadie. It's only because this is the kind of place he would have taken you. It's only natural that you'd want to share it with him. I had no idea where the voice came from, but I recognized it was not the voice of Leon's memory. It didn't really matter; it seemed to surround me with a tranquility that I'd never before experienced. I only wish it had warned me about what the next few hours would hold. But then, it wouldn't have left me with that lovely sea of calm at that exact moment, as it was.

"Do you think we'd better find Mabel and Miz Eudora?" Hattie asked once we'd carted all our belongings to the assigned rooms.

One passing glance at the rockers on the front porch overlooking the lake was all I needed to answer that question. "They'll be fine. If they get into a squabble, there are enough clergy and church leaders on these grounds to handle them better than you or I could." I took a seat in one of the rockers, propped my feet on the porch's ledge and surveyed the view that lay before me, with the intention of allowing nothing to interrupt the scene before me. "Besides, there's no Ingle's on the grounds."

That comment drew a large chuckle from Hattie, who'd been the instigator for Miz Eudora having earned her acclaimed reputation from the Ingle's grocery store back home in Smackass Gap.

"This is, after all," I reminded her, "the United Methodist Conference Center, ***not*** New York City. How could they possibly get themselves into trouble here?" I sensed the growing apprehension still in Hattie's expression. "Relax, it's okay. There's plenty of security, trams and trains frequenting the grounds. They're in the safest place they could be."

With that, it was only a few seconds before I had lulled myself into a private world of recluse, void of anything or anyone around me, including the roses, the lake, the mountains and Hattie Crow. I'm not sure how long I had indulged myself in the luxury of that lost world when my euphoria was brusquely and unpleasantly disrupted by two fire engines blasting their sirens as they sped up the lone street that led into Lake Junaluska.

I watched in silence as they pulled to a grinding halt in front of the Lambuth Inn. It was at that exact moment that I noticed the fire alarm was also blaring from the walls of the hotel behind me and the management was shuffling residents out in an orderly manner.

"Where's Miz Eudora?" I roared toward Hattie's chair. "Have you seen her or Mabel?"

The blank stare in her eyes told me all I needed to know.

"I CAN'T BELIEVE we walked all the way up that mountain and neither Hattie, nor Sadie, are even here," fussed Mabel. "How am I supposed to get freshened up?"

"That was only a small hill," replied Miz Eudora. "We told them we'd meet them at the auditorium. They had no reason to sit in their rooms and wait for us. If you were so 'all-fired' anxious to get to your room, you should have gone with Sadie to start with and let Hattie enjoy the Rose Walk with me."

Refusing to admit her ploy to be seen, knowing all eyes would be on the Rose Walk as the thirteen hundred women arrived, Mabel informed her sister-in-law, "Someone needed to make sure you got to the right place. We couldn't take a chance of you getting lost here."

"Lost?" Miz Eudora repeated angrily. "Lost? Land sake's, Mabel, I've got so much mountain blood in me that you couldn't lose me in these Great Smoky Mountains."

"I wouldn't call it 'so much mountain blood.' I think, in truth, you're a bear. A regular old black bear. ***That's*** why you can find your way around these mountains so well. Instinct. Black bear instinct."

Miz Eudora said nothing as she headed around the corner and toward the stairs.

"I'll tell you one thing," declared Mabel, "I'm not walking down those steps. One time was enough for me." She stopped at the elevators and pushed a button to summons a car.

Miz Eudora kept walking and was met by a polite younger woman who'd taken to the "charming little old lady in the purple fur coat" earlier while strolling along the Rose Walk. "Fancy meeting you here," said the woman. She introduced two friends who immediately had to have their photo taken with Miz Eudora and "the coat." "Why don't you take the elevator with us?" she suggested, linking arms with Miz Eudora and leading her back toward the waiting area for elevators.

"Thank you kindly, ma'am, but I think I'll walk," replied Miz Eudora. "I'll meet you downstairs."

"No, no, you don't want to do that," insisted one of the other women, this one approaching middle age. "It's way too many steps."

"She's right," agreed the third friend. "That would take you half the day and you'd be so tired, you wouldn't be able to enjoy the afternoon's sessions."

"You absolutely don't want to do that," continued the first woman. "I've heard the song leader this time is absolutely divine and you surely don't want to miss hearing her inspiring music."

"They say she has the voice of an angel," shared the second woman.

"And looks like one, too," added the third woman.

A grimace appeared in Mabel's expression that turned her already-sour face into a replica of a prune.

"I'll be alright," began Miz Eudora.

"She's never ridden on an elevator," interjected Mabel, who was listening with a touch of jealousy. "She's scared."

"If I'm not a'feared of you, Mabel Toast Jarvis, I'm sure as shootin' not going to be a'feared of some little box that goes up and down. Besides, even if I were scared, I'm old enough to speak for myself."

"Eudora, you don't have the good graces to carry on a decent conversation with these ladies. I'm only trying to keep you from embarrassing yourself."

"I don't know why that should bother you so. ***You*** certainly don't mind embarrassing myself."

"Oh, honestly, Eudora, you're impossible. Impossible, do you hear me? Whatever did I do to deserve spending the end of my life caring for you? I should put you in a home, that's what I should do."

"I already have a home and the problem is, you

put yourself in ***my*** home way too often. If you'd realize you weren't welcome, we wouldn't have this problem." Miz Eudora took a step closer to Mabel. "Furthermore, I'll bet you're just trying to get me on the elevator because your feet are too lazy to carry your rump down the steps. Why, I've been trompin' up and down mountains every day of my life since I could walk. These few little steps aren't going to keep me from getting where I want to go."

She shook her head in disgust. "P'SHAA! If you'd have been a real Rumph or Jarvis instead of half a one, we'd have already been to the auditorium."

"I'll have you know that I ***am*** a whole Rumph," Mabel retaliated angrily, "I mean Jarvis. It doesn't matter whether you like it or not, my name written on a dotted line has just as much say-so as yours."

"Well, I'll give you this much," Eudora conceded, backing away. "Your last name is Jarvis and you are definitely a whole rump. They don't get much 'wholer' than yours, on or off the dotted line."

"Impossible, I tell you, IMPOSSIBLE!" Mabel stormed.

By the time their banter ended, the first elevator had filled up and the buzzer sounded, indicating the doors were closing and it would soon be on its way.

"Now look!" scorned Mabel. "Everyone else is already gone." A bell, signaling another elevator's approach caught her attention. "Here," she directed as she reached out her cane, which she'd brought "solely for ease of walking up and down the steep inclines," and stuck it between the opening doors while assuring their entry into "the oversized moving lunchbox," as Eudora had called it. "Hurry up and get in before the doors close and we miss this one, too."

Miz Eudora gave a disgruntled huff as she took a big step over the opening in the floor, looking concerned that she might fall through. The doors automatically closed and the elevator car gave a slight jolt as it began its slow descent toward the ground floor.

"See there? Nothing to it," said Mabel, appearing to be the seasoned pro of elevators.

Before Miz Eudora had a chance to respond, the elevator jerked to a sudden stop as the lights went out and air stopped moving through the vent.

"What on earth?" belted Mabel.

"What's wrong?" asked Eudora, her boisterous voice maximized due to the complete darkness and silence that surrounded them.

"What's wrong is that you piddled around and we didn't get on the other elevator with all the other women!"

"What's wrong with that? With all of them on it, someone might have tripped over us in the dark."

"Good heavens, Eudora! Don't you understand anything? We must have stopped between floors."

"Why'd we do that? Why would anyone want to get off between floors? Besides, there's no one on here to get off there."

"HMMPH!" Mabel blasted disparagingly. "Don't you know ***anything*** about elevators?"

"You mean it doesn't usually do this?"

"No! Not unless you're in a James Bond movie or someth…oh, never mind. You've never seen one of those movies."

"Maybe there's a ghost. I have seen Casper when I was watching Chip and Dale one time at someone's house."

"HMMPH!" Mabel repeated, ignoring the senselessness of her sister-in-law. She began to grope for the panel on the wall, fumbling for buttons. "I sure wish I had paid attention to how many floors were in this hotel. Then I could try to figure out which button to push for the alarm."

"Alarm? Why do you need to push an alarm? We're not on fire, are we?"

"Don't you know anything, Eudora Rumph? If we don't push the alarm, then no one will realize we're in here."

"Those women in the other elevator…," began Miz Eudora.

"Those women were so excited to get to their shopping that they won't notice we're not there until one of them gets trigger happy with her camera again," interrupted Mabel, "and that won't be until at least dinnertime. Now hush up so I can concentrate on the alarm button."

"For your information," Eudora noted, "there's seventeen floors in this hotel. I saw a sign when we came in that said so."

"That means there are only sixteen floors in this elevator, because there's never a thirteenth floor in a hotel. Leastways, not one for customers and the elevator won't stop there."

"Maybe there's a ghost and that's why we did stop there."

"Honestly! Will you stop it with your nonsense about a ghost? I've got to figure out how to get us out of here, no thanks to you."

"And there's a red button on the bottom left under all the numbered buttons that says, 'In case of an emergency, push this button,'" Miz Eudora informed her.

"How'd you know that?" quizzed Mabel. "You've never been on an elevator before."

"Well, I figured if'n I was going to be on one, I might as well find out everything about it that I could. There wasn't much to look at in here before the lights went out. It was like that time Sadie offered to take us to the movie and you fiddled around and made us late. We took one step inside the theater and it went dark. Hattie tripped over that poor man's foot and knocked somebody's popcorn in the floor while Sadie fell in another man's lap because she slipped when you knocked that drink over. It's a good thing it was her that fell in his lap instead of you because,"

"I've got to find that button," insisted Mabel, not daring to admit that ***had*** she been able to see, for once she'd have hugged her sister-in-law. Or least she would have hugged her before the statement about it being a good thing she didn't fall in the man's lap.

Miz Eudora took three steps, let her fingers walk along the wall until she found the button, and pushed it. She rang the alarm not once, not twice, but three times.

"What do you think you're doing?" Mabel asked indignantly. "Chiming the Holy Trinity with the elevator alarm? Once was enough. You didn't need to tell the entire world we're in here."

"Just because it sounded like we're inside a bell tower from in here, how do you know they heard it out there? I want to make sure they know we're here. I also read on the sign when we came in the building that they're having chicken pot pie and carrot cake for supper. I want to make sure I don't miss either one."

"How can you think about your stomach at a time like this?"

"The same way you do all the rest of the time. At least I know what I'm gonna be missin' before I start thinkin' about it!"

Within a few more seconds, the lights came back on and the air once more began to circulate.

"Does that mean we're going to get out now?" asked Miz Eudora.

"I'm not sure, but at least we can breathe in here now." Mabel looked all around the elevator as she shook her head in disbelief. "I can't believe there isn't a telephone in here. I thought all elevators had a phone inside them."

"It wouldn't do you any good if'n it did," replied Miz Eudora. "Neither Sadie nor Hattie are home to answer if you call them. And you heard Sadie, her cell phone doesn't work here. Nobody else gives a flip about talking to you."

"Not them, you...you...Gracious alive, I'd call the operator. That's why they have telephones in the elevator. So that you can call the...What are you doing?" she asked as she saw Miz Eudora's pointer finger again hit the alarm button.

"I'm calling somebody. Somebody ought to be able to hear that."

"They must know we're stuck in here by now. You don't need to keep ringing that thing."

"It was a long way to that check-in desk downstairs. If the lady working there hears this, I'll bet she'll call that operator for us."

To be sure, Miz Eudora rang the alarm again,

but this time she let her finger sit on it for a good thirty seconds. Satisfied that she'd done all she could, she reached for the side rail, knelt down and rolled onto the floor.

"Now what do you think you're doing?" Mabel inquired.

"I'm going to take a nap. I didn't get much sleep last night for being so excited about coming here. I was too excited to sleep. Being hung up in this elevator with you isn't too exciting, so I can sleep now."

"You certainly can't sleep in here," Mabel said.

"I certainly can, if'n you stop that infernal squawkin,'" Miz Eudora replied. "It's good and cool in here now, just like an early fall evening. Best kind of sleeping weather." She closed her eyes and was out like a light, like the light in the elevator had been minutes earlier, to be precise.

Mabel, seeing it worked for Miz Eudora, took hold of the side rail and attempted to kneel herself. Finding that to be an impossibility, due to her bad knees – or so she said to herself – she tried to sit down. Fearing she'd fall and cause the elevator car to go crashing down the shaft, she spent the next while in silence trying to decide how she was going to come out of this like the beautiful heroic creature of a lady she was. She had wanted to make an impression, but this was definitely not what she'd had in mind.

Miz Eudora had been out for a good forty-five

minutes when a man's voice called out, "Are you okay in there?"

"Yes," answered Miz Eudora.

Her answer was countered out by Mabel's, "No! No, we're not alright."

"How many of you are in there?"

"Two," answered Mabel, sounding even more panicked now than she had earlier.

"Two unless you count Mabel as two people. Then there's three of us. If you ask me, she's more trouble than any three people I've ever seen. Maybe you'd better say four."

"Is anyone having an emergency?"

"Yes, sir," answered Miz Eudora. "We're stuck in an elevator and I'd sure like it if you could get me out of here. Being shut up with Mabel is about the worst thing you can imagine."

"Yes, ma'am, I understand," replied a kind male voice.

"You do?" Miz Eudora hollered back, puzzled. "Have you been shut up in an elevator with Mabel, too?"

"No, you ninny!" exclaimed Mabel. "He just means that he understands the horrible dilemma of being stuck in this thing, not being stuck in it with me."

"Then he doesn't understand the half of it!" Miz Eudora blared.

The elevator gave a sudden jerk.

"Land sakes, what are they trying to do?" asked Miz Eudora. "Jump start us?"

"Are you ladies still okay in there?" the man inquired. "No one's having a heart attack or anything? Do either of you need immediate assistance?"

"We're still fine," called Miz Eudora. "Thank goodness Mabel decided not to drink that second bottle of water. Otherwise, you'd have to be sending a bed pan in here."

"Eudora Rumph! Don't be saying stuff like that."

"Why not? It's the truth. You know you can't hold your bladder very well."

"I'll have you know I'm holding my bladder and my…I'm fine."

"You still okay in there?"

"We are," answered Mabel.

"We're working as hard as we can to get you out. Hopefully we'll have you out of there in fifteen more minutes."

Miz Eudora started to lie back down.

"Now what are you doing?" Mabel asked.

"I'm going to finish my beauty sleep. It wouldn't hurt to you start one."

"HMMPH!" Mabel exclaimed.

The elevator gave another sudden jerk, this time lunging several feet down.

"Ahhh-Whooop!" screamed Mabel, in that distinctive way as only she could do.

"Are you still holding it, Mabel?" asked Miz Eudora.

"Holding what?"

"Your…your…,"

The door was suddenly pried open a couple of inches and the kind rescuer's face was now visible. "Just a couple of more minutes, ladies, and we'll have you out of there."

After one more lunge of a couple of feet and another deafening "Ahhh-Whooop!" out of Mabel, the door opened approximately four feet. The problem was that it was also still approximately four feet from the elevator to the next floor of the Lambuth Inn.

"Can you ladies climb out?" the man, whom the ladies now recognized as a fireman, inquired. "If you can hold your arms up, I'll grab hold and pull you out."

He took a peek into the elevator and saw the two women. "It would probably be easiest if the largest one came out first," he instructed.

"Mabel could barely get up the hill. That's why we're on this blasted elevator anyway. She couldn't walk any further. If she can't walk, how do you think she can climb? You know what we say in Smackass Gap. 'You've gotta crawl a-fore you walk and you've gotta walk a-fore you climb.' Pa was awfully proud of me 'cause I crawled ***and*** climbed first."

"Eudora, would you please shut up and get me out of here?" fumed Mabel.

"Mister, can you open the door a little wider. I'm not sure Mabel will fit through there. She's a whole rump, not a half a one, you see."

"You're going to see something in a minute if you don't get me out of here," ranted Mabel.

"Why don't you take your cane and try to pole vault out of here?" suggested Miz Eudora.

"Pole vault? Eudora Rumph, I do believe the lack of oxygen in here has made your brain even more senile than it already was. I'll hold my hands up and you push me. The fireman can get me the rest of the way."

"What are you going to do with your cane?" asked Miz Eudora as she reached for Mabel's backside and started pushing. "Never mind. I've got a great place for it."

"Eudora, will you just concentrate on pushing?"

"Have you got a helper up there, Mister?" Miz Eudora yelled.

"Yes, ma'am. There's four of us here ready to pull her out once you get her far enough up."

"That's a good thing, but do you happen to have a crane on that fire truck?"

"No, but would it help if we brought the ladder? We could drop it down there and you two ladies could climb up."

"Land sake's, no!" exclaimed Miz Eudora. "Mabel would probably break all the rungs."

"I'm going to 'rung' your neck if you don't start pushing me out."

"Get ready," Miz Eudora yelled up the shaft. "She's a-comin'!"

Miz Eudora took hold of the side rail, got to her knees and used her back to hoist Mabel up high enough that the men were able to pull her up to safety.

"She's a healthy one, alright," sighed one of the firemen quietly.

"I hope you're alright, ma'am," offered the fireman, who appeared to be in charge, once both of Mabel's feet were planted on the floor. "It gets dark when the elevator stops and some people panic."

"Land sakes, those few minutes wadn't nothing," Miz Eudora replied, a large dose of assurance in her voice. "Mabel's spent most of her life in the dark."

The handsome young fireman in charge laughed as he reached a hand down to pull Miz Eudora from the elevator shaft. "Do we need to call an ambulance for either of you?" he asked.

"No!" shouted Mabel, still concerned about escaping this escapade gracefully.

Miz Eudora held her arms as high as she could while two of the men pulled her up until she could put her feet on the third floor of the Lambuth Inn.

"Thank you kindly," acknowledged Miz Eudora. "We'll be on our way now. I hope you fellers get her fixed real soon."

"Someone from maintenance is working on it right now. It will be back up and running in no time."

"Good, then some other poor person can enjoy all the fun and games," joked Miz Eudora. "Say, you don't happen to know whether that elevator has a ghost or not do you?"

Mabel shoved Miz Eudora forward with her cane as they quickly shuffled toward the back steps and walked around to the front of the building to get on the sidewalk.

"What in the world?" asked Miz Eudora when she saw the crowd of people outside the Lambuth Inn all staring up at the building. That's when she also noticed the two fire trucks parked at the front entrance, their lights flashing wildly. She spotted Sadie and Hattie and made her way through the crowd to them.

"What happened?" Mabel, who followed her, inquired of the pair. "The building isn't on fire is it?"

"No," said Sadie, giving each of the women a hug.

"Two people are trapped in an elevator inside and when we couldn't find the two of you, we were afraid it might be you."

"You mean there's two more…," Miz Eudora began, but was interrupted when Mabel stomped on her toe. "Oh, I'm so sorry," she apologized. "I must have lost my balance."

"Speaking of losing things," began Miz Eudora, "did you get out with your cane?"

"My trusty cane is right here, ready to walk down to the Sunset Café for a bite."

"I'm with her," seconded a man nearby. "Most all of us missed our lunch because of those two. The staff paraded us all out of the dining hall the minute that first alarm went off."

"There's one thing for sure. When that alarm goes off, nobody misses it. It nearly scared me to death."

People began to tell where they were and how the "inconvenience" affected them.

"I'll have to admit it was the loudest thing I've ever heard, with it blaring off the walls of the dining hall the way it did."

"If you think it was loud in the dining hall," Miz Eudora commented, "you'd should'a been in the elevator. That was the,"

"In the elevator?" Hattie repeated, cutting Miz Eudora off.

"Yes, we," Miz Eudora began to explain.

"Didn't it turn out to be a gorgeous afternoon?" Mabel quickly asked, trying to change the subject.

"Can you believe our luck?" complained one of the preachers next to them. "Why'd that have to happen right in the middle of lunch? Not only did we not get to finish eating, but we couldn't go back to our rooms to retrieve our car keys, which meant our golf clubs were locked up in the trunk."

"What a bummer!" agreed another minister. "We could have spent the entire afternoon on the golf course, and instead, all we got to do was sit in rockers and watch time go by."

"I think that's one of the things that God tells us to do," replied a non-golfer.

"That's right," said one of the golfers' wives. "Nowhere in the Bible does it say, 'Thou shalt play golf instead of smelling the roses.'"

Touché! I wanted to applaud her reasoning, which because of the Rose Walk was perfectly literal in its theology, but decided against it. However, I did find it interesting that "men of the cloth" were not exempt from having "words" with their spouses.

"Dear Sadie!" This time it was Leon's voice that she heard. ***"Don't you remember that was the reason for us even discovering Smackass Gap? I was leading a marital retreat at Hinton Rural Life Center for clergy and church staff members."***

I had to admit I'd forgotten that tidbit of the story surrounding our "finding" – ***or rather God's leading us to*** – Smackass Gap.

My attention focused back to the breaking news at hand. I'd apparently missed a few comments, but was able to pick right back up with the story when I heard Sadie ask, "So what did you think of your first elevator ride, Miz Eudora?"

It seemed Miz Eudora and Mabel had turned into a pair of celebrities as people began to hear of their notable experience that was now the talk of Lake Junaluska.

"I'll bet it'll be...what did you call it...'a blue moon' before you ever get on another elevator," said the polite woman who'd tried to get her on the elevator originally.

"I didn't know it wasn't supposed to be that a-way. That is, until Mabel started a-carryin' on so. I don't know as I've ever seen her so scared. 'Course, I didn't see her then, either, cause it was pitch black in there."

"What did you do?" came another question, directed to Mabel.

Mabel was still fanning herself, more from humiliation than heat, so Eudora spoke for her. "I took myself a good afternoon nap. I'm sorry the rest of you didn't get one. Mabel huffed and puffed so much, though, that she likened to have sucked up all the air. It's a wonder I didn't suffocate in there." She laughed heartily. "But I'll bet it ***will*** be a blue moon before Mabel ever gets on another elevator. Eh, Mabel? You take up walking with me and you might only be half a rump."

I fully expected her to poke Mabel in the ribs with that statement, but instead, Miz Eudora must have noticed the same degradation that I did on her sister-in-law's face. Strangely as it seemed, she actually reached out to her in kindness. "Don't worry, Mabel," soothed Miz Eudora, as she adjusted her hat on her head with her new red-and-purple hat pin. "I'll see to it that you have a part in the service before the day's over, and that everyone will see you. I'm sure they'll even all know your name by the time they go home. And you're welcome to go ahead and sit with us. Preacher Jake said we should all hold our heads up and represent First Church, Smackass with great pride."

Maybe* that's *why she's being so agreeable. Preacher Jake must have had a word or two of his own with her regarding Mabel. It's about time, I resolved. Although, secretly, I wasn't sure that bout of getting stuck in the elevator for a couple of hours together did any harm.

TWENTY-SEVEN

Sweet Hour of Prayer

THAT WAS THE day that I discovered exactly how obsessed Mabel was with fame. Ordinarily she'd have been concerned - ***rightly***, I might add - with the manner in which Miz Eudora might see to that promise, but I quickly discovered that she was ruthlessly handicapped by a compulsive disorder when it came to being the center of attention. Until then, I'd had no idea of the severity of her condition.

Although Mabel had sulked during the entire ride from Smackass Gap, she now rushed to the restroom to check her appearance in the mirror. Personally, I hoped the matter of "Mabel's appearance" would prove as simple as Miz Eudora made it seem. But, knowing her, there was an underlying lesson to be learned for her sister-in-law.

My fears vanished with the first note of the organ's prelude. No exaggerations had been made when it came to the beauty of the sounds floating across the water. My heart was truly filled with glorious melodies which, when the auditorium filled with ladies, soared straight up to the heavens. The guest speaker was inspiring in her words and her insights, making me greatly relieved that the Spirit needed no help from Miz Eudora's borrowed "spirit" this day.

I was so caught up in the moment that I was oblivious to Mabel's bobbing head and light snoring. I didn't even notice Miz Eudora pull the long stickpin from her hat until I heard Mabel scream "Dear God!" as she flew upright in her seat and landed on her feet in a standing position. Before she had time to balk, Miz Eudora whispered that it was time for her to pray.

"We join our hearts in silence," Mabel began, in her loudest voice and right on cue.

The speaker stopped in midsentence as attendees began to look around and see that one of their members felt an urgent call to prayer. I, on the other hand, saw that it was an urgent call to Miz Eudora's "well-adjusted" hatpin, and not to prayer, that sent Mabel into action during the service.

Just about the time she got wound up was also about the time she got good and awake enough to realize that she'd interrupted the entire service. With no way to gracefully get out of her predicament, Mabel concluded her talk with God as quickly, yet reverently, as she was able and took her seat. She didn't dare look in the direction of Miz Eudora, but I was sure we'd all hear about it on the way back to Clay County.

As far as I was concerned, Mabel couldn't complain too much. Miz Eudora had promised her a chance to be seen and heard and that had, indeed, happened. The speaker finished her sermon, Miz Eudora helped serve the communion – which consisted of grape juice instead of wine – and all ended with the ladies saying it was the most enthralling Spiritual Renewal retreat they'd ever experienced.

I had to hand it to Miz Eudora. After the initial shock of what was going on, every head was definitely bowed and every eye was surely closed during that prayer, a goal that many ministers seek from their congregation every Sunday, but never fully attain. No one dared look up, or in the direction of a neighbor, for fear of bursting into raucous laughter.

You had to admit, Miz Eudora held true to her word. By the time we left Lake Junaluska, Mabel Toast Jarvis was a household word to all in attendance. There was no doubt that she, or at least her participation in the service, would be known throughout every United Methodist Church, as well as their neighboring churches, in Western North Carolina by the next week. There was also no doubt that she would not dare fall asleep during one of Preacher Jake's sermons in the coming months.

The melody in my heart was nothing but joyful

as we departed Lake Junaluska and I slowly drove my three passengers past the lake and the Rose Walk, my soul awakened and stirred. A look in the rearview mirror, where I saw Mabel in the backseat, showed that she, too, was awakened and stirred. Except her spiritual renewal was visibly overshadowed by ninety sweet minutes (the time it would take us to get home) of prayer – ***even better than a whoppin' hour's worth!*** – for how to get one up on her dear sister-in-law.

Hattie and Miz Eudora conversed happily as if nothing had happened over the course of the past two days except a vibrant renewal of spirits. I saw that for Miz Eudora, though, that renewal meant a revitalization of everything concerned with her. She was "goin' on" about her new Christmas line of "Smack from the Gap" that she was going to release.

"I think I'll even have a fashion show for all my Red Hatter friends to see all my beautiful new creations. And I've already got the perfect title for it. Listen up, everyone!" she ordered, an effort which was totally unnecessary - as Hattie and I were already listening and Mabel was silent in her fuming - yet she wanted to make sure we didn't miss her important announcement. "I'm going to call it 'Beautiful Star of Bethlehem' after Pa's favorite Christmas carol. I can see it now. I'll have Red Hat Nanny make me a big red star hat to go with my outfit and I'll have all the ladies paradin' around the square of Hayesville, showin' off my new collection. I'll get Theona to model the petite sizes. Hattie, you can model the busty sizes and Mabel, you can…,"

There was a hefty pause as Miz Eudora drew a blank, the sudden concern written all over her face.

"I'm not sure I can afford that much fabric," she finally continued. "Mabel, how's about you singin' ***Beautiful Star of Bethlehem*** while the rest of the ladies show off the clothes? I'll even get Grover Swicegood to be in charge of building us a runway so's the ladies will look like real models and I'm sure Rob Tiger will help us get the word out."

Miz Eudora smiled and rested her hands in her lap, satisfied with all her arrangements as she leaned over and whispered to me, "And Sadie, you be in charge of finding the elevator."

I knew not what next Christmas would hold, but I was sure that on the back side of it, there would be lots of gratifying "precious memories" and one "beautiful star"- Miz Eudora Rumph.

PRECIOUS MEMORIES

Precious mem'ries, unseen angels,
sent from somewhere to my soul;
How they linger, ever near me,
and the sacred past unfolds.

CHORUS: Precious mem'ries, how they linger,
how they ever flood my soul;
In the stillness of the midnight,
precious sacred scenes unfold.

Precious father, loving mother,
fly across the lonely years;
And old home scenes of my childhood,
in fond memory appear.
CHORUS

As I travel down life's pathway,
know not what the years may hold;
As I ponder, hope grows fonder,
precious mem'ries flood my soul.
CHORUS

J.B.F. Wright

A Final Thanks

Kudos to my dear friends, and stitchery talents, Leona Burdock of The Crooked Needle in Findlay, Ohio; Ruth Wiertzema of the Red Bird Missionary Conference in Beverly, Kentucky; and to Peggy Donald ("Red Hat Nanny"), hat maker extraordinaire.

Their hands, led by their creative genius, make the "Smack from the Gap" Collection of Miz Eudora Originals a reality. You'll note that Leona designed, sewed and quilted the "real" Miz Eudora quilt, and also the crazy quilt skirt and quilted jacket on the *Precious Memories* cover. In addition, she designs my one-of-a-kind shirts and jackets. Peggy made my purple hat that is so incredibly spectacular that I could take flight in it, and is my "official" hatmaker. Lastly, Ruth styled the "bags" embroidered with Miz Eudora's caricature, and also makes the "Bling It Your Way" capes and purses.

Without these three women, my endless ideas would still be floating around in my head. However, due to their combined gifts and talents, you can also own a part of Miz Eudora's "wardrobe" from her blamed old "Smack from the Gap" cedar chest.

Thank you - Leona, Ruth and Peggy - for sharing your many gifts. I give thanks for your many talents, but most especially, for the blessing of your friendship.

CR?

You Asked...

Miz Eudora Rumph receives many, many questions during her appearance tour. In an attempt to keep from being asked the same questions repeatedly, she has decided to answer the three most popular ones here for all her readers. "And remember," warns Miz Eudora, "there are no dumb questions, ***nor*** dumb answers."

What's it like in the purple fopher coat?

A little warmer than it is out of it.

Do you wear a fat suit under Miz Eudora's clothes?

Land's sakes, no! I'm Miz Eudora Rumph, not Santa Claus. Fat suit, I reckon!

Is there really a Mabel?

Well, duh! You couldn't dream up anything like her in your worst nightmare. That's just like all you readers who didn't believe there was really a place named Smackass Gap. There are simply some things you absolutely cannot make up.

The Woman Behind the Fopher Coat

We've so often been asked, "What's she really like?" that we've invited three of Catherine's dear childhood friends – all of whom have reconnected in the past year and are members of Miz Eudora's Sparklin' Shiners – to give you the real scoop, "from way back when" on "the person behind the coat."

We'd like to thank Chris Williams Efird, Deb Rodgers Farris and Barbara Brooks Taylor for allowing Miz Eudora's readers the personal insights on the following four pages.

"Catherine, the woman behind the coat is the girl that I sat beside in Advanced English and enjoyed her stories then. I always remember her piano playing in Chorus and all our school events. Oh, and that beautiful auburn hair that we all wanted. She was someone who always pushed the limits of perfection, never satisfied with ordinary, looking for the best in others while not accepting anything less in herself.

Recently going on the trip to Smackass Gap with her and the Sparklin' Shiners just made me realize that there will never be enough "Catherine" to go around. She wants everyone to be happy and will work tirelessly to make that happen. The trip started out on a bad note with all kinds of adversity, but before the 48 hours were up, she had ridden the bus with us, sang songs, told stories and made us all forget our troubles and that feeling spread throughout the group like soft butter!

Which is exactly what she will do for you when you read her books. Her voice on the page can carry you to a place where times are simple and people are good, all the while making you laugh and cry.

The woman in the Fopher Coat is a lady and our childhood friend. When she dons the coat as Miz Eudora she becomes a virtual "Pied Piper" of storytelling that will bless your heart as only our Catherine can do!

Catherine, I will never forget the trip. I enjoyed just being around you, Barbara and Debbie. We proved that friends are forever!"

Christine W Efird

"The woman behind the coat was the quiet, petite red-head that set the standards for both academics and music in school. She managed to stay out of trouble yet was always in the midst of everything. Just how does that work? (Miz Eudora was obviously already being formulated.) And, for those of you who don't know, it is 'Catherine' with a 'C' . . . not Kat, not Kathy, not Cathy, but Catherine!"

Deb Rodgers Farris

Our friendship started as young children when Catherine and I shared playtime while our grandmothers visited. In school, she was quiet as a church mouse, (NO, I'm not lying!) studious, and always polite. Mostly I remember that I was in awe of her musical talent. Catherine played the piano beautifully and her fingers glided effortlessly across the keyboard. I remember watching her feet tapping the foot pedals and wondering, 'How does she know just when to tap the pedal?' Catherine was voted the Most Intellectual our 8th grade year. She was very upset and cried and cried because she wanted to be the Most Talented instead! I just assured her "You couldn't get both" and "There's no doubt that you were the most Talented!" And I have no doubt that she was the Most Intellectual, also.

In the past year, we have rekindled our friendship. I'm still in awe of her and have to admit I find her absolutely amazing! Her zest for life, her energy, talent, kindness, and humor are such an inspiration to me and others. I believe in divine intervention and there's no doubt that God had a part in reconnecting us again. And for this I thank HIM. I treasure the time I get to spend with my friend. She may wear a purple faux-fur (fopher coat) in character as Miz Eudora, but in real life, she is so Real, so True, so Caring!

Barbara Brooks Taylor (Smokin' Barb)

Sincere thanks to John Barden for his “Smack from the Gap” sketches featured in this book.

Meet Miz Eudora

Want to see Miz Eudora in person?

She is available for your next event or conference - with or without Mabel - and sometimes appears with The Purple Stallion, singer extraordaire. On rare special occasions, Hattie Crow may even be seen sharing the stage with Miz Eudora!

Also check out Miz Eudora's monthly newsletter to follow her shennanigans, whereabouts and book release dates.

www.mizeudora.com

ABOUT THE AUTHOR

Catherine Ritch Guess is the author of nineteen books, all of the inspirational genre, which include fiction, non-fiction and children's titles. In addition, she is a published composer and a frequent speaker/musician for a wide range of conferences and events.

She is currently working on a non-fiction on eminent domain, and completing five novels, one of which is ***Beautiful Star of Bethlehem,*** a fun Christmas tale for the next volume in The Winsome Ways of Miz Eudora Rumph.

Her most treasured activity is spending time with her family at home on her grandfather's land in Indian Trail, North Carolina.

www.ciridmus.com